The Immortality Chronicles

WINDRIFT BOOKS

Edited by Carol Davis (http://caroldavisauthor.com/a-better-look-editing-services)

Cover art and design by Adam Hall (http://www.aroundthepages.com)

Print and ebook formatting by Therin Knite (http://www.knitedaydesign.com/)

The Immortality Chronicles is part of The Future Chronicles series produced by Samuel Peralta (www.samuelperalta.com).

978-0-9939832-4-5

The Immortality
Chronicles

STORY SYNOPSES

The Antares Cigar Shoppe (*John Gregory Hancock*)
One might wonder how a robot is made, what levers make it work, or for what purpose it was intended. But no one ever wonders how old a robot is.

Rememorations (*Paul B. Kohler*)
Decades after receiving an immortality endowment, Nathan Duncan returns to the Lazarus Center for Extended Living to discover that his treatment was not all he was promised. The routine maintenance he requires will affect his past every bit as much as his future. Now, Nathan can't help wondering: is it the man that makes the memories, or vice versa?

The Scout (*D. Robert Pease*)
In the not-too-distant future, humanity is conducting a frantic search for the next step in human evolution. Everlasting life is within its grasp, but one man needs it more than anyone else. It's the key to ending his already-immortal life.

The Control (*Will Swardstrom*)
A moment exists for everyone—a moment between disaster and victory. It was there, in that moment, where I lived. Always waiting. Always letting my fate be determined by others. Always hovering between a rousing triumph and a crushing

catastrophe. I was that moment. But my moment was not to be under my control. My name is Bek and I am immortal.

The Essence of Jamie's Father (*Gareth Foy*)
Scientists say the Earth will be destroyed in a billion years as the sun expands to engulf it. They are wrong: Earth doesn't have that long. But there is a key for humanity to escape its Sun, and start solving the biggest of mysteries: Essence, and Jamie's father holds the key.

The Backup (*Patricia Gilliam*)
After being shot during a press conference, Nick Mathis wakes up alone in a lab over nine hundred miles away. Unsure of whom he can trust, he seeks out his best friend from childhood—and draws his killer to them both.

Legacy (*David Bruns*)
At what point does a man with cybernetic enhancements cease to be human? Over the past two hundred years, Edward Stemm has replaced 82.5% of his organic body with bionic improvements. A bad day in court makes him wonder about the remaining 17.5%.

A Severance of Souls (*Drew Avera*)
To save the human race, what would you give up, what would you sacrifice? Would you sacrifice your humanity?

Room 42 (*D.K. Cassidy*)
In a future where humans can no longer die naturally, Dr. Vivian Toujours is fueled by a desire to return a sense of normal-

cy to the world. The breakthrough she strives to perfect is the hope of a weary, timeworn humanity, but her motivation is much more personal – namely, the occupant of Room 42.

Eternity Today (*Thomas Robins*)
New Year's Day is a day for recovery, a day for making plans for the future, a day that never ends. The universe is caught in loop, continually resetting to New Year's Day. And what will happen to humanity, when people realize there are no lasting consequences for their actions?

The House on the Cliff (*E.E. Giorgi*)
A mercenary returns to his home after almost losing his life in the war he fought for another country. The technology that saved him gave him a curse, one that he willingly accepted so that he could see, for one more time, his true love.

A Long Horizon (*Harlow C. Fallon*)
Kate boards a ship for a fresh start in Virginia Colony, free from the drudgery of her life in London. But something from her nightmares lurks below the waves. When it rises from the sea to take her, Kate finds herself on a journey spanning millions of miles and nine hundred years. Her new world is no longer Virginia, but a planet the entity inside her calls home.

CONTENTS

FOREWORD
by Samuel Peralta

*"We all die. The goal isn't to live forever, the
goal is to create something that will."*
– Chuck Palahniuk

Underneath the incandescent bulb, the vertical inscription inside the oval outline came into sharp relief –

*A folded cloth, a vulture, an owl, a quail chick, a flowering reed,
a lion.*

My name, inscribed on the back of a scarab, a beetle form carved in soapstone, glazed in aquamarine and fired to fingernail hardness. Another of my father's souvenirs, this one was from an excursion to Cairo, to a conference under the auspices of the National Museum.

My younger brother had one too. I looked over his shoulder in envy – in the oval shen ring that encircled the hieroglyphic symbols, his longer name required one more symbol than mine did.

Our scarabs were probably carved around the year of our births, scant decades ago – but there are scarabs that date from the time of the Middle Kingdom, from the age of the pharaohs and the building of the pyramids.

Fascinated by this discovery, my brother and I wrote poems and stories in spurious hieroglyphics, referring to a photocopy of a page from our school's Encyclopedia Britannica that showed the various symbols and what purported to be their English equivalents. We drew on onion-skin paper, rolled them into scrolls as if they were papyrus, and pretended that our compositions would outlast Ozymandias.

I've long forgotten where I'd kept those childhood scribblings. But I still pretend – sitting here behind this flat screen, typing a modern hieroglyphics with my wireless keyboard – that my words might find a permanence more lasting than my life. Or is it hope?

We live a life of contradictions, we writers. We seclude ourselves from the world, perfecting our creations – and then release them like doves, hoping that the world embraces them, and through them, ourselves. We seek, in this, the only way we know to live forever – through our words.

Maybe we haven't changed so much, over the ages.

In the British Museum, there is a fragile papyrus from the 19th dynasty of ancient Egypt, accession number 10684. Mounted behind glass, it is a fractured and fragile parchment, marked with black ink. The verses on its front are hymns to an ancient god.

Flip the papyrus, however, and on the reverse you find one of the oldest surviving passages about writers.

Within a longer treatise exhorting apprentices not to give up on, but to hold true to their writing, there is, in my rendition, this marvelous observation:

When a man dies, his body is interred;
And all his kindred too will one day lay to rest.
But his words, those will be his commemoration,
Intoned in the mouths of others…
Unlike temples, more lasting;
Unlike towers, more perfect;
Unlike monuments, immortal.

www.amazon.com/author/samuelperalta

The Antares Cigar Shoppe

by John Gregory Hancock

GASTON SAT IN HIS USUAL SPOT on the bench just inside the cigar shoppe. The shoppe itself was wedged into a half-circle of retail buildings that curved in a graceful arc from the traveler hostels, and ultimately emptied onto a broad collection of ticket turnstiles leading to the east. Ornately fashioned gates of metal (really sculptures by any sane definition) opened to the rocket pads. Light-duty sentinels stood at the kiosks, relaxed because there was really no threat to deter. Hadn't been, for as long as anyone could remember.

The village where Gaston had found himself catered to the interstellar trade. Travelers consisted of families, business agents, and the occasional religious pilgrim. The number of transient persons far outnumbered the locals, though the ratio fluctuated.

But even local people were themselves transient, making

or losing their fortunes and relocating somewhere else down the line.

Universal credits passed from hand to hand. Products and services that a traveler had forgotten, and wanted, were offered for sale. There were plenty of taverns for people who actually wanted to forget the things they had left behind, or to celebrate what awaited them at new destinations.

There was a back door to the cigar shoppe, but it emptied onto nothing but sand and dirt. Gaston faced the entrance instead, and calculated the total number of dust motes as they were revealed by a shaft of orange light.

The number was without significance. He discarded the information.

Mr. Arsenault, who acted as owner, crossed in front of Gaston and pressed a small black button at the entrance. An ionizer expelled the dust particles through a semi-permeable membrane. The security barrier automatically rolled into the top frame of the store like an antique roll-top desk would have, on Earth, long ago.

The Antares Cigar Shoppe was open for business.

Gaston hummed to himself and leaned back to watch Mr. Arsenault perform the myriad tiny chores one does when readying a shoppe for customers. These were mostly silent, arcane and needlessly busy things. Gaston caught his eye and politely nodded. Mr. Arsenault smiled shyly before returning to work.

Gaston always stationed himself at the bench because he enjoyed chatting with travelers, if they felt like it. You never knew who would. In case no one stopped by, he enjoyed chatting just with Mr. Arsenault.

This morning's disconnected parade along the arc was

heavier than usual. Some were in a dreadful hurry, having forgotten to set alarms or having slept through wake-up calls pre-arranged at their hostels.

Others comfortably savored their time, looking at scenery, absorbing memories. Dawdling.

Gaston considered the travelers to be *his* scenery.

"Do you think we'll see many sales?" Mr. Arsenault asked, nervously sitting down on the bench next to Gaston, their legs accidentally touching. They both looked out onto the walkway instead of at each other.

Gaston reflected, "Well, there are eighteen scheduled launches this cycle. Factoring in various seating counts dependent on manufacturer, there is a potential for six to seven thousand passengers. Of those…"

Mr. Arsenault looked at Gaston and sighed. "I was just shooting the breeze, Gaston. You don't have to actually predict anything."

Gaston's smile dropped fractionally.

Mr. Arsenault rubbed his large hands against his knees and hesitated as if about to say something. Gaston waited, but was ungifted with whatever treasure was percolating inside the owner's head.

Over the roofs of the shoppes across the arc peeked an assortment of nosecones and fuselages, standing straight at attention.

"Those two look like M-class," Mr. Arsenault began.

"Actually M-Theta class…" Gaston interrupted, then drifted off when he caught the withering look of Mr. Arsenault out of the corner of his viz-screen.

Not for the first time, Gaston reminded himself to listen

more, and stop ending conversations before they began. "But it's true there is little difference to the naked eye," he offered as consolation.

Mr. Arsenault responded by pushing against his knees and levering himself off the bench. He walked to the counter deeper inside the shoppe.

He opened his private humidor underneath the counter and selected a slim perfecto, then added a small selection of other cigars to his breast pocket. He returned to stand next to the bench with a cutter and a tiny yet clever lighter.

Gaston gazed out onto the moving street. For a moment, he saw a river of blood flowing deep, as high as people's calves.

No. Not yet.

He closed his eyes and mentally turned a virtual switch in his head to shut off the image.

When he opened them again, he saw the orange light of Antares bathing everything in apricot. Even the exhaust streams of coiled smoke that pushed rockets away from the encumbering planet were stained in color. He relaxed.

The shadows shone a brilliant blue against the light, unlike the grey shadows of ancient Earth. It reminded Gaston of the Maxfield Parrish painting *Night Is Fled*. He repeatedly viewed the art nouveau image in his databanks. It was one of his favorites. No one living could have seen it so they could discuss its beauty together. That should have made him sad; instead he just felt empty.

Today was launch optimal: no capricious gusts, no predicted rainstorms, and limitless visibility. The complex gravitational interrelationship between red supergiant Antares and its companion blue dwarf Antares B made Curie Prime an ideal planet for a rocket port. It was one of many places in the galaxy where multiple wormholes could remain coherent.

A gaunt young man in an expensive suit stood still on the walkway, allowing it to move him past the shoppes as he gawked at the assorted items for sale. Mr. Arsenault waved his unlit cigar at him, holding it between his fingers as if it were already lit and he were already enjoying it.

"Say, is that a Delphian Ultra?" the man asked as he stepped off. The walkway continued on without him.

"No, it's a Badeaux. But the aroma is far superior to a Delphian, I promise you," Mr. Arsenault answered, using his fingers to pantomime waving nonexistent smoke to his nostrils.

Gaston noted the precise moment the man had made his decision to step off the walkway. He observed a slight change in expression, the tightening of irises and accelerated breathing. The number of neurons involved in creating one microsecond of differential choice was staggering, he observed. A human brain employed countless temporary synaptic configurations when making any decision. The afterimages of the resulting patterns remained as vestigial ghosts in the cerebral cortex.

"Great morning for a rocket trip," Gaston offered amiably, waving a metal-clad hand with articulated fingers.

The man paused at the edge of the shoppe and stared at Gaston. Mr. Arsenault recovered the incident quickly by extending the cigar to him.

"Do you know much about the Badeaux? No? Let me explain the source of its magnificent aroma. Harvested at the precise peak of maturity, the leaves are delicately aged over steam produced from slowly roasting silkworms. The essence of their secretions in death adds a tantalizing lift to the palate, which mixes deliciously with the tang of exotic Rigellian tobacco leaves," Mr. Arsenault said, imposing himself between the man and Gaston, redirecting the man's attention back to the product.

The owner continued to extol the virtues of the cigar with a hypnotic rhythm, like a seductive siren calling to a lost sailor. He finally paused, and the customer nearly fell forward, unaware he had been incrementally leaning in closer and closer, drifting along the stream of finely crafted words.

Gaston had experienced this spiel before, but he never tired of it. There was always a variation, a shading of a word here, an accent on a syllable there. He treasured hearing it.

Still, he discarded it from his memory for being too repetitious.

Mr. Arsenault used a small brass guillotine to remove the cap end of the perfecto. He activated a lighter and sensuously rolled the foot of the cigar over the tiny flame, lightly heating the tobacco inside. The man was mesmerized by the process.

The owner handed it gently to the customer as if it were a holy religious totem. The young man seemed afraid to take it for fear of dropping it.

"No, go ahead and place it in your mouth. That's it. Don't worry, it's just a free sample for a new customer."

Mr. Arsenault placed the lighter just beyond the end of the cigar and demonstrated how to draw in the flame, in case the man had no idea of the proper way to smoke a fine cigar.

Gaston was briefly fascinated by how the flame reshaped

itself in the random patterns of the man's breath. But it was close enough to previous observations that he decided to discard the image.

The customer closed his eyes in pleasure as the flavor of the smoke acquainted itself with his palate.

Then he pointed at the bench where Gaston sat. "Where did you get that?" he asked.

Like dogs and small children will, Gaston looked at the end of the man's finger, instead of where he was pointing.

Mr. Arsenault shrugged and said apologetically, "He came with the store. When I started the business, he was already here. I haven't the heart or the ability to remove him." Then he laughed lightly. "But weren't we just talking about cigars?" He glanced out of the corner of his eye to make sure Gaston was not upset.

Gaston had heard that chestnut of deflection so many times, he was no longer actually offended. Instead, he pretended not to notice and patted the space next to him on the bench. "Here's a comfortable place to sit and enjoy your cigar, Mr....?"

"Montreuil. Jean Montreuil." He hesitated briefly, then, with a nod to the store owner, he gingerly sat down next to Gaston. The owner strolled back to the counter, knowing that a customer enjoying a cigar was as good a billboard as one could have.

"Are you traveling today?" Gaston asked politely. He made sure to rotate in his most genial expression. He resisted the urge to lean in closer.

"Yes, I'm scheduled to arrive on Tau Ceti this evening. Or their evening. There is an arrangement of marriage waiting for me on the second planet." His expression turned to equal parts excitement and dread.

"Oh? Are you Neo-shintolic, then?" Gaston chose one of a handful of current religions that practiced arranged marriages.

"I personally am not very religious at all. But my bride-to-be's family is orthodox, and rather insistent upon custom."

Montreuil drew on the cigar and staged a minor celebration as he managed to puff a wobbling ring. It spun slowly until the integrity of the circle distorted and it dissipated in the air.

"Remarkable. Then you are graciously honoring her religion, as a gesture of political goodwill?" Gaston asked, hoping that this was a new cultural variant.

"Political?" Mr. Montreuil's eyebrows drew together as he posed the question to himself. After another exhalation of fragrant smoke, he answered. "Depends on how you define political. The dowry is sinfully large. The number of marriageable men on Tau Ceti is low. Some sort of mining mishap, or asteroid strike, I've been led to believe. My future father-in-law owns one of the more profitable mines," he said, being very transparent as to what the marriage would mean to his own fortunes as the eventual inheritor of the mine.

Gaston compared that information to actual data. The shortage of men at Montreuil's destination was exaggerated. The daughter was likely Gabrielle Trunduel, whose father was the owner of Trunduel Enterprises. Her image was markedly, almost painfully plain, judging by accepted human standards, and her father had not been completely honest with Mr. Montreuil. Instead, he had withheld information to achieve a desired outcome. An old strategy, but a new permutation, taking advantage of an interstellar knowledge deficit. Gaston decided to flag it and keep an eye on it.

Montreuil glanced at his chronometer and reluctantly got up, taking a few more rushed draws before he extinguished the cigar in the provided collector. He did arrange to carry a large box of the special cigars as a gift for his future father-in-law.

As he was leaving, Gaston stopped him. "You know, Mr. Montreuil..."

"Yes?"

"Wanting to be loved is not a crime."

"Meaning?" The young man canted his hip and stared at Gaston.

"Meaning, you will meet all sorts of people there. What they are is often not their fault. Pay attention instead to *who* they are. All life is precious. Let your first instinct be to show kindness."

The man screwed up his face to retort something angry, but the meaning of the message filtered through. He nodded in assent and stepped back onto the walkway, strolling quickly to add speed.

First checkmark of the day.

The owner opened the collector to retrieve the discarded cigar and proceeded to finish the remainder. No sense it going to waste.

He rubbed his hands nervously. "Why did you pick this bench, my store?" Mr. Arsenault wondered aloud. Gaston felt that that was just a small piece of the question he had really wanted to ask earlier, but had been afraid to. "Wouldn't you meet more people in a restaurant at the rocket hub itself?" His face was impassive, but his eyes glimmered as he awaited the answer.

"Are you wishing me to move on?" Gaston asked.

"No, no, that's not it at all." The owner waved his arms in frustration.

"Mr. Arsenault, this location, this very store, this precise bench. It's all the best sort of invitation to talk, to observe. A beautiful and relaxed pause in an otherwise hurried day," Gaston explained.

Only partially relieved, the owner agreed. "True. One should never rush a good cigar."

"Precisely."

* * *

Lunchtime. Or what passed for it in a place with a rocket port where travelers operated on circadian rhythms separated not just by time zones, but galactic neighborhoods. The 12:18 rocket to the Andromeda wormhole blasted off on time, rumbling the ground.

Gaston observed its gradual gain on escape velocity, the greased easing as it surpassed it, and the distant *thunk* it made as it slipped into the corresponding opening in space-time. There was a series of portals in synchronous orbit around the planet. Each had its own specific flavor of *thunk*.

Average people performed acts of great bravery, or foolhardiness, traveling in modes which stretched the boundaries of their understanding of the laws of physics. By any normal logic, wormholes shouldn't work at all. That didn't stop them.

A rush of passengers had just disembarked from an arriving rocket. One piece of the crowd, a family, paused to borrow part of the bench and allow their little girl a rest for her stubby legs. Walking, even on the treadway, appeared to be a chore for her labored lungs. The mother and father stood close by with another child, an adolescent boy. The girl appeared roughly eight Earth standard revolutions old. It was difficult to gauge exactly, because Gaston recognized the telltale signs of Down syndrome.

She climbed cheerfully up next to Gaston with no preamble at all, and stared directly at him for a long time, inspecting his mirrored visor, his metal limbs. She laughed, and her grin was an amazingly beautiful thing. Gaston knew already he was going to keep this memory.

"Who're you?" she asked with a slight lisp. She did not say, *What are you?*, which he appreciated.

He rotated projections to put on his most kindly face. "Gaston," he replied. "And who are *you*?"

"Chantal," she answered boldly, acting as if her family were not really there to rescue her at any moment from the strange thing at the other end of the bench.

But he could see through the bravado to her struggle with curiosity. She was burning to know. He altered the direction of the conversation before she could ask the inevitable and obvious question, the one that adults were usually too polite to bring up. Politeness, he knew, was a skill that took time to learn. Children almost never mastered it, but made up for it with increased adorableness.

"Let me ask *you* a question. Do you dream, Chantal?"

"Yes, of course, silly Gaston. Everybody dreams." She rolled her eyes and laughed. She didn't just laugh with her face. Her whole body was involved.

"Can you remember one to tell me? I collect them."

She held her finger to her lips in melodramatic fashion to let him know she was thinking. She bounced it off her lips a couple of times.

"A bear was chasing me around a tree." She formed her hands into claws and hunched up her shoulders to look formidable. "And I ran and ran until my feet turned into roller skates made of tumblebugs. Only they weren't really roller skates because they didn't roll but they lifted me off the ground until the bear passed right under me. He couldn't see me so he kept running until he disappeared far down the trail."

"I see. Was it a grizzly bear?"

"What's a grizzly bear?"

"Here," Gaston said as he lifted up the palm of his hand. The hologram projected a segmented ribbon containing photos of different kinds of bears as it rotated in a circle. He flicked at one picture and it enlarged in the center of the circle on a disc. "Is this the kind of bear it was?"

"No. The bear was fuzzy pink," she directed seriously.

A glowing line passed through the hologram of the grizzly bear from top to bottom. As it passed through, it turned the fur pink.

"Oh! And it had seven legs!" She nodded with certainty.

"Seven? Really? How did it walk?" Gaston laughed. "Okay. Three more legs coming up."

The image sprouted the improbable legs.

"And it had a golden dress on…" Chantal was trying very hard not to smile, but the corners of her mouth betrayed her, quirking up ever so slightly.

"Did it maybe also have butterfly wings?" Gaston asked oh-so-seriously in return.

"No, they were dragonfly wings. All shiny and see-through."

The hologram lifted up off Gaston's palm and hovered in flight. It winked at the little girl. Chantal clapped her hands with delight.

"Was this your dream bear?"

"No, not at all, but isn't this one much prettier?" she asked.

"Yes, it is, in fact," Gaston said, storing the memory of the image and especially the interchange with the girl.

"C'mon, Chantal, we have to catch a *rocket*," said her brother.

The girl flounced off the bench and waved backwards over the top of her head without really looking back. "G'bye, Gaston!" she squealed joyously.

"Wait, Chantal!" he called as he plugged in a carbon block to the matter printer. "Don't you want your doll?"

The little girl ran back, breathless. A few seconds later, the printer kicked out a cloth pink bear with dragonfly wings.

"Oooooh," Chantal said as she examined it from every angle.

"Okay, sweetie, thank the man…robot…thing," said her mother.

Gaston didn't bother correcting her.

* * *

Three bright million years ago,
a madman plied his vicious war
Drank darkened blood
from vanquished suns
Struck wide his iron-bladed fist
Swung dread and cruel
his strengthened arms
Planets, stars, and harried men
fled wormhole armies evermore

—Lamentations of the Purge, Tsu'ar Venadi

* * *

Dusk.

There was no real night. The gargantuan curve of Antares never quite left the horizon. It just dipped lower, diminishing its influence. Bluish shadows unfolded longer, turning more purple.

It was a time for easily mistaking one thing for another in the muddled play of light. Briefly Antares B, the companion star, could be seen hanging in the sky, the apparent size of a credit coin. Compared to the primary star it was faded and barely blue, like a reflection in a smudged window.

The Antares Cigar Shoppe did not close, not just yet. For now came the second tide, the neighboring shoppe owners. After they shuttered down their collapsing doors and twisted their keys into oversized locks, some carried their bags and satchels to the Cigar Shoppe for an evening smoke.

Gaston retained tiny recognition spaces in his mind for each of them. Some had families they were neglecting by staying. To them it was worth it; a man (or a woman, or a thing) sought ways to unwind at the end of the day. To chat, maybe drink from a concealed flask and share a fine cigar.

Mr. Arsenault and Gaston sat close together on the bench while the rest sat on scavenged boxes or crates or collapsible chairs they'd brought with them. Mrs. Plouffe preferred to stand, no matter how late into the night her visit went. She was a tough older woman with legs like tree trunks and a solid torso. She had probably been pretty in her day, and some of that still sifted through, especially if she laughed.

Mr. Arsenault made the rounds with cigars and lighters, always taking care of others before he came back to the bench. He kept in reserve a special smile for Gaston, and a sideways glance or two most nights. Tonight he still seemed bottled up, still wanting to address something between them, when and if they had some time alone.

But right now was the group, the 'club' they sometimes called it. Often they'd chatter and talk, raising their voices to be heard over each other, and sometimes they'd become tangled in awkward silence as a topic would falter, none of them knowing what topic to broach next or whose turn it was to jump in.

Sitting in groups like this, in the deepening dark of evenings, was something so utterly human that it had been unconsciously practiced on hundreds of worlds throughout the galaxy. An unintentional thread of connection that maybe only Gaston realized.

Perhaps those who were mortal clung jealously to every moment, understanding their fleeting nature which would wilt under the inexorable march of time and the heat of various suns.

"Let's play *Faux ou Vrai*—false or true, then," Mrs. Plouffe suggested after one of those awkward silences had stretched on a bit long. "I'll start. *Faux ou vrai*: I was once an exotic pole dancer, making money from tips."

This brought some laughter, which made her face redden. There were a few coughs and the rest quieted down.

Mr. Lemieux said, "I will say true. You do have smolder-ing...eyes."

But when they voted, most thought it was not true, *faux*.

"Well, which is it, Mrs. Plouffe?" pressed Mr. Navarre.

She pulled herself up straighter and patted her hair. "*Vrai*. True. When I was very young, with little money, I danced in a rocket port on Rimroude, the fourth planet in the XC117 system. I was the best earner," she laughed, "but I got out as soon as I could, and used my money to open up my shoppe."

The rest of the group applauded. Mr. Pascale even request-ed a demonstration, which earned him a slap on the arm.

They played the game, going around the circle, until it fell on Gaston.

"Wait. Does Gaston get to play?" Mr. Navarre objected. "I mean, can a robot lie, Mr. Arsenault?"

Mr. Arsenault shrugged and looked at Gaston, motioning for him to answer.

"Well, that's an interesting question. I could tell you that I never lie, which could be a lie, but you wouldn't be able to tell. Why not let me play, and you can find out?"

Everyone nodded, though Mr. Navarre just stared.

Gaston put his hands behind his head and turned a virtual switch in his mind that no one could see. "*Faux ou vrai:* Mr. Arsenault invented wormhole travel."

"What?" Mr. Arsenault leapt off the bench and turned to face Gaston.

"*Faux*, obviously," declared Mr. Navarre. "Well, I think we now know robots can lie, at least for the purpose of the game. I know you're pulling our leg. Wormholes are natural phenomena that occur when space folds in on itself. Everyone knows that."

That made Mr. Arsenault shake his head as he sat back down. He inched slightly away from Gaston, looking as if he'd been betrayed.

"*Faux,*" voted Mrs. Plouffe as well. The rest followed suit.

"I think I win the game," Gaston said. "Because it's *vrai*. True."

"I did *not* invent wormholes," Mr. Arsenault insisted.

Gaston moved his metal-clad arms. "No, of course not. But the person who invented them was also named Mr. Arsenault."

The merchants all glared at Gaston.

"Okay, this will take some time to explain."

The listeners shifted in their hodgepodge of seats.

Gaston leaned forward. "Many years ago, a boy was born, naked like any other, but there was one thing different. He couldn't die."

"What?" blurted Mr. Lemieux, nearly dropping his lit cigar in the sand, much to the amusement of everyone else.

"He didn't notice at first, until his family and friends grew older and sicker and fell away from him, while his stubborn heart beat on. In the era in which he was born, people were ignorant and superstitious. Was he a demon? they wondered. An angel? A vampire? He didn't know what he was, either. Suspicions festered, and there were no welcoming places for him. Some feared him, many hated him, because they didn't understand. They tried to take him apart to discover his secret. They attempted to kill him. Each time he suffered great torture and pain until he could make his escape. Over time, he grew smarter. He vowed to never be at someone else's mercy again.

"He trained in every discipline of war. He learned strategy and the use of power from the masters of each of his lifetimes. Machiavelli, Sun Tzu, Hitler…"

Mr. Navarre objected, "Who are these people? I've never heard of them."

"Their names have been lost for millions of years. They were iconic masters of war and programs of inflicted suffering."

In the haphazard circle, they looked warily at each other at the word 'suffering.'

"He became the greatest warlord his world had ever known. Or never wanted to know. But it was not enough. He wanted more. As science and weapon-making progressed, he kept up. He amassed wealth and power behind the scenes, choosing to exist in the shadows while his proxies proceeded under his explicit orchestration. What he didn't know, he obtained from those he coerced or enslaved. Eventually, his top scientist happened upon the technology to make wormholes."

"I assume his name was Arsenault," said Mr. Arsenault.

Gaston nodded.

It was now as night as it would ever be on Curie Prime.

Gaston pointed to the stars visible on the side of the canopy of sky not dominated by Antares. There weren't just a few stars visible, like there had been on old Earth. There were trillions and trillions, numbers larger than could be conceived.

"All those stars. The warlord coveted them. He hungered to own them. Time did not limit him. Once he had in place a wormhole network, his lackeys colonized or terraformed planets across the galaxy. It took centuries, until all known livable space was his to rule."

"I feel like there is a 'but' to this story," Mr. Lemieux noted.

"Yes," Gaston continued. "Even immortality is not perfect. It's been claimed that a human brain is only partially utilized, with a lot of growing space to take on new memories and thoughts."

"I've heard it's twenty percent," said Mrs. Plouffe, "although my husband uses a lot less than that."

Many in the circle laughed, knowing her husband.

"After a thousand years, the warlord ran into a wall. The brain is an amazing organ, but even an immortal one has a storage limit. His neurons and synaptic pathways had overwritten themselves too many times. His immortal ability to regenerate began to spontaneously reformat gray matter containing important information, gradually corrupting his mind's ability to remember and even function. He became insane," Gaston said.

"Wasn't he already insane? I mean, the desire to control everything?" asked Mr. Navarre.

"Yes, in a way. Once the situation became clear, he made his scientists devote all their attention to a solution. But they couldn't alter his cells to store more. Every experiment ended up with the cell replacing itself with a fresh, new cell. There is a theoretical maximum boundary of knowledge that can exist in a confinement the size of a human skull. A normal lifespan would never trip this boundary. But an immortal life would have to, at some point."

"So what happened?" asked Mr. Arsenault as he lit up a new cigar.

"The warlord developed uncontrollable brain injury. It was really brain renewal, of course, but his memories were being lost or scrambled at random. This resulted in increasingly erratic behavior and irrational rage. All the worlds he had built across the galaxy became targets for his bloodlust. There was a massive purge on planet after planet. His warriors feared him or were so misguidedly loyal that they followed his directives without question. Further, as best he could, he tightened his inner circle to prevent leaks about what was happening to him."

"But I don't remember reading about any purges," Mrs. Plouffe objected. Others in the group nodded along with her.

"How far back does the historical record go?" Gaston asked her.

"I don't know, maybe ten thousand years?" She glanced at the others present to get a confirmation.

"Sounds about right to me," said Mr. Lemieux.

"Well, these events occurred millions of years ago," Gaston explained.

"So this happened before written records?" Mr. Navarre asked.

Gaston bowed and rolled his shoulders apologetically. "*Vrai,*" he nearly whispered.

Mr. Lemieux looked around the group. "There is no way to verify or disprove it, then."

"I knew letting the robot play was a bad idea," added Mr. Navarre. "Anyone else want to keep playing? I don't."

The topic changed uncomfortably and the game was abandoned. No one wanted to cross Mr. Navarre. He had a habit of escalating disagreements.

The group eventually spoke the small talk of goodbyes, and gathered up their items to go to their homes or to the sleeping spaces above or behind or below their shoppes. Mr. Arsenault waited until it was only he and Gaston left behind, and rolled down the front gate. They both walked into the shoppe, then walked down to the apartment below the building.

As they were walking, Gaston flipped the virtual switch in his head.

Now. It is time.

He allowed the recording to overtake him.

The river of blood flowed deep, as high as a person's calf. The warlord stood in the street, his armor bathed in drying blood. This was one of the last planets with human life. Life seeded by him in centuries past. All he could think was, 'Why?' What was the point? On his orders the warriors had traveled the wormhole highways and helped him destroy life on planet after planet.

He vibrated in blind fury, in contempt and confusion. He couldn't concentrate on anything but death, and thirst for killing. There was a feral animal in his breast.

He saw red everywhere. It churned in him, the bile and the anger. It filled his mind until his eyes reacted and filmed over.

As he watched, a man wearing the uniform of his science di-

vision walked up to him and said words. Just words. He thought he should recognize the words, but he could not. The words had no meaning. He had forgotten words. He had lost the way of them.

The man bowed, and then rose up to caress him and kiss him gently on the cheek. At first, he pulled back in alarm. Then he did remember something. Scenes like this, being held like this, maybe by this same man. Kissed and even loved. And then those connected thoughts unraveled until he was left with nothing but breath and pressure.

The kissing man pulled something out of his uniform, said more words empty of meaning.

Something was jabbed into his neck.

His body, trained by centuries of fighting, reacted instinctively. The warlord let out a guttural and savage scream. Swifter than thought, his weapon sliced off the man's head. The body crumpled into the gore in the street. The head spun and landed at his feet. He watched it happen without comprehending.

Then he began to feel strange. Something opened a discreet window in his mind. A recorded voice in his head recited instructions, and on some level, his mind obeyed, even though he did not yet understand the words.

His mind opened. And opened again, like a piece of intricate origami unfolding. A great breeze traveled through him, cleansing and beautiful. His thoughts traveled beyond him, to a waiting repository of data. It was a comprehensive library of all recorded history, greater than the largest libraries ever constructed.

He touched the first file, and it rebooted his mind, overwriting the empty and jumbled cells with a robust template of streamlined understanding. At first, he was overjoyed to be able to think clearly.

The plans were there for the clever mechanism that had been implanted in him by the man at his feet. It explained that there was no more room inside the warlord's head, but a whole universe outside of it. The scientist had found a way to connect the warlord's brain to the matter of asteroids, planets, and nebula dust. He had designed a virtual wormhole that would work inside the warlord's head to store his memories outside the limited skull box that held his brain.

In the data repository he found a data trail about himself, through the words and the thoughts of others, in a million books and articles. Photographs of the mindless purge stared starkly back at him. Antiseptic data. No bias, only truth.

He UNDERSTOOD.

He wept, for he knew now that he had become insane.

He reached into the blood and lifted up the head of what he realized was his scientist, his lover, his savior. Lifeless, the face dripped blood from the off-center mustache that the warlord remembered loving once.

He collapsed to his knees, holding the head to his breast while his warriors looked on in bewilderment.

There were only a handful of survivors.

Would it be enough?

It must be.

It had to be.

Gaston stood watching Mr. Arsenault put things away in the apartment below the shoppe. He looked everywhere but at Gaston.

"What did you want to ask me today?"

Mr. Arsenault shrugged. His struggle played over his face.

"Why do you continue to sit here, day after day?"

"You already asked me that. I mean, what did you *really* want to ask?"

"Well, I mean… Why would you stay here with *me*? I'm just a cigar shoppe owner."

Gaston walked over to him and held the man's face in his articulated metal fingers. "No one is ever 'just' anything. If you haven't figured out by now why I stick around, I don't feel inclined to tell you. Except for this."

Gaston lifted the mirror visor from his face and kissed dear sweet Mr. Arsenault, with his off-center mustache. And he was kissed back, for quite a long time.

"Love is the only thing that becomes more valuable the more you remember it," Gaston said.

Gently, he reached behind Mr. Arsenault's neck and tapped a discrete button to shut him down for the night. With a twist, he removed the robot's head and held it to his chest and rocked.

"And I have a whole planet devoted just to remembering you," Gaston whispered, "and how you saved me, long ago."

The parts of Mr. Arsenault were lovingly packed away in a special box to recharge until tomorrow.

When he was done, Gaston removed the metal devices and plastics attached to his body. Where they had been embedded into his skin, he watched as his pierced flesh regenerated.

The dead cells fell to the floor and became dust.

No one asks why a robot doesn't age.

Gaston erased the unimportant memories of his day. Then, one by one, he shuttled the ones he wanted to treasure into the virtual wormhole leading to his backup, which for the last several decades had been a gas giant planet in the Europa cluster.

A WORD FROM
JOHN GREGORY HANCOCK

John Gregory Hancock has been a newspaper graphic designer for several decades. He's lived in so many cities and towns he's lost count.

His visual sense feeds into his writing. Often, his dreams fuel his imagination, becoming the touchpoint of his tales.

He is but a simple storyteller, in the grand human tradition of old men found spinning yarns at village campfires. His characters tell him what to say, and he chooses those tales he wants to repeat.

Like many of his characters, life has shaped and unshaped him.

He lives with his wife Jill (who puts up with him, beyond all logic) and a fantastically brilliant son, David (who whips him fairly soundly in video games).

They are hopelessly landlocked in Southwest Ohio, far away from either ocean or desert. Or glacier, come to that.

http://www.amazon.com/John-Gregory-Hancock/e/B00B8EC-QMW/

Rememorations
by Paul B. Kohler

THE SIGN on the door read *THE LAZARUS CENTER FOR EXTENDED LIVING* in brushed silver letters. Although it looked somewhat familiar, Nathan couldn't be entirely sure he was in the right place. He hesitated briefly before grasping the antique brass handle and walking into a richly decorated anteroom. Besides the newer snow-white carpet, the room looked like it hadn't been updated in centuries. The warm sensation of being surrounded by aged wood panel walls and antiquated leather-bound furniture was comforting, and he felt the twinkling of déjà vu course through him.

The sound of the door latching behind him made him jump. When he turned toward the sound, he found a woman sitting behind a desk, staring back at him. She smiled and nodded her head in greeting.

"It's good to see you again, Mr. Duncan," she said.

Nathan nodded, frantically sprinting through his memory for her name. He knew he'd met her before, when he'd first visited the center. *Has to be close to 70 years since I first walked into this place,* he thought.

"Yes. Good to see you…again." He paused. "I'm sorry, but for the life of me, I can't remember your name," Nathan said.

"That's quite alright, Mr. Duncan. I'm Nancy. I remember you from your initial enrollment back in 2065. I have your records right here," Nancy said. A holo-screen appeared in mid-air over her right shoulder, showing Nathan's profile and scrolling statistics.

"2065? Are you sure? That's what? Eighty-three years ago?" Nathan asked, his cheeks flushing with embarrassment.

"Yes, sir. It was mid-April, to be exact. I remember you were battling quite a case of hay fever at the time, and couldn't wait to join our organization. By the way, how are your allergies?"

Nathan thought for a moment. Allergies. He remembered having the ceaseless nose drip and the stuffy head that usually accompanied it, every spring, but it had been so long since he'd had to live with any of that.

"I…I haven't had a problem with allergies since…" He paused in an attempt to recall when he'd last suffered his annual hay fever.

"I'd guess that you haven't had the seasonal symptoms since you walked out that door all those years ago," Nancy said with a smile.

Nathan smiled again, wishing he'd not waited so long between visits. "Yes, I'm sure you're right."

Nancy stood and walked around her desk. As she approached, Nathan silently gasped at her beauty. She looked like she was in her 30s, slim and curvy in all the right places. Her shoulder-length auburn hair shone brightly, and her hazel eyes would pierce even the most skeptical customer's doubt. She might have been the best "equipped" saleswoman Nathan had seen in decades.

"If you'd like to follow me, Mr. Duncan. The doctor will be with you shortly." Nancy strode through another antique wooden door that led to a long corridor. Nathan happily followed.

Walking through the passageway was like stepping through time. Not into the past, however, but into the future. The walls were lined from floor to ceiling in stainless steel, and the ceiling was a solid sheet of light. He had trouble discerning whether there was actually something solid there, or just a luminous glow. The floor was a rubber textured surface that resembled concrete, but it cushioned each step, not unlike walking on firm, therapeutic foam.

Spaced every five meters along the corridor walls on either side were doors of opaque glass. As they passed each one, Nathan tried to peer inside. Shadowy silhouettes stirred inside each of the rooms. He had another bout of déjà vu as they approached the first solid door in the corridor.

Nancy tapped at a barely visible touchpad near the edge of the door and within seconds the door flickered from solid to clear, and then dissolved. "If you'd like to wait inside, the doctor will be with you shortly."

Nathan nodded and stepped past her and into the quaint waiting room. Once he was inside, Nancy tapped again at the panel. The opening in the doorway solidified to a faint teal color, but remained transparent. Nathan refocused on his surroundings and sat in one of two chairs positioned on opposite sides of a long table situated at the center of the room. An oddly shaped chair that closely resembled a bed sat near one of the corners. It looked remarkably comfortable. As he sat, memories leaked into his consciousness. He began to recall details of his initial trip to the center, and the personnel who had worked there. The face of the doctor, or administrator, rather, that he had first met with filled his mind. His face began to coalesce, and just as Nathan was about to pull his name from deep memory storage, the door disappeared. Nathan looked up as the exact same visage walked in.

"Ah, Mr. Duncan. It's very good to see you, although you are a few years overdue for your scheduled maintenance appointment."

Nathan nodded. "Yeah, kind of unavoidable. I was going through…let's just say I was dealing with some personal issues."

"Life does throw us curve balls from time to time," the doctor said as he reviewed information on an ocular plate resting on his brow. "And it looks like you've come in just in time."

"Did I cut it that close?" Nathan asked.

"I wouldn't say it was tight, but you are certainly overdue for your procedure. Tell me, Mr. Duncan. How are you feeling?"

"I feel good. I feel like a man in his mid-thirties, I guess? I try to exercise regularly—to maintain appearances, and to stave off my indulgences," Nathan said.

"Indulgences? Care to elaborate?"

"After my fourth wife passed, I...began drinking again. It's nothing I can't control, but it does help with the lonely nights."

"You say...again? Have you had previous bouts of drinking?" asked the doctor, reviewing the data in his readout.

Nathan bowed his head slightly. "Yeah, I had a bout, as you call it, after my second wife died."

The doctor scanned through the data until he found what he was looking for. "Ah, yes. The robbery. It was in...2099. Was it the loss of your wife the caused you to start drinking, or was it something to do with the crime?"

Nathan felt like he was being interrogated and instinctively threw up his guard. "It was nothing in particular, just a coping mechanism. Can you tell me that outliving most everyone in this world is easy for you?" Nathan snapped.

"Relax, Mr. Duncan. I'm not judging you. I'm just gathering information for your treatment," the doctor said. "Might I inquire about your multiple marriages? You mentioned you recently divorced your fourth wife."

"Yeah," Nathan began. "But it's nothing to worry about. You see, I'm afraid to be alone. So, I marry. I learned a long time ago that divorcing is so much easier on the soul than experiencing the death of someone you love."

Dr. Morrow nodded his head but remained silent.

Nathan leaned back and looked up at the glowing ceiling. The moments ticked away as the doctor typed at an invisible keyboard to record information. After several minutes of uncomfortable silence, the doctor spoke.

"How is your memory, Mr. Duncan?"

"I, uh. It's okay, I guess. I have trouble remembering things from time to time. Like, I know we've met, but I just can't remember your name," Nathan said.

The doctor nodded his head. "I expect so, Mr. Duncan. You are close to three years beyond your applicable rejuvenation appointment. I wouldn't expect anything less than significant memory loss. I'm Dr. Morrow. I was your administrator when you first came in, back in 2065."

"Dr. Morrow. I knew it! I had it on the tip of my tongue. I don't think my mind is going. It's just a little slow sometimes."

"Understandable," Dr. Morrow said as he entered more information. "Would you mind if we run a few tests before we proceed? I'll only need a small sample of your DNA."

"Yeah, sure. Do you think there's something wrong?" Nathan asked.

"Oh, no. It's nothing like that. We just want to analyze the nanite count in your DNA. We need to verify that the 24th pair of chromosomes is functioning properly. Now, if you could place your hand on the center of the table."

Nathan did so, and a moment later, he felt a sharp warming sensation in the palm of his hand.

"Okay, Mr. Duncan. If you'd like, you can relax on the chaise for a bit. These tests shouldn't take more than an hour," the doctor said before walking out.

As the door reformed into a new tangerine hue, Nathan glanced at the swooped chair in the corner and muttered, "Ah, what the hell." He eased himself into the chair and reclined. Staring up at the ceiling, he wondered where the lighting was coming from. The entire ceiling glowed evenly without a direct pinpoint source. Within moments, he drifted off to sleep.

* * *

As I walked into the office, an uncontrollable sneeze burst past my lips, and a fine mist of phlegm sprayed across the room. Embarrassed, I smiled nervously at the attractive receptionist. "Sorry about that, Ms....?"

"I'm Nancy. I understand the pollen count is above average this year."

"Pleased to meet you, Nancy," I said as I dabbed at the corners of my nose with a tissue before stuffing it into my pocket. "There must be something different. I can't seem to stop sneezing. It's only like this for a few months of the year. The rest of the time, I'm quite a normal guy." I winked.

Nancy returned my smile, and it appeared quite genuine. "Now, then, Mr. Duncan. Do you have any questions before we process your payment?"

I cleared my throat before answering. "As a matter of fact, I do. About the payment. Is the full amount due now, or can I spread it out over, say, a few installments?"

"I'm sorry, Mr. Duncan, but are you having trouble coming up with the agreed amount?" Nancy asked, concerned.

"No, it's not that. It's just that I was thinking of having my wife administered at the same time. You see, she's already a number of years older than me. Five, to be exact. And I know that if I go through with this procedure, my aging will cease, but hers won't. I'm sure you understand."

Nancy nodded at my predicament. "I do, Mr. Duncan, but the procedure must be paid for in advance. That's been our policy from the very beginning. If we gave you immortality on credit and you decided to default, we would have no way to…repossess what you've purchased. The procedure is irreversible." Nancy paused long enough for the information to register. "Perhaps in a few years, you can afford the credits. Then you can bring your wife in."

I bowed my head. "I, um. I don't think that'll be possible. I've already had to scrape up just about every credit we have just for this one procedure. By the time I squirrel away enough for her transition, she might have aged too far past her prime."

"Age becomes much less relevant once immortality comes into play. Have the two of you discussed this?"

I nodded. "In great depth, actually. I tried to have her go first, but she insisted that it be me."

"Perhaps, then, we could delay your treatment until a more appropriate time when you can afford both?"

"We've talked about that as well. My wife, Beverly, insists that I go through with the procedure today. I've tried talking to her about waiting a few years, but she won't hear of it." I shrugged my shoulders. "So, here I am."

Nancy listened intently to my explanation as she guided me to one of the multiple procedure rooms at the facility.

"Well, then, Mr. Duncan, it sounds like you have everything in order. If you'd like to have a seat," Nancy said as she motioned me into a room, "Dr. Morrow will be right in."

"It appears, Mr. Duncan, that your credit transfer has been completed. All that's left is your DNA signature before we can proceed."

Dr. Morrow motioned toward the palm scanner embedded into the tabletop. I placed my hand on the scanner, palm side down, and waited nervously.

"There's no need to worry, Mr. Duncan. This scan is quite similar to the one we used to prepare your serum. This final scan simply authorizes us to administer the 24th pair of chromosomes to your DNA sequence."

As the doctor explained, the scanner glowed red, turning to green as the palm of my hand increased in temperature.

The doctor then produced a thin vial from his breast pocket and held it out. "Last chance, Mr. Duncan."

I only hesitated for a moment before accepting the vial from him. "All I do is drink this and I'm good?"

"Yes, that's about it. We do, however, request that you remain on-site for the first thirty minutes."

"Why is that? In case something goes wrong?"

"Not exactly. There will be…unusual side effects that, how can I say this, may come as a surprise to you. But don't worry. They're all normal and non-invasive."

"Such as?" I asked. "I have to say, Doc, I think you could've told me this before I paid you 500,000 credits."

"No, no. It's nothing like that." Dr. Morrow chuckled. "It's just, well, you'll see. It's completely painless, just a little unsettling for some. For starters, your nasal drip will clear up almost instantly. There's typically some drowsiness and mild disorientation."

"So, a little sleepy and woozy. Well, then, the cost might be worth it, just for the relief alone," I joked as I removed the rubber stopper from the vial. "Here goes nothing," I said as I placed the edge of the vial to my lips and tilted my head back.

* * *

Dr. Morrow gently shook Nathan awake. "Mr. Duncan. Can you hear me? Mr. Duncan. We have your test results."

Nathan opened his eyes, and saw that the glow of the ceiling had dimmed considerably. He looked around the room, and remembered where he was.

"How—how long was I asleep?" he asked.

"Oh, about forty-five minutes. Did you have a relaxing dream?" asked the doctor.

"It really wasn't a dream, per se. It was more like…I don't know. Like I was reliving part of my past."

Dr. Morrow nodded knowingly. "Ah, yes. Which memory did you re-experience?"

"It was when we first met. It was the day I first came into the center. I know it was nearly a century ago, but it felt like it was yesterday. It was so clear."

"For all intents and purposes, it *was* yesterday, in your mind. You see, this chaise lounge is more than just a place to relax. It's what we've coined as the rememoration machine. We use it to summon lost or forgotten memories for our clientele."

"Did you intend for me to remember my initial visit?" Nathan asked.

"No, not specifically. That was by your own doing. Lying on the chaise is kind of like lucid dreaming, but within your own past realities." Dr. Morrow motioned for Nathan to come sit at the table.

"So, I could bring up any memory I want? What if it's something I've forgotten? How would I know to remember it?" Nathan asked as he sat across from the doctor.

"It gets a little complicated, but yes, you can mentally direct the device to retrieve even the most quarantined memory you possess." Dr. Morrow paused as he tapped away at his invisible keyboard. "Much of this discussion is a perfect segue into your test results."

Nathan leaned forward. "Which are?"

"Mr. Duncan, do you remember our discussion regarding the limitations of immortality? We discussed it in depth during your initiation seminar."

"I—I didn't get that far in the memory, but I still remember some of what was discussed. Why?"

"It has to do with your mind, and its ability to remember things. Or, more technically, to process stimuli. The human mind has limitations. It was never 'designed' to remember more than a hundred and fifty years or so of perpetual memories. At least not in our current biological understanding. Our brains may contain additional storage space, but we've yet to discover or tap that resource. When we discovered the secret to longer life, we had to adapt to that limitation."

"I think I follow. Isn't that what the 24th pair of chromosomes was supposed to take care of?" Nathan asked.

"Not quite. Those were integrated so that our bodies stop aging, or more specifically, our bodies can heal themselves. No more molecular degeneration. Your mind is a different animal altogether. Consider your old personal computer. Do you remember what happened when the hard drive got full of files and documents?"

"It's been a while since I've used one, but the computer would slow down," Nathan said.

"That's right. The overall performance would suffer until you deleted some files, and defragmented the hard drive. Our minds work in a similar fashion. After a century and a half of memories, we begin to respond or react much more slowly than normal."

"I think I get it. So, you want me to forget some things? Then why the chair? Doesn't it just make me remember the memories I've already forgotten?"

"Precisely. Your mind needs more than to just forget. Memories need to be removed completely. The rememoration machine will help you with that. In order for you to select which memories to remove, you will need to recall and decide which ones you no longer need."

Nathan leaned back and contemplated what the doctor was suggesting. "Just how many memories do I need to forget?"

"After closely reviewing your test results with my colleagues, we agree that you have two options. Both of which have their own merits and disadvantages." Dr. Morrow clasped his hands together and stared intently at Nathan.

"I, um. Okay, let me have it. What are they?"

"The first option is to go into your mind and selectively extricate thirty to fifty percent of your stored memories. This reduction will free up approximately forty to fifty years of continued memorization before the procedure needs to be repeated. The overall procedure will take approximately eighteen hours, spread over six visits to the lab."

"Fifty percent of my memories just gone? Will I even remember who I am?" Nathan asked. "And how will you know which memories to eliminate?"

"Fifty percent is only an estimate. Some memories are obviously more extensive than others, and may free up extra space. Your core memories will remain intact. You will still be Nathan Duncan." Dr. Morrow paused to moisten his lips. "As for which memories we eliminate, that is completely up to you. That's why it takes such an extended period of time. You will have to recall individual memories during each session, and then choose whether to keep or remove the memory. Unfortunately, the procedure can become quite emotional."

"And the second option? The first one doesn't sound terribly appealing."

Dr. Morrow smiled politely. "Option two is much more straightforward. Consider again the antiquated computer hard drive. With option one, you would in essence be selecting individual files to be deleted. With option two, you will be deleting an entire file directory."

"Like deleting an entire year?" Nathan asked.

"Sort of. With option two, we would go in and delete the memory of a single individual from your mind. In doing so, all memories associated with that person would also be lost. Option two is a much simpler task, and it can be performed in a single session which takes about an hour."

"It sounds like option two makes the most sense all around. It's easier, it's faster. What are the consequences?"

Dr. Morrow's smile faded. "There really is only one unfavorable outcome. There is no way to determine just how your life will change by removing all memories associated with any one person. Results are dependent on who the person was that is being removed. There's no way to determine the cumulative effect because our clients can't remember what they technically never experienced."

Nathan nodded. "And how long before I'll need another procedure if I choose option two?"

"We've seen results in the neighborhood of seventy to

eighty years." Dr. Morrow leaned forward. "There is one more thing to think about. The cost."

"Cost? It's not covered by my original initiation fee?"

"I'm sorry, Mr. Duncan, but no. Maintenance procedures are extra. It was covered in your commencement seminar and initiation contract."

"Well, how much, then?" Nathan demanded.

"Option one will cost you 300,000 credits, while option two will cost you 75,000 credits."

"Are you kidding? That's nearly the same amount I paid to get into this exclusive club in the first place."

"Like I said, Mr. Duncan. It's an intense procedure."

Nathan bolted from his chair. He stood hovering over Dr. Morrow, pulse quickening as beads of sweat rose to the surface of his forehead. "Here's what I think. I think you sold me an illusion of immortality, where you promised me that I could live forever, and now you're telling me I actually cannot without spending more credits."

"In essence, Mr. Duncan, you are right on both accounts," Dr. Morrow began. "Yes, you will continue to live, potentially forever. However, if you want to live a happy and coherent life, it will cost you. If you choose not to have either of these two procedures done, your life will continue as it has, but your memory and mental acuity will continue to slow, sometimes faltering. We are, however, continually working on groundbreaking research which utilizes an advanced form of nanotechnology that will hopefully expand the memory capacity of the human mind. Unfortunately, the technology is complicated and is still quite a distance away from completion."

"How far away are we talking?" Nathan asked.

"Unfortunately, I'm not at liberty to discuss our current research status. But I assure you that we're making every effort to bring this solution to our clientele as soon as possible."

Still standing, Nathan leaned against the cold metal wall as he digested this massive wrinkle. After several minutes of silence, Dr. Morrow spoke.

"Mr. Duncan," he began.

"Call me Nathan."

"Alright. Nathan, please understand you don't have to make this decision right now. If you like, you could go home and think through the options that I've presented. If you come back in a day or two, or even a week, no severe memory issues will occur."

Nathan nodded his head, but didn't say a word. He continued to lean against the wall in stoic contemplation.

"Nathan?"

"I, um. If you don't mind, could I have another go at your rememoration machine?" Nathan asked as he nodded toward the chaise lounge in the corner. "Maybe if I could cycle through some past memories, it might help me decide."

Dr. Morrow smiled. "Absolutely, Nathan. Really, that's what it's there for. My only suggestion is that you start with an early memory, and cycle through as many as you can get through without dwelling on any single point for too long."

"How do I do that?"

"Imagine that you are remembering your first visit here again. When you feel that you've re-experienced as much as you need, just think the words *fast-forward* and the rememoration machine will advance you and your memory ahead. It's a little tricky to get used to, but once you get the hang of it, you'll be able to slide through many years of your life in a matter of minutes."

"Sounds easy enough. How much time can I have?" Nathan asked.

"Take as much time as you need, but I imagine that you will need only a limited amount of time before your decision is clear."

"What makes you say that?"

"Experience, mainly. Also, you are in your first generation of immortality. Once you get the hang of controlling the pace of your memories, you'll be able to fly through your life before you know it," Dr. Morrow said as he stepped out into the corridor.

Nathan stared at the reappeared door for a minute before he settled into the lounge chair. As he lay back, he tried to recap all the information that he'd just received, but within moments, sleep had swallowed him whole.

* * *

A peculiar haze obscured my vision, but I could hear voices— or a single voice, rather, in the distance. As I focused on the words being spoken, I began to understand. The voice was mine. I was at Beverly's memorial. I was delivering her eulogy, and the room was silent.

"...Beverly was the love of my life, and I, like many of you, am lost without her. She was the most giving, the most caring person

I've ever known. She made many sacrifices to better the lives of those around her.

"One of her particular gifts was such a selfless act, she saved me in more ways than I can truly say. She gave me a long life, and she was the reason for me to live. Then, shortly after this amazing act of kindness, she was diagnosed with a virulent disease. She vowed to fight for her life, but she only lived a short six months after her diagnosis of MDS, and four of those were spent bedridden in the hospital. She continued her fight after undergoing a bone marrow transplant and contracting a lung infection. I stayed with her, sleeping in the same room, until a few months ago, when Beverly was admitted to the ICU with pneumonia. She was unconscious for almost the entire time. I held her hand often and stroked her hair. I massaged her legs and feet, and talked to her. I told her that I loved her every hour of every day. The cruelest part of her ordeal was that she was so close to me, but couldn't say a word. Just a few weeks before, she had been talking with me and the nurses, planning some spring activities, and dreaming of her future. Then last Friday, her heart stopped for the first time. By Sunday, it was clear that she would not recover. On Monday I held and kissed her hand for the last time.

"I forever want her near me. To feel her arms wrapped around me, squeezing me—feeling her cheek pressed against mine. To say: Bev, I love you. My life is complete with you by my side. My beloved, I will miss you forever and can't wait for the day when we can be together—to hold each other and share our love again.

"Beverly has gone into the light and is now free..."

fast-forward

As I wandered aimlessly along the city sidewalks, the soles of my feet were nearly frozen by the rain. People would see me and cross to the other side of the street, avoiding contact. It had been months since I had spoken with anyone directly. My beard had grown in, scraggly and unkempt. The standard string of condolences had filtered through, but I didn't respond to any of them. All I wanted was my wife back—my old life back. Now, all I could do was wait for eternity and its punishment of self-pity and suffering.

A car slipped along the road, its tires carving through the standing puddles in its path. As it neared, it swerved in an attempt to avoid drenching me, but it was too late. I saw it coming and did nothing to avoid it. Seemingly in slow motion, I watched the driver as he passed and a look of concern was clearly present on his face. Now soaked, I turned at the next corner and headed for Homer Bridge.

As I ascended the steep incline, I felt invigorated for the first time since Beverly left this world. It wouldn't be much longer before I could be with her again.

Despite the late hour, the traffic on the bridge was heavy. Several times, cars swerved into oncoming traffic to avoid hitting me. Those drivers didn't know that they needn't have worried, because it would have saved me the long climb to the top.

As I crested the approach ramp, I saw a break in the traffic. After the next truck passed, I would be clear to take my final steps back to Beverly. I wiped the moisture from my eyes—a mix of tears and fallen rain. I stepped up to the protective railing and looked out across Cadre River and wondered…

fast-forward

Staccato beeps cut through the black. The room was dark, and I was lying down. Beep, beep. Beep, beep.

I blinked away the darkness, only to have it replaced with blurred light from all directions. I leaned my head from side to side, but still couldn't focus. The pain that was present was strong, but bearable. I tried to raise my hand and scratch the side of my nose, but my arm was lashed tightly to my chest. I tried to raise my other hand, but it was also incapacitated. The itch—it was driving me crazy. I forced my head hard to the right and rubbed my nose against the pillow beneath my head. As I did, the tubes running into my nostrils dislodged and the beeping was now accompanied by a hissing sound. Beep, beep—hiss.

"Hello there, sleepyhead," came a voice from my left. The voice was female, soft and comforting.

I whipped my head toward the source, but the plaster covering my left shoulder prevented me from looking in that direction.

"Take it easy, mister. You're okay now. You're going to be up and about before you know it," she said.

"Mpah id ghapgn?" I tried to speak, but the thick tube stuck down my throat prevented it.

A warm hand soothed my forearm. "Shh, shh. Just relax. The tracheal tube is in place because you had a collapsed lung. You couldn't breathe on your own for several days. The doctor thinks we can remove it later today, though, so that's good news."

I blinked rapidly and with each beat of my eyelids, the blur began to subside. I looked down at myself and noticed that my body was covered in plaster, from the tips of my toes all the way up to my left shoulder.

"I have to say, you are one lucky man. If that boat hadn't spot-

ted you as you fell, you very well might have frozen to death. But here you are, and your prognosis is quite remarkable. I've never seen a person heal as quickly as you have. You truly are a special individual," the woman said as she slid the oxygen tubes back into my nose. "I'm Nurse Sadusky, but you can call me Addison." She smiled. "That is, if you could speak. And at your rate, that won't be too far off."

fast-forward

"I can't. Just let it go, would ya!" I screamed.

"No, I won't! Nathan, how long have we been at this? Twelve months? Look how far you've come. The doctor told you that you might never walk again, and last week, you took your first steps. So what if we helped? That's a tremendous achievement. I think you've got this. Now get your pansy ass up and try again," Addison demanded.

"Can't I just rest for a bit? I'm so tired," I cried, and rolled away from the nurse who had been with me every step of the way.

"Okay, I'll give you five minutes," she agreed. "But after that, I want to see you pull yourself up on those bars and give me five steps."

"Five? I only took one last week. I'll give you two, and you'll be happy with it," I said, hoping my stern attitude would relieve her persistence, even just a little bit.

"Only two steps? What do you think this is, some kind of country dance class? I need four from you and then we'll call it a day." Addison stared deep into my eyes, and I could see that she was easing her drill sergeant stance with every obstacle I threw up.

"How about we meet in the middle? I'll push for three steps

and then I'll let you give me a sponge bath," I said, trying to turn on the charm.

"You think me giving you a sponge bath is my reward for helping you walk again?" she asked as she sidled up to me and begin to lift me back to the rails. "I think you owe me much more for everything that I've had to endure since..." She broke off.

Addison pulled me up and placed my hands on the rails. Before she could back away from me, I leaned in and gently kissed her cheek.

"Hey, mister. There'll be none of that on my watch."

"Well, when does your watch end?" I said just inches from her lips.

"When I can get you to walk, unassisted. That's when." She smiled.

I knew right then that I would walk again. She was the driving force behind it all.

"Now, move!" she demanded.

fast-forward

"I now pronounce you husband and wife. You may kiss your bride," proclaimed the minister.

I lifted Addison's veil and kissed her passionately in front of several hundred of our closest friends. Then we turned and walked effortlessly down the aisle.

"I love you, Addi. If it weren't for you, I wouldn't be here right now, and walking gracefully, to boot," I said.

"And I love you, babe. You've also saved me, in so many ways," she replied.

As we walked past our guests, I wondered if marrying again was the smart thing to do…or just the right thing to do right now.

fast-forward

I paced anxiously outside the bathroom door. The sound coming from the other side of the door was stomach-turning.

"Are you going to be alright in there?" I asked. I knew the answer before she said it.

"I'mm gon' be fiiiine, babby. Why doncha go and warm up the sheets an' I'll be right out," Addison slurred—from the bathroom floor, no doubt.

I grabbed my pillow and walked toward the hall. As I passed the bathroom, I paused. "Listen, I think you need some rest. I'm going to sleep downstairs tonight. We can talk about this in the morning." Then I waited.

I could hear her spit into the toilet before she responded. "But, baaaby, I wan' you tooooniiight." And then, more grotesque splashing into the toilet.

fast-forward

"Happy anniversary, babe. Let's toast to eight exciting years. And then let's do shots for eight more," Addison stammered, obviously having already consumed a few too many flutes of champagne for the evening.

"It's been an exciting eight years, that's for sure," I said, not sure how to cut Addi off without inciting another incident. "Let's finish the bottle now, and then move the rest of the celebration home," I suggested, hoping to placate her indulgences.

"Oh, please, Daddy. Can't we stay out late just once?" she cooed. "I promise to be a good girl, Daddy."

I smiled on the surface, but deep inside, I worried for her. She'd promised me, yet again, just last month that she had her drinking under control. Yet here we were, on the precipice of an uncontrollable situation.

fast-forward

"I want to thank you, asshole, for supporting me like you have," Addison spat.

"Do you have to constantly belittle me like that? It's not my fault that you lost your job. One would think that showing up to the hospital drunk would be a career-limiting move," I replied, feeling no remorse.

"Well, to hell with you. You were right there drinking with me, or did you forget?"

"I remember. I also remember telling you that you'd had too much, and that you can't control yourself. Many times."

Addison stomped into the kitchen. I'd known this argument would come eventually, and after 15 years of marriage, I was constantly looking for the right time to get out. Unfortunately, Addi was always one step ahead of me, knowing that I would delay asking for a divorce if she was unable to support herself.

Soon. It had to be soon.

fast-forward

After 18 years, 18 very difficult years, I knew tonight was the night that I would end it. My agelessness could no longer take her disregard for life. She failed to understand just how precious every moment was. She'd been aware of my condition for several years now, and seemed to despise me because of it. She somehow expected me to swoop in and treat her to immortality as well, but I couldn't bring myself to do it. Her total disregard for anyone but herself would make her an ugly immortalitarian. No, tonight, after dinner, I was going to ask for a divorce.

"Where are we going tonight?" Addison asked. "I hope someplace good. I'm starved!"

"I was thinking that we'd walk into midtown and try that Cuban place," I said.

"Ooh. That sounds divine." She slid her arm into mine. "Honey, can we talk about something?"

"Sure. What's on your mind?"

"I know the last few years have been rough, and I'm going to make a change," she said.

I continued to stare ahead as we walked. I'd known she would try to woo me into another trap. "What kind of change?" I asked, not sure that I wanted to hear her latest excuse.

"Today, I stopped by the AA office and signed up. I know my drinking has been hard on both of us, and I feel that I can really stick with this, if you'll still have me."

Shit. Now what was I going to do? I couldn't very well ask for a divorce now. And she, no doubt, knew that. Was I so transparent?

As we continued to walk along the dark streets of midtown, my mind was completely focused on what I was going to do. I failed to notice the shadowy figure come up behind us until it was too late.

"You two, stop right there! Don't turn around or I'll shoot. I have a gun."

Instinctively, I turned to the stranger behind us. He did in fact have a gun, and it was pointed right at my face.

"I said, don't turn around! Now give me all your money. And while you're at it, give me all your jewelry," the robber demanded.

I slowly pulled my wallet from my pocket and motioned for Addison to do the same. She shook her head, almost unnoticeably.

NO! my eyes screamed at her, but it was too late.

"I am not going to give you anything, sweetie, and you know why? Because my husband here—he can't be killed. He's immortal, so it doesn't matter what you do to him."

"Don't listen to her," I begged. "Here. Take my wallet, and here's my watch. It's a Tag."

"So, he's immortal, huh? What about you?" he asked Addison, now pointing the pistol at her.

"Here! I have your money," I said, nearly shoving my wallet in his face.

He snatched the wallet out of my hand and stuck it in his coat pocket. "Thanks. Now, I also want what Miss Smartass has, and it ain't the money anymore," he said, looking Addi up and down.

Addison tried to step behind me, but the robber grabbed her, nearly missing her arm. His grip couldn't hold as she yanked away. As she began to run, the report from his gun nearly deafened me and I watched Addison drop to the ground, blood quickly soaking her blouse.

"No!" I screamed as I bolted up from the rememoration machine.

* * *

"How long will the procedure take?" Nathan asked.

THE IMMORTALITY CHRONICLES

"Well, that's a relatively difficult question to answer," replied the doctor. "There are several factors that need to be considered. If the memories of your second wife are extensive, it could take upwards of a few hours. If the memories are shallow and lack connection to your overall personality and your life, it could be less than an hour. Don't worry, you'll be asleep the whole time. When you wake, your mind should be as fresh as it was in 2065, and you'll be active and alert for at least another 75 years."

Nathan nodded as a look of concern crossed his brow. "Am I making the right decision, Doc?"

"This decision isn't an easy one to make. I can't influence you one way or another. It's completely up to you. There is really no wrong decision here. Only the right decision for you. If you'd like, we can reschedule this for another day, but I would not suggest that."

"No, no. I think I'm making the right choice. Let's do this before I change my mind."

"Alright, Mr. Duncan, drink this vial, then lean back and relax. The next time we meet, you'll be a new man. Again."

Nathan did as directed. After consuming the flavorless serum, he leaned back on the chaise and was asleep within minutes.

* * *

Nathan began to stir, first opening one eye and then the other. He felt completely relaxed and fully rested. As his eyes adjusted to the dimmed light, he noticed that his mind felt clear.

Using the controls at the side of the rememoration machine, Nathan tilted the backrest to an upright position before he attempted to swing his feet to the floor. Unfortunately, his legs remained stationary. He tried again, but quickly realized that he had no muscular control from the waist down. Refusing to give up, he used both hands to lift his right leg from the surface of the chair and swung it out. The momentum of the dead weight dropping to the ground pulled the rest of his body with it. He flailed his arms, trying to break his fall, but it was no use.

His body smacked the floor like a baseball bat slapping a side of beef. Mere seconds later, the door vanished and in walked Dr. Morrow.

"Nathan! Are you all right?" he said, rushing to Nathan's side.

"I, uh, seem to have lost the ability to use my legs. Is this a typical reaction to the procedure?"

Dr. Morrow helped Nathan back into the lounge chair. "Unfortunately, no. Everything is quite in order."

"How is losing the ability to move my legs normal?"

"As promised, Nathan. You are as fit as a man in his mid-30s, just as you were before the procedure. The only difference now is that your ability to store information has been drastically improved by the removal of Addison from your memory."

"Who is Addison?"

"Nathan, I cannot in good conscience tell you who Addison was, because she was just removed from your mind."

Nathan continued to poke and prod at his lifeless legs before leaning back in disgust. "Okay, I get that. But why can't I move my legs?"

Dr. Morrow bobbed his head slowly. "By removing Addison, all of your memories associated with her were also eliminated."

"Again, I'll ask. Why can't I move my legs?" Nathan said, frustration beginning to surface in his tone.

Dr. Morrow pulled a chair next to the rememoration machine and sat down. "Nathan, how many times have you been married?"

"Three."

"Do you remember Beverly?"

Nathan closed his eyes, drawing the image of his first wife in his mind. "I do. She died in 2080."

"And do you remember what happened after that? Take your time."

"Of course I do. I jumped off a bridge. I tried to kill myself," Nathan said, tears beginning to leak from the corners of his eyes.

"And how about right after that? What do you recall?"

"I, um. I...I can't remember a whole lot," he said, wiping his eyes dry.

"You see, after your suicide attempt, you had to learn to walk all over again. Addison was heavily involved with that process. By removing her from your mind, you inadvertently removed those muscle memories. Unfortunately, until the procedure was complete, we had no idea..."

Nathan listened to Dr. Morrow's words, but his vision began to tilt from side to side as the effects of the information ebbed into his consciousness. Beads of sweat broke out across his forehead, and dizziness tugged at his equilibrium.

"I don't understand. What are you telling me?"

"Nathan, you are a paraplegic."

A WORD FROM
PAUL B. KOHLER

When I first heard about The Immortality Chronicles, I knew instantly that I wanted to be included. I would have loved to write a story that could fit into the topic of eternal life. Visions of distant future worlds filled my mind. After actually being confirmed as one of the selected authors, the sweating began. Having read many of the previous Future Chronicles editions, I felt a little out of my league as there have been some pretty phenomenal writers included. And here I was - a relatively green newcomer to the world of sci-fi. I asked myself: Self? Can you do this? You know you can't phone it in. You're going to have to really write something here.

So, the planning began, and the panic closely followed. With each now story concept I came up with, the less I felt myself as a real writer. I would brainstorm on any one of the myriad of ideas, just to shoot them down inside of ten minutes. What I quickly realized was that I hated the thought of Immortality. Each time I tried to figure out something cool and sleek about the ability, I swiftly discovered how much hell my life would be like to live beyond everyone I know and love.

After umpteen attempts at a happy story in the Immortality theme, I turned my views slightly and started looking at the negative aspects. I wasn't at all surprised that I had even more ideas come rushing in than I did when I was trying to write a happy/fuzzy story. And with each new story idea, the brainstorming sessions become much longer, with far more intriguing aspects to Immortality. So much so that I had a pretty difficult time narrowing my story choice down to the one that you just read. Before I started writing "Rememorations", I had five extremely viable story concepts to choose from. Part of me contemplated pulling out of the anthology all together so that I could write all of them for my own Immortality story book. It was that difficult. But, after narrowing down the list to the most intriguing concept, I knew I had the right story.

And so, "Rememorations" began. I wrote the first draft in one sitting - something that I have never done before. After that first draft was out, I let it sit a week or two - fermenting. When I picked it up and reread it, I knew it had lots of potential, but I wanted to hear from others before I took the scalpel to it. The first reader for all my stories, my wife, read it and thought it was great as it was. She's so kind, but I knew that it still needed work. After a few rewrites, I tossed it to the first editor - my best friend, Kyle. He did his magic, and I knew it was close. I gave it a few more passes before giving the entire second half of the story a haircut. I ended up shaving nearly 1,000 words from the story, and it made all the difference.

That is the story about the story that you just read. I hope you enjoyed it, and would consider reading some of my other work.

You can see all of my books, as well as blog and twitter links on my Author page at Amazon. The link is *http://www.amazon.com/author/paulkohler*

The Scout
by D. Robert Pease

I'D BEEN KILLED a hundred times, and I wished just once it'd stick. Perhaps tonight was the night.

Across the millennia and thousands of worlds, I'd finally been found. Hunted down and cornered on this godforsaken world at the edge of a godforsaken galaxy far from a home I knew I'd never see again.

"You want another?"

I glanced up to see the bartender standing over me, a bottle tipped toward my glass.

"Probably shouldn't."

"Ah, why not? You look like you could use another."

I shook my head.

"Just as well. You couldn't handle it anyway." The chrome-skinned bartender gave me a sly smile.

I chuckled at the robot and sighed. "Go ahead." Someone

had done an amazing job on this guy's AI. Either that, or I didn't want to leave and face whatever was out there in the dark alleys of New York.

The robot poured me the drink, then moved on to his next customer. The bar was half-full of guys like me, who most likely didn't have anyone to go home to—or at least, anyone they cared to go home to. Here we all sat, in a crowd, but all alone. I glanced back at the bartender. Of course I probably had more in common with the circuits and processors that made up this robot than I did the flesh and blood men who sat around trying to quiet the screams in their heads of the billions of creatures they'd massacred all over the universe... Okay, maybe that last bit was just me.

"I've seen you in here before, haven't I?"

A slender man whose skin hung loose on his bones like his worn suit jacket nodded toward me.

I just nodded back, not in the mood for chitchat.

He slid over a couple of bar stools anyway. "Hard to believe, isn't it?"

"What's that?"

He bobbed his head toward the room. "This is what it's come to."

I grunted, not enjoying the intrusion into my dark thoughts.

"Humanity pulls itself out of the slime, builds what folks a few hundred years ago would have thought to be a utopian society, and yet here we are, doing the same thing guys have done for centuries."

"Annoying those who want to be left alone?"

"Exactly." He cupped his beer with calloused hands, staring

into the amber light bouncing through the dirty glass. "Why do we feel so alone?"

I nodded grimly. It never ceased to amaze me how these creatures, whose entire existence was merely a blink of an eye compared to my own, would feel just as keenly the pointlessness of life.

"Do you ever wonder if there's something more?"

How much had this guy had to drink tonight?

"I mean, my mother used to talk about heaven, like that's where we truly belong. Maybe..." His gaze drifted off as he whispered, "Maybe she was on to something."

"Listen." I set my glass down on the bar. "I've seen more than you can imagine. Lived longer than you'd guess, and I can tell you there isn't anything more. The sooner you deal with that idea, the sooner you can find some kind of meaning in *this* life."

His soft smile, which had appeared at the memory of his mother, faded. "Yeah, I suppose you're right." He grew quiet and went back to staring into his beer.

I hated this planet with all its contradictions—all its false hope for a future that would never be. Why were these stupid humans so hopeful and so depressed all at the same time?

In the end, it didn't matter. I had a job to do. And somewhere, perhaps in this very bar, was a creature whose sole purpose was to see me fail. I sensed a dull resonance that could only be Hunter—like a ping off a wireless transponder—but I couldn't gauge distance or location. He could be anyone, or anything, and when he found me he would take pleasure in ripping me limb from limb.

It was the same on every planet. Sometimes Hunter found me and killed me in the most unpleasant ways. Sometimes I failed to deliver to Master a world worthy of her conquest, and she did even *more* unpleasant things to me. But every once in a while, I succeeded. I helped mold some despicable creatures into an army whose might nearly matched that of the Muradine. During those rare occasions I'd given Master an opportunity to achieve the highest acclaim back on our home world. Each time she'd promised me the next success would be my last, and she'd give me my greatest desire: a permanent death.

Earth held more promise than any other world I'd scouted, but first I had to crack the puzzle that was humanity. This crazy race seemed to defy all that was proper and all that should be in a universe that, to the unskilled eye, seemed without order. But within the disorder I'd discovered a pattern—a natural progression all life seemed to follow. Not here. Not on this watery world. No matter how I labored, applying the knowledge I'd gleaned over millennia, men would not be molded into the worthy opponents I knew they were so capable of being.

Something in their flesh resisted.

Understand this: mankind was nearly as accomplished at doling out death as any species I'd discovered. Their minds raged with turmoil. The history of this planet they called Earth was filled with war after war. But always they stopped short. Always they held back. I was running out of time to discover why.

My partner in misery didn't notice when I stood. Any joy he'd hoped to find in this life was draining onto the sticky floor beneath his stool.

I had that affect on people.

One last glance at the patrons in the bar revealed no signs of Hunter. I pulled up my collar and headed for the door.

Outside, the air was cool. A wisp of cloud between the skyscrapers passed over the nearly full moon. How I hated this planet, with its lonely cratered moon—nothing like home. Nothing like the immense sphere that unraveled around me, no matter where I stood on its inner surface, with its star, much warmer than this one, always gleaming in the same place overhead. Never dark. Never cold.

Sometimes I worried I'd lose that memory, but like everything else I'd experienced in my blasted unending life, it was burned into digital storage, never to be erased, never letting me live in peace. I shook my head. It was going to be one of those nights.

Pulling my coat tight around me, I dialed up my light sensors and headed down the street. Not that I'd be able to see Hunter. Not until it was too late, at least.

Even at this late hour the streets were teeming with people, both living and robotic. Bright lights flashed, displaying every kind of entertainment possible. In a world where folks hardly needed to work—where robot-kind did all the manufacturing, cooking, cleaning and every other labor that required lifting a finger—mankind had a whole bunch of free time. Instead of figuring out better and more efficient ways to kill each other, they spent their time involved in anything that took their minds off the meaninglessness of it all. This was where I'd failed. This was where *she* would find me guilty.

The hair on the back of my neck stood on end and I glanced over my shoulder, sure Hunter would be there. I wasn't sure who'd sent him, only that he'd come. If Master had sent him because she already knew of my failure, then Hunter would wait for a moment that was just right to cause me the most pain. If it were some other member of the Muradine, then a blessed death could follow. Of course, I hoped for the latter, but it was always the former. Master didn't give her subjects a long leash. She had to know I'd failed.

Picking up my pace, I headed for Central Park. If Hunter tracked me now, there was only one place I'd be safe.

* * *

Like mankind, I had a proclivity for places of solitude— places that resembled the way things had once been. It hadn't taken much influence on my part to have the land set aside for a park all those hundreds of years ago, a place for me to recharge—literally. Even as I entered the well-lit paths between centuries-old trees, I felt the energy of the cosmos surging through my limbs. The ground all around me hummed, giving me strength.

The moonlight glinted off the reservoir in the middle of the park, highlighting the surface as it began to vibrate. Droplets of water separated from the lake and streamed toward me. I basked while the liquid power poured over and through me. The few people nearby slowed for a moment, then went on as if they hadn't seen anything unusual. Thus was the strength of my glamour—or the weakness of their minds.

Time stilled until it was just the deep, cool water and me. The lake churned and was thrown back as I stepped into its depths. Geysers thundered twenty feet into the air. I walked until the surface of the lake was over my head. The churning cauldron above collapsed, smothering me in its cold embrace. Time continued on—with those outside unaware that a creature from another world had passed by. A thin line of blazing light appeared before me, and I strode forward through the water, allowing the glow to bathe me just as the water did. The line widened while I pushed into the light. The water stayed behind.

I was home. At least as much of a home as a gypsy who endlessly wandered the stars could hope for.

Home was my respite from the world outside. I'd moved it from place to place around the Earth as the need arose, but it had been in Central Park for a few hundred years now. I suspected I wouldn't be moving again and hoped that perhaps, one day soon, it would become my tomb.

Of course that would never happen, because she wouldn't allow it.

It was meant to be a simple task. Master, who was on the cusp of being empress, had created me to be the perfect scout and sent me across the universe in search of worlds that had the makings of greatness. This little blue planet was to be my highest achievement, the world that would propel her to ultimate power.

For millennia I was on track. I helped mold humanity into creatures who constantly warred with one another. I laughed when they called World War I the war to end all wars—for there would be many, many more.

The main difficulty was, their skill in battle had more to do with the weakness of their flesh than their prowess at killing. That was the standard course on the worlds I'd developed in the past. The next step was always an enhancement of the flesh and the mind—a putting aside of weak tissue for something much stronger, something worthy of Master's interest.

Here, my failure becomes apparent. At every turn, humanity resisted an upgrade.

* * *

Lights flared to life as I walked down a long silver hallway. The power of the universe still coursed through me. I thought back to before I'd built my lab—before I had begun to use its framework to focus the cosmic rays pouring through the planet from the deep reaches of space. My constant weakness was almost unbearable at times. That Master had left me in that state—that she somehow gained pleasure from dropping me off on some half-formed world so far from home—

I stopped, pressing my hands against the orbs these humans called eyes. No, I wouldn't allow the fury to overtake me again. I'd put that aside eons ago.

The door to my lab opened and I strode in. My gaze immediately fell on the robot lying on the table. It was perfect in every way—indiscernible from a natural-born human. Under intense scrutiny, even dissection, it would be seen as human. Only if its cells were viewed under an electron microscope would the truth be known. Billions of tiny nano-bots made up its biological structure, designed to allow infinite variation in its form at will...if it had a will, that was. I could program it to talk like a human, interact like a human, but in the end it would be a facsimile. It would still be an imposter. I shook my head. I'd done this on hundreds of planets. Nudging the technology along. But something was different here.

I turned to the small cage in the corner. A grubby woman huddled there, her face hidden beneath a mound of matted hair. She used to cringe when I opened her door. Now she gazed at me dully.

Pushing aside her hair, I saw the sensor band was still in place. Those first months, she had torn it off at every chance, but now she was truly broken. I felt a twinge of sadness for this despicable being. Why did these humans move me at times? They were so weak. So unworthy of pity, and yet...

I grimaced. The years were finally taking their toll on me.

"Perhaps today will be the day you'll be free."

She made no response.

I closed the cage and moved over to the computer terminal next to the robot. There, I stared at a stream of numbers rolling up the screen. Patterns that showed some semblance of the consciousness locked inside the woman in the cage, even if she displayed no outside appearance of being aware.

What nightmares she endured.

This technology *should* be sufficient. Humanity had already mapped the brain down to the smallest level. They knew what memory looked like. They had delved deep into the subconscious and learned the secrets of how a human life came to be self-aware. But some barrier stood in the way of mapping that to an artificial life form. I'd worked for centuries to help them along. I'd done it on other worlds with much less effort. So why couldn't I bring humanity to the next stage, one that would make them a truly formidable opponent?

"Computer, initiate transfer."

A slight crackle from the paper sheet under the robot and a soft moan from the cage told me it was working. The display on the screen lit up. I'd done this long enough to see patterns, to know the difference between pain and pleasure. The test subject was definitely not enjoying the process. A second monitor presented the robot's brain activity. A simple stream of zeros scrolled up the screen. Then some numbers changed. More and more, until patterns began to emerge. Patterns that started to match the ones on the other display. Within moments both monitors showed the same scrolling code. The robot was now synced with the woman.

I let it run for a few more minutes, let the transfer bake into the hardware. "Computer, sever the connection."

Glancing back and forth between the two monitors, I watched as the patterns diverged. The human's thought waves softened. Her pain diminished. The robot's pattern continued to show the same pain and fear—but something else, too. Something I hadn't seen before. Was it independent thought? The minutes ticked by, and I began to hope. Perhaps I'd done it. Perhaps this time—

The numbers on the screen went haywire. A massive spike of agony rolled through the code. The robot on the table bucked once, twice, and grew still.

Rows of zeros on the monitor mocked me, shouting out my failure.

Master wouldn't like this at all.

* * *

Back out in the streets of New York, I searched for my next test subject. The rational side of me said I'd done this a hundred times before, without success. But perhaps this one would be different.

The screaming still haunted me. Though it was only a pattern of numbers on a screen, I felt the horrendous agony of the life I'd attempted to transfer into the robot. Something had fought against the process. It was almost as if—

I stopped short. A man walking behind me yelped as he swerved around.

All of my human test subjects, every single one, had been part of the experiment unwillingly. Yes, most of them came for the promise of a warm meal after spending long, cold nights out in the brutal New York winter, but once they saw what I wanted from them, every man and woman had rebelled—even the children. Perhaps willingness was the key. Maybe something within the human psyche fought so intensely against being used in such a way that their consciousness refused to be transferred.

I turned on my heel and headed back down the street. A few blocks east of Central Park sat a dive bar frequented by students from the nearby liberal arts college. As I ducked through an alley, I adjusted my appearance. A blue T-shirt with jeans and a blazer complemented my now early-thirties face, one that bore the dangerous smile and scruffy whiskers co-eds got all dreamy over.

It was a Thursday night; still, the place had a nice crowd.

After a quick scan of the room, I headed for the bar. Once again, I was getting drinks from a bar-bot. No apologies here; I'm an alien with a taste for alcohol, and these Earthlings seemed to have mastered its manufacture better than the natives of any other planet I'd scouted—enough to make this hellish world worthwhile…almost.

Running my gaze over the room, I scanned for the telltale signs. There would be some, especially in a crowd of kids like this—early twenties, ready, willing, and even excited about the latest fad.

It only took a few moments to find a couple of girls seated at a table near the back wall. A petite blonde with signature blue and red lights flashing just under the skin of her cheek and forehead was in deep conversation with her redheaded girlfriend. Her skin was so pale as to be almost translucent—another effect of the flashing lights running through the circuitry implanted in her face. As I watched, the girls swapped faces. Their hair didn't change, but the smaller nose of the blonde elongated slightly and her lips filled out while the redhead's face did the opposite. They squealed in delight at the transformation.

I stood, drink in hand, and strode toward the table. "Why would girls with obviously perfect skin have DermaYoung implants?" The young ladies looked up, their smiles frozen on their faces. "Don't get me wrong. It's a noble quest."

The redhead with the blonde's face pinched her eyebrows together. "Noble quest?"

"The fountain of youth. Immortality."

The blonde chimed in. "We're having a bit of fun, but who

wouldn't want to live forever?" Her words were slurred together. She'd been hitting it a bit too hard tonight.

I, for one.

Blondie nodded when I gestured toward an extra seat. "Where do you girls go to school?"

"Over at Lancaster," the redhead said.

"A fine institution." I paused for a moment, glancing at the blonde, who batted eyelashes over glassy, bloodshot eyes. I'd picked the right face to wear tonight. Both girls' faces returned back to their own.

"I'm sorry, where are my manners? I'm Dr. Hunt from Hardy Scientific."

"I'm Raquel," the redhead said, reaching for my hand.

"And I'm Suzanne." The blonde grappled for my hands before her friend could claim them. "What d'you teach?"

I gave her hands a squeeze and released them. Raquel smiled slightly at that. "I'm in research, mostly. Although I do have several grad students working under me."

"*Under* you, huh?" Raquel laughed. "What are you researching?"

"Well, I guess you might say immortality."

Suzanne's flushed face lit up. "So, you're in cosmetics?"

"Not exactly. I work in consciousness transference."

She registered nothing. In fact, she looked like she was about to pass out.

"Taking the you out of you and putting it into something more...robust."

The blonde's eyes glazed over and she laid her head on the table. "I don't get it," she mumbled.

"Well, it's—"

Suzanne closed her eyes and immediately began to snore.

I winked at Raquel. "Seems your friend has had a bit too much to drink."

She laughed. "I guess some girls can't handle their liquor."

"And you?"

"I guess you'll have to find out."

I took the hint and motioned for the bar-bot.

"So, consciousness transference, huh? As a psychology major, I find the whole subject fascinating. I actually went to a lecture not too long ago by a Dr. Winslow. Have you heard of him?"

I nodded. In fact, I'd been feeding Dr. Winslow anonymous information for years, attempting to influence his research in the right direction. But he was struggling to put it all together.

The bar-bot arrived and I nodded toward Raquel.

"A White Russian, please."

I laughed. "My favorite drink. Make it two."

The bot nodded and turned away.

"So, your lecture?"

"He talked all about consciousness transference. How the only way we'll ever move forward as a species is if we get rid of these bodies. But—" She frowned, trying to remember. "He had come to a dead end, and began to research purely biological transference—deciding it would be impossible to transfer our minds into robots. He thought that perhaps we could grow new bodies in a lab and upload ourselves into them when our own bodies wear out."

I shook my head at that. "So shortsighted."

"That's what I thought." Raquel's face lit up. "These organic shells we live in can still be killed. If our minds can only be stored in a flesh-and-blood body—"

"We are all one global pandemic away from being wiped out." This girl definitely knew her stuff.

She rested her hand on mine. "So, how about you? Are you any closer to figuring it out?"

"Actually, I am."

"So you're going to show this Dr. Winslow he's got it all wrong?"

"That's the plan." I squeezed her hand. "Do you want to see what I'm working on?"

"Right now?"

"Sure. My lab's not too far away."

She glanced at her friend, who had a nice puddle of drool forming on the table beneath her face. "Why not? It's not every day I get to see the work of a real genius."

I laughed. "I don't know about that, but I think you'll find it at least slightly interesting. I'm only working on next evolutionary step for the whole human race."

"Such modesty." She stood, still holding my hand. "Let's go, Doctor."

We headed for the door, passing the bar-bot moving toward the table with our drinks. I grabbed the glass and downed its contents.

* * *

If I continued for any length of time with this new strategy in my experiments, namely using willing subjects, I'd need to figure out a better way to get them to my lab without having to resort to post-hypnotic suggestion. Raquel stood in the gleaming room wide-eyed, with no idea how she'd gotten there. I made sure not to frighten her—at least not at first.

She spun around, taking it all in. I smirked when her gaze drifted past the cage in the corner, oblivious of my last test subject still inside. The human mind was so malleable. Weak bodies and weak minds…exactly the opposite of what Master had sent me to this planet to find—or cultivate.

"Your lab is amazing! We have something like this on campus, but I've—" Raquel shrieked when she noticed the robot on the table. "Is she dead?"

"It's quite alright." I moved toward the table. "She's not dead. She's simply not alive."

"Not alive?" Raquel's eyes grew wide as she glanced around.

"What I mean to say is, she's a robot."

Raquel stopped seeking a possible escape and reached a hand toward the robot. "But it's…it's so real."

"I am very good at what I do."

"She's beautiful."

I smiled. "The way I see it, if you're going to live forever, you might as well do it in style."

She touched the skin on the robot's exposed arm, which was draped over its stomach. "So, consciousness transference is copying the mind—including memories, emotions, everything—and uploading them to this robot, a body that won't wear out?"

"That's what I'm after."

Raquel continued to caress the robot's arm in reverence. "Would you still be…human? I mean, what about the soul?"

There was that word. It was actually something I'd put a great deal of thought into. The people on nearly every world I'd visited had had some form of religion. Worshipping the stars around them. The land. Mountains. Oceans. Many had myths of immortality of some kind or another, often growing out of the influence of my work on their planet, but none of them spoke of having a part of them that lived on outside their bodies after death. Only on Earth was this the case; here, many religions talked of an afterlife based on this thing called the soul.

"Your soul, of course, is only a manifestation of your mind, your will and emotions. It's who you are up here." I pointed to my forehead. "Precisely what we're talking about."

She stood transfixed by the robot. "So you could transfer my soul into this…"

"Yes." I paused. "Well, in theory."

"I'm not sure I could do it." Raquel stepped away from the table. "I mean, it's kind of creepy."

"How old are you, Raquel?"

"Twenty."

"How long until the cosmetics no longer work?"

"I…"

"You are beautiful, but in reality, how long do you have until your beauty fades?"

"Thirty, forty years, maybe."

More like twenty, I thought. "So, thirty or forty years and your body starts to wear out. You wake in the morning with ever-increasing bags under your eyes. Parts of you sag, while other parts bulge outward. Sure, you can fight it off. You can spend hours a day at the gym. Eat salads at every meal. Try all the latest creams and gadgets." I gestured toward her DermaYoung implant. "This body of yours is fragile under the best of circumstances."

I turned toward the robot. "That's where she comes into play. You said she was beautiful. When you are hunched with age, and your skin is so spotted and wrinkled you hardly recognize yourself in the mirror, she will appear exactly as you see her now."

A gleam appeared in Raquel's eyes.

"This body is self-repairing, impervious to everything but the most severe trauma, nearly indestructible."

She laughed nervously. "Where do I sign up?"

I smiled. "Slow down. I said I was *almost* ready. There are still some tests to run. Of course…" I eyed Raquel. "I could use some help to speed up the process."

She studied the robot again, her eyes drifting up and down the figure, taking in the firm shape of its body, the flawless perfection of its face.

"I…I guess if it's for science, how could I say no?"

* * *

Raquel sat on a stool at the foot of the robot. She smiled nervously, but there was definitely a gleam of anticipation in her eyes.

"This may be a little uncomfortable." I placed the metal sensor array on her head. "Sorry if I mess up your hair."

Raquel smiled weakly. "Will it hurt?"

"No. Only a slight tingling of electricity at the node locations, but nothing painful, I assure you."

She took a deep breath and nodded.

"The process is actually quite straightforward. Sensors shoot tiny magnetic currents through your head, imaging a physical map of the brain and the neural activity down to the individual neuron level. The real breakthrough couldn't happen until processors had reached a point when the computer could map all the electrical activity at the speed the human brain creates it."

I'd been waiting a very long time for computers to reach this capability... Well, waiting might not be the best word for it, but we can't let that little secret get out.

"Okay, here we go."

Raquel closed her eyes as I initiated the transfer. Her eyelids fluttered when the magnetic field coursed through her cranium, but she took several deep breaths and remained calm.

As before, both screens lit up with rows of letters and numbers scrolling upwards. Almost immediately I noticed a difference. The two monitors synced up much more quickly than I'd ever seen before. After only a few moments the screens displayed an identical pattern. And that pattern showed no pain. Some fear, but excitement as well.

The robot shifted slightly. I severed the connection with Raquel and shut down her sensor array. Her monitor went dark, but the robot continued to show a comfortable pattern.

Raquel opened her eyes and glanced down at her hands, turning them over. "Did it—?"

I waved to quiet her. The screen displayed a change in pattern from the copy of Raquel, indicating unique thought. A finger twitched on the robot.

"I thought I was going to be in the robot." Raquel's face showed disappointment as she stared at the robot on the table.

"Right now I'm working on making a copy."

"So a copy of me is in that—?"

"That is yet to be—"

"Her face!" Raquel pointed.

Sure enough, the features on the robot's face were changing. Bit by bit, they molded themselves into an exact representation of Raquel. More than that, the robot's once brown hair turned a deep red. Its skin grew pale, and I swear it lost a few inches in height. The robot sat up, opened its eyes, and stared straight at Raquel...then screamed. It grabbed its head with both hands and fell back against the table with a thud.

A quick glance at the screen showed rolling zeros.

I slammed my fists on the desk. "Why is this so hard? I'm running out of time!"

"Out of time?" Raquel raised an eyebrow at me. "Investors?"

"Something like that." Master expected a report from me soon. All her plans relied on my producing a world to elevate her standing in the Muradine. If she invaded before humanity was a worthy opponent, then she would suffer great shame. That, of course, would manifest itself in never-ending suffering on my part.

Then there was Hunter. He was still out there. If I didn't get this done before he killed me, she would be furious, and, again, I would regret it for all of eternity. There was a very low possibility for success on my part. I used to relish those odds. Not anymore.

Raquel had a peculiar expression on her face.

"Why are you smiling?" I asked.

"It didn't work, because I have a *soul*."

I shook my head. "I think it's a bit more complicated than that."

"Why?"

"Because there's no such thing as a soul. Only the weak dream of a life after this one." I looked her straight in the eyes, but she continued to smile. "This is all there is." *And that's more than enough for me.*

"You think I'm weak *because* I believe in something that can't be seen, some world beyond our ability to measure?" She sat up straighter on the stool. "You think humans are slow-witted to have faith in a soul that will go on living, even when this body wears out?"

Some floodgate inside her had opened, like she'd been bottling up her feelings on the matter for far too long. "Like you, I once believed in a science that studied only what can be discovered with our five senses. I say I'm strong because I believe in the invisible."

Her voice deepened, and echoed off the sterile walls of my lab. "I have a confidence that says we cannot possibly know all that's out there. It takes so much more to stand in front of you and say, 'Yes, I don't know if there is a life after this one, but I choose to believe there is.'"

Her skin began to shimmer. Darker grays and silver bubbled to the surface. "I choose the harder path, belief in something beyond science. Something above the rational." Her voice lowered to a growl. "That does not make me weak. Oh, quite the opposite. I am stronger than you could ever imagine."

Red hair changed to black. Her delicate face squared off, sprouting stubble.

"You!" I staggered back, catching my balance on the desk.

"After all these millennia, I finally caught up to you."

Hunter stood before me—a creature of pure destruction, built for one purpose—death. There would be no escape tonight.

I smiled. "What took you so long?"

* * *

"You are a most intriguing prey." Hunter, who hardly resembled a human, let alone the beautiful redhead he'd been moments earlier, circled the robot. "I've been admiring your handiwork since the dawn of civilization on this watery world."

"You've been here, all this time?"

"What is time for us immortals, eh?" Something resembling a smile split his face—a face with six black eyes blinking back at me. "I've never encountered a scout so dedicated to its master. The lengths you will go to—"

"I only observe." Even as the words left my mouth I knew he wouldn't buy it—couldn't buy it based on the very existence of the lab we stood within.

"Do not misunderstand me. I admire your dedication—to the point of restraining my hand, even when the evidence was sufficient to warrant your destruction. Even when the complete downfall of your master was assured."

A glimmer of hope filled me. If Master was brought down… then she couldn't resurrect me. Death would finally be mine.

"Only now, I'm not so sure." Hunter had circled around until he stood only a few feet away from me. A smooth tentacle uncoiled from his body and touched my cheek. "Something strange has happened to me over all these millennia. Watching you. Experiencing these beings who are so different than any other found in the universe."

I stepped back from Hunter's touch. "They're not that different." But he was right. There was something about humanity I'd never discovered before.

"My master also desires worlds worthy of his attention—civilizations to be destroyed that will assure his place above all others. But this world, these humans—"

"Are pathetic." I spit the words out. "I've never failed so miserably at molding a race into beings fit to be conquered." No sense attempting to hide my true purpose here.

"Not for lack of trying." Hunter smiled as he caressed the robot with the tip of his tentacle. "Their bodies are so weak—their weapons useless. Earth is in a constant state of near ecological disaster. You said it yourself: the right virus would destroy them. In a matter of weeks, you or I could wipe every living thing off the face of the planet."

I nodded my head. Thus was the shame of my endeavors. "If I only had more time—"

"Don't you see? Nowhere else in the universe are there beings of such contradiction. One man rises to power and attempts to conquer the world. Another spends months on his back painting the ceiling of the Sistine Chapel. One tries to destroy an entire race in an act of terrible genocide, while another labors in the most wretched conditions her entire life to save orphaned children. There are those who would kill millions without a thought, but others who would die to save only one. Their music, their art, their idealistic belief is in something better—their quest is for a world where good triumphs over evil. Even those who would be called monsters have goodness inside of them. I've seen a cold-blooded killer who would give anything for his pet dog. Where does this come from?"

"It's all about perspective, I guess."

Hunter had touched on something I'd never dared put into words.

"The ultimate *good* on our world is the destruction of others," I said. "Humans would call that evil."

Hunter turned in a pirouette, changing back to the redhead, Raquel. "Not all humans." He paused, batting green eyes at me. "What do *you* think? Are we evil, or good?"

I glanced away. He was definitely trying to manipulate me. "There's no way to answer that. It's all relative."

"Is it?"

"Without some kind of outside determination, yes."

"What does your heart tell you? After all these years with humanity, what is right, and what is wrong?"

He had no idea the nights I'd pondered that very question. Never before, on any other world, had I thought what I did for Master could be labeled as wrong or evil.

I fought against the words that surged inside me—against the desire to finally speak. To confess to the horror I had become—the horror I had always been.

"What was all that talk about a soul?"

He smiled. "You're changing the subject."

"Am I?"

"Don't you see?" He motioned toward the robot. "You couldn't transfer my consciousness into your little friend here."

"I know. I've been having issues."

"With humans. But as you can see…" The redhead's face shifted for a moment to Hunter's. "I'm not human."

He was right, of course. There was nothing substantively different between the makeup of the robot on the table and Hunter. Both consisted of billions of microscopic nano-bots, all working together as a unit. "So, you think you've somehow acquired a *soul* while hanging out on this planet?"

"Honestly, I don't know what to think. But something has changed. Our whole civilization, back to before we transitioned to these bodies, has been about expansion at any cost. Taking what we need from those who are too weak to keep it. This is our right. There is no purer motivation."

"But now you question that very foundation?"

He nodded. "I think you do too."

Before I came to this world, it would have been impossible for me to even contemplate such a thought, but I would deny it no longer. "My heart says we *are* wholly evil. That the blood we've poured out over the vast reaches of the universe brands us as completely irredeemable and devoid of anything good."

That was what haunted me. The blessing of immortality was nothing more than a curse. For all eternity, I would be haunted by the intimate knowledge of my own evil.

Hunter smiled.

"You find this humorous? What kind of sick game are you playing?"

"Don't you see? How could we agree? You and I are pinnacles of evolution—the ultimate survivors. Are we just getting soft in our old age?"

"We've been old for a very long time."

Hunter nodded. "So, you and I reach the same conclusion at the same time, after all these lifetimes? No, there's something about this world…"

"Something worth saving." I said the words I'd never dared think. It was treason.

"Something worth dying for."

"I've wanted nothing more than to die for millennia." I spit the words out.

"As have I, but what nobility can be found in a death without meaning?" He glanced at the robot on the table.

I closed my eyes, feeling the immense weight of years heaped upon me, crushing the air from my lungs. "But this life… What kind of life is this?"

He placed his hand on my arm. "You can't truly live until you find something worth dying for."

My breath caught in my chest as I looked into his eyes, Raquel's eyes. "The only worthy death is one granted after a job well done." How hollow my words sounded.

"How much greater would be a life laid down for those who cannot save themselves. How wretched are these humans. How desperately in need of someone to champion their cause."

Something built within me that hadn't existed since Master had first commissioned me as Scout. Something I hadn't thought I'd ever feel again: a sense of purpose.

"So, what do we do? Humanity is so weak. It could take ten thousand years to make them strong enough to resist the empire."

"Our hope isn't in strength, but in weakness."

Hunter saw the puzzled expression on my face.

"If we convinced the Muradine of Earth's insignificance, of how utterly embarrassing it would be to conquer—"

"Then they would never invade."

"Precisely."

An excitement surged through me. "I'll prepare my report." I spun around, heading for the terminal. "Master—"

The lights went out, bathing the lab in darkness.

"*Master* is displeased with you."

It was a voice I'd truly hoped to never hear again.

A pale green glow filled the far end of the lab, and a form shimmered into being. A terrible black and silver figure glowed with a slick green sheen. "You have been a bad boy, Scout."

I dropped to my knees. "No, I—"

A blur to my left cut me off. Even as Hunter lunged past, his shape changed from the frail redhead to a beast meant for one purpose: killing. Limbs elongated into blades two meters long. Muscles rippled along his back legs as he charged forward, driving his weapons toward the center of the shadowy form. That he would dare attack a member of the royal family—

The shadow coalesced into a humanoid shape and stepped aside. Hunter crashed into the wall behind. In a flash of green light, Master spun and placed her hand on the back of his head. Light coursed down Master's arm and Hunter exploded into a cloud of dust. The tiny nanite cells ripped apart and scattered across the floor.

Master turned to me, her face still in shadow, her body changing every moment, from humanoid, to a creature with several heads and appendages, to a formless blob. I couldn't focus on her.

"I failed you." This would be my undoing.

"This world is not ready?"

I imagined the joy she would take in punishing me and

shook my head. "They may never be an opponent worthy of the Muradine."

Her ever-changing form moved toward me.

Somehow I had to make her leave and never come back. "Do with me what you will. It's impossible—"

"Enough." Her voice rumbled through the room. Slowly she undulated along the floor. "You have been a valuable scout, but I would be weak if I allowed you to continue living."

The words I had longed to hear, had yearned for all these millennia, smote me over the head.

"Your work here has been nothing short of pathetic. You are useless to me, and the end has come." Towering over me, she slowly snaked a blob of mechanical flesh toward me, the tip coming to rest under my chin.

"As much as it pains me, stand and receive your reward. I suppose you have served me well on other worlds." Her appendage slithered around my neck and lifted me to my feet.

"Goodbye, Scout." Her tentacle squeezed, and my mind went black.

* * *

Intense heat awoke me from darkness. I pushed into my cells, which filled a shallow depression in the ground, and formed myself into the shape I now felt most comfortable in. Standing upon two shaky legs I breathed deep the moist air. I smiled. This should have been her most heinous punishment, promising death at last but instead casting me onto some newly made world to begin my eons-long struggle once more.

In that, she had misjudged.

No longer would I be dedicated to building a world *she* would one day deem worthy of conquest. I had a new purpose—a new master.

I looked up into a dark, star-filled sky. Somewhere out there was a small blue orb—and on that planet, a people unlike any other in the universe.

A people worth dying for… Or, even, a people worth never dying for.

A WORD FROM D. ROBERT PEASE

With new planets discovered, on a seemingly daily basis, many in the Goldilocks Zone (not too hot, and not too cold) it doesn't seem unreasonable to think there are planets besides our own that harbor life. And it's not a huge step to think there might be creatures on other worlds with intelligence far beyond our own. But if that's the case, why haven't they discovered us yet?

One answer could be, maybe they have. Some have proposed that we as a species haven't reached a level worthy of notice by advanced beings. If this is the case, what measure is being used to define our worth? What line must we cross before an alien race takes notice of us?

In the Star Trek universe, this was warp drive capability—humans invent warp drive, and the Vulcans show up. But even with warp drive, humans would still be, well, human. Our potential to process thought, and understand the universe around us, hasn't really changed since the first humans walked the planet. Sure technology has improved, but our brain capacity hasn't.

It is widely speculated that the next step in human evolution will be when we make the jump from organic bodies to the digital realm. When our minds are uploaded to computers that have processing power far beyond our three-pounds of gray matter.

Is that what the aliens are waiting for? Are they just biding their time until we are creatures they can relate to, communicate with? But, what would happen if they grew impatient? Maybe they'd work to help us out a little?

That's what I'm exploring in "The Scout". It's a look at one alien, and his work on Earth to help mankind reach the point where we are worthy of notice by the rulers of his home-world. The only problem, for us, is that notice isn't something we really want.

"The Scout" is self-contained, but is also prequel short story to my sci-fi trilogy The Exodus Chronicles. The first book, Enslaved, will be out early next year. I also write sci-fi and fantasy for kids through adults. You can learn more at *www.drobertpease.com* or subscribe to my newsletter here—*www.drobertpease.com/mailinglist*—where you can get free copies of my stories, and learn about new releases.

The Control
by Will Swardstrom

THERE EXISTS FOR EVERYONE a moment.

It's so small, you can almost miss it, but it's important. Vitally important. In that moment, all can be lost, or all can be saved. It is that moment that stands between victory and anarchy.

In music, you hear it when the song swells, building bit by bit until eventually the music reaches a cliff. All the instruments drop out. The vocalist may act as a bridge of sorts across the chasm of silence, but the moment is solely dependent on the other musicians. The impetus is on the piano, percussion, and the collection of other instruments to count, to keep a steady but silent beat internally, only to resume playing at precisely the right time.

Should the band hit the mark, the song sends shivers up

your spine. It brings the crowd to their feet, and gives the piece an air of authority it didn't have before.

If the musicians miss the landing, there may be no salvation. Their chance is gone, now just part of a disjointed past. Whatever the song sounded like before that infinitesimal break, it now has the sound of ruin. For the audience, the failure of a solitary moment within the song only accelerates their desire for the end. It cannot come soon enough.

But in that moment, neither has happened. The musicians have not yet succeeded or failed. Both options await them, depending on their internal clocks. The overwhelming joy of everyone rejoining at the perfect moment is balanced with the abject fear of failure.

It was there, in that moment, where I lived. Always waiting. Always letting my fate be determined by others. Always hovering between a rousing triumph and a crushing catastrophe. I was that moment. But my moment was never under my control. I was always under *his* control. Throughout the moments of my life, though, I became the man I am, and I am not ashamed of it.

Those were the moments I truly remembered. Over time I learned that names and dates are utterly forgettable. I can't tell you the name of the man who decided whether or not I deserved to board one of the few lifeboats on the night of April 14, 1912. I don't remember what day of the week it was when I was chosen to be one of the first to experience the guillotine during the peak of the French Revolution. I have no idea what clothes I was wearing when I was part of the crowd that decided the fate of Jesus of Nazareth.

What I can tell you is how I felt. For a brief moment, I thought I was the master of life and death. I was not. As was so often the case over the past few millennia, the result turned out to be death, but over and over I was brought back due to a gift. A curse. An experiment.

Whatever you want to call it, immortality has followed me.

My name is Bek. I have been alive for nearly five thousand years.

I live for those moments, but I have come to realize that the truly special moments happen too infrequently. My sense of mortality has grown too thin and I have found I don't have the same thrill about my life anymore.

My only wish is to finally die. To experience an end. When I was younger—in my first life—I would have craved a life like this. A life apart from all the rest, where death held no reign over me, and I could live like there was no tomorrow.

Instead, I simply move from one experience to another. I cannot die as everyone else does.

My master will not permit it. Instead, I am forced to live. Again and again, my life is forfeit to satisfy his curiosity. For a long time, I thought the irregularity of my existence was a blessing. Instead, I have come to understand that it is a curse. Over and over I have tried to end my life, only to be brought back again and again. Different place, different body, but it's still me.

Human technology has not done this. It was a gift of the gods. At least that's what the pharaoh told me at the time. He offered any of his servants to the gods to appease them, and I was selected.

Gods.

Just another name for aliens.

Of course, I didn't understand this for a very long time. In fact, I was thousands of years old by the time I recognized my "creator" for what he was.

He said his name was Osiris. Is that his real name? Five thousand years ago I would have sworn to you it was. Just like dates, the name really doesn't matter. He was a god, and then he wasn't. All I know is that to him, I'm just part of a grand experiment.

It was a warm day (but weren't they all in ancient Egypt?) when I was called into the pharaoh's palace to meet with the vizier.

"Bek!" called a palace guard.

I walked over to him quickly. That was when I used to care about what happened to me.

"Yes? What can I do to please the king today?"

"You can start by wiping that grin off your face. You are requested at the palace. The vizier needs you."

I quickly found myself at the palace with about twenty other men, all about my size, waiting to be seen. I knew better than to talk to any of them. I had been called to see the vizier, not them. When we were all finally called before the vizier, we were instructed to line up. The vizier inspected each of us, dismissing a handful as he went. In the back of the room, I glimpsed a cloaked figure, but again, I knew to not say anything.

Eventually there were about ten men left in the room.

The cloaked figure stepped forward to address us.

"I have selected each of you from afar. I have chosen each

of you to show the power of the gods." He paused. "You may wonder who I am."

Slowly and purposefully, he slid back his hood, revealing a glowing presence. It shone so brightly, each of us had to look away. But before I did, I caught a brief glimpse of dark green skin on the most glorious face I'd ever witnessed in my short life. I knew who he was before he even had a chance to tell us.

"Osiris," I gasped under my breath.

Apparently it wasn't quiet enough, because the god approached me. Suddenly I was afraid. Osiris was known for much, including his role in the afterlife.

"Yes," he said quietly. "I am Osiris. Who are you that you are so wise?"

"I...I am Bek."

"Bek."

"Yes," I said as boldly as I dared. I was speaking to a god, but I wanted him to grant me his favor. My answer was short, but it offered him what he wanted.

Osiris laughed. It was loud, filling the entire chamber with echoes upon echoes of deep roars and howls that somehow came from the being in front of me. The men on either side of me shook with fear. For whatever reason, I was unafraid. The laughter somehow reached inside of me and touched something. I felt...peace. While the other men were a hair away from cowering, I stood tall, proud that Osiris had chosen to address me. I had pleased him, somehow, and who was I to question a god?

Suddenly, I was alone in the room with Osiris. Gone were the vizier and the other men I had shared the chamber with.

In fact, the room was different somehow. Like it was the same room, just in a different location. It took me centuries, but I eventually learned it was Osiris' ship, occupying space above the earth and designed to look just like a royal chamber room in ancient Egypt. That day, however, I was awestruck by everything surrounding me.

"Bek, I have chosen you to be favored among all men. As the god of resurrection, I wish for all men to witness my miraculous rebirth in the body of a man," Osiris said. He put his hood back over his head, so the light receded, but kept his face visible. He locked eyes with me and at that moment, I felt greater than any man who had ever lived. "Your life will be a beacon throughout the ages, endless and steady. You are blessed among men, for you are no longer a mortal man, but are immortal, a step closer to the gods themselves."

I don't remember weeping, but I wouldn't have been surprised had I spontaneously burst into tears. A favor from the gods was truly magnificent. That I would be chosen was the pinnacle of my life.

Little did I know that my life up until that point was miniscule compared to what was to come.

What happened next was so minor, I didn't give it much thought for years, but I came to understand that what Osiris did to me was what gave me eternal life. As I stood there, looking into his eyes, I felt a sharp but brief pain in my neck. I don't even remember his hand moving there, but Osiris had a gauntlet of sorts, made of gold and shining jewels. Knowing what I know now, I came to understand that it concealed some sort of handheld syringe.

He left his hand there for a moment, then pulled it away and took a step back, as if he was admiring his creation.

"Bek, you are now perfect. Man will no longer have dominion over you. I will guide you through the ages of earth still to come. You will be my constant as the tides of humanity rise and fall. I will see you again soon."

Before I could even open my mouth, the world disappeared around me, and I found myself standing in my home. The bed was next to me, and I lay down, desperate to sleep. And sleep I did. It was the first time I'd slept as an immortal man.

* * *

In my life, I've experienced many things. The birth of my first son. The birth of my one hundredth son. The rise of Rome. The fall of Rome. The creation of sliced bread and the advent of television. I've been privileged enough to shake hands with Charlemagne, Napoleon Bonaparte, and Winston Churchill. I fought at the Battle of Hastings, the Battle of the Alamo, and the Battle of the Bulge. I have lived more than any man before and surely more than any man after me.

As I said, I have died many times, but each time I reawaken in another body. Every time, a perfect body given to me by Osiris.

That first body, though…that one was mine. Given to me by parents whose names I have long since forgotten. The only memory I have of when I was a small boy is of playing along the Nile River. Every year the river would flood, bringing life to the once dormant riverbed. One day I was playing among the reeds along the riverbank with a few of my friends when my mother called to me.

"Bek, make sure when the sun is just over the big pyramid that you head home for dinner. Do you understand?"

I nodded, desperate to resume my playtime with my friends.

"Are you sure you understand?"

"Yes, Mother. I understand," I said, my eyes on a ball that my friends had brought with them to the river that day. "Can I go play now?"

She smiled, the love from mother to son clear in that one small gesture. "Yes, my son. Go play. Enjoy the day, but come when I asked, all right?"

"Okay!" I shouted back, barely registering the words she'd spoken. Years later I would regret not heeding those words the first time. Instead, I went to play, not ever looking back at the pyramids off in the distance. The sun began to set over the Great Pyramid and I kept running and kicking the ball with my friends. Before I knew it, my mother was out calling to me again.

"Bek, it's time to come to dinner."

"Coming, Mother!" I shouted back, but I continued to play among the papyrus. I ran and laughed, my friends and I enjoying the last rays of sun on a bright spring day in Egypt. At the time I thought it was a precious thing, the sun on my back and the wind in my face. Before I realized it, much time had passed and when I turned to run towards my friends, I found my mother standing before me.

"Bek."

I hung my head. I knew I had disappointed her.

She walked towards me and took my head in her hands. I heard my friends scatter and for a few moments, only my mother and I were alive. The world could have faded away; I wouldn't have noticed. She was my entire world and I had let her down. She crouched down to look me in the eye. I couldn't avoid the tears welling up as she spoke to me. Never will I forget her words.

"Bek, my dear son. Life is a wonderful thing. I love to see you enjoying the time you have and friends that you can play with each day," she said, capturing my attention with her soft eyes. I can still remember that look to this day, along with the slight brush of her hand across my cheek as she wiped my tears. "If you ever remember anything, please remember this: your word is your bond. It makes you who you are. When you grow up to be a man, a promise kept or unkept shows everyone the type of person you really are. For good or bad, for better or for worse, if you promise something to someone, you must follow through on that promise. The words you say will not matter, unless you back them up with your actions."

As a small boy, I didn't comprehend what she had said to me that day as twilight came to the Nile River. The words went into my mind and stayed there, but I didn't think about them until much later. It was one of the few things I could remember about my mother. Her words that day formed the basis for the man I would be…again…and again…and again…and again.

* * *

I awoke with a start, my head pounding like a fist hammering on the door.

Except it was literally a fist hammering on my door.

"Bek! You get your sorry behind out of bed and to the work site! The foreman says all hands are needed today, and that means you," growled the voice on the other side. It was a friend at the time, another whose name has escaped the confines of my mental storage over the years.

I dragged myself off the stiff bed and prepared for the day. A few times, my head felt like it was about to explode, but that was no excuse. The foreman would have me whipped if I didn't show. Better to suffer a headache than deal with pain on my backside as well.

Within the hour I was hauling bricks for the new monument—me, and hundreds of my closest friends. We'd all heard stories about how the Great Pyramid had been constructed, and the pharaoh wanted this one to be as close to that one in quality as he could get. A few hours in and I had already soaked through the few articles of clothing I had worn to the work site.

As I was getting another stone ready to transport, I caught a shape out of the corner of my eye. My breath caught for an instant when I saw Osiris talking to the foreman. Perhaps he was here to take me with him. Perhaps he would stop the work for the day. Perhaps…

The foreman stepped up and called out to all the men working that day. "Okay, you grunts. Orders from the top— everyone must double their block totals until further notice."

This was one of those moments. I didn't realize it, but I was about to be tested with forces beyond my control.

Osiris wasn't there to save me. He was there to kill me. Well…my body.

We doubled production. Food, water, and breaks were not doubled. I am proud to admit I lasted longer than many on my work gang, but within a week, most of us had collapsed along the route to the new monument. The heat, combined with the lack of vital resources such as water, doomed us from the start. Egypt wasn't the most forgiving of places.

It was about midday of the sixth day after the production order. I thought I could make it. I thought my body was stronger. I thought it was just a test.

It was, but I was wrong about my body. I collapsed from severe dehydration and malnutrition. I wasn't dead when I fell, but an hour in the sun, unattended to by a doctor, ensured a painful end.

Except…it wasn't.

The moment…that one brief instant between this life and the next…happened on Osiris' ship. I stopped breathing on Earth, under the naked sun, before the Old Kingdom of Egypt even came to be. But I didn't die. Not really.

My body stopped working, but my consciousness was immediately transferred to another one. It was a strange feeling, but not unpleasant. In fact, there was a bit of euphoria as I moved from one body to another.

How did I know I had gained a new body? I didn't at first, but when I opened my eyes I found myself lying on the floor of Osiris' chamber. I looked down and found myself naked. I reached down and touched my arms and my legs. My skin and muscles bounced back with the elasticity that hydration and health provided. My body was different, but my mind was the same. It was clouded, though. It cleared instantly when a voice rang out in the room.

"Welcome back, my son!"

I looked up, momentarily concerned about my lack of dress, but then realized I was in front of a god, and if he wasn't concerned, I should not be, either. I was too stunned to speak, though.

Osiris gestured to my right and I saw a small pile of neatly folded clothes. I understood he wanted me to put them on, and he addressed me as I did so.

"How was it? The process of dying, and being resurrected—how was it?" Osiris asked.

So that was what had happened. It made sense. Osiris was the god of resurrection, but I hadn't put it all together quite yet.

I finished dressing while I gathered my thoughts. I spoke my mind, unaware at the time that I didn't have to be honest with Osiris.

"It was glorious, my lord. In one moment, I found my body too weak to continue. The effects of the sun had been wearing on me and the overseers were not providing us enough water. Thankfully, you have chosen to resurrect my spirit into a new body, much like your wife resurrected you," I said. "I do regret I failed you in your appointed task for the pharaoh. But I am grateful you chose to give me another chance."

Osiris smiled, his white teeth a stark contrast to his greenish skin. He was happy, and that made me happy.

"No, my son. You have not failed me. No matter what you do, you will never fail me," he said.

I didn't know what to say, so I kept my mouth shut.

"Bek. I had the foremen push you and your friends to test the limits of what you were capable of. I knew that no matter what happened, you and I would meet again here, safe from the ravages of death. That is the gift I gave you. You possess a life eternal now," Osiris said.

"Eternal life, my lord?"

"Yes," Osiris said, and waved a hand. To his left, a dais rose out of the ground. On it was a bronze medallion. It had a very Egyptian look to it, but was mysterious in other ways. It was attached to a flexible leather lanyard. "Take this. I will always be able to find you, but this will give you added protection. As long as you wear it, I will be there. You will surely live again, as long as you carry this with you."

I reached for it, making sure not to actually touch Osiris. It was one thing to accept a gift; it was another altogether to dare to make physical contact with a god.

"Thank you. This gift…it is more than I could ask for," I said.

Osiris held up his hand. "Do not thank me, Bek. Your death and resurrection today were easy. Painless. Maybe even pleasurable. I think you will have to die again and again, and I cannot say each death will be as seamless as the one you just experienced. Are you prepared for that? Will you live an eternal life for me? Are you willing to accept the consequences of that choice?"

Who would turn down everlasting life? I didn't that day. I wouldn't for a long time, but he was right. Death stopped being easy. Thousands of years later, I wish with everything I am that I had refused his offer.

"I will serve you in whatever way I can," I said.

Osiris touched a bracelet on his wrist, and he vanished. My eyes saw a smiling god in one moment, and a rocky terrain the next. I swiveled around, trying to find the familiar sights of the monuments to the pharaohs in the distance. No monuments. Just mountains. A cool breeze blew through my clothes. I shivered, and saw for the first time something I could never have imagined, something I did not know the name of until later.

Snow.

* * *

I barely lasted five days. I didn't know it then, but Osiris had dropped my newly regenerated body right in the middle of the modern-day Canadian territory of Nunavut. Even now, several thousand years later, only a handful of people live there. The Inuit, though, never found me during that short stretch. I managed to find a cave, but the clothes Osiris had given me were the same small loincloth and tunic I had worn in Egypt—not quite the proper attire for the near-Arctic.

That was probably exactly what Osiris had in mind.

"Back so soon?" Osiris asked after I had died and returned to his care.

Nowadays, I might have a few choice words for the guy. Back then, he was still very much a god in my eyes. I was silent, praying he would look favorably upon me in my next life.

Osiris offered a wry smile as he advanced towards me in his vast chamber. Once again, I was lying in the middle of the large room, naked as the day I was brought into the world. I sat up and immediately found the pile of clothes nearby. I dressed and secretly wished for more. Even with a new body, I still felt a chill from the past few days.

"It might surprise you to know that less than a half day's journey to the north of your cave, there was a dead carnivore. Alive, it would have been five times your mass. Had you found it, skinned it, and appropriated the meat and bone from the creature, you would have had an outer covering, a source of food, and tools. You could have lived in that environment for decades."

I was astonished. "How was I to know that?"

"There was no way for you to have known, Bek. But I didn't put you down there to sit in a cave and hope for salvation."

I considered that for a moment. "I am guaranteed to live again, correct?" Osiris nodded. "So, I am tasked with living as much as I can. Sitting and waiting for the end is not in your master plan."

"That is correct, Bek," Osiris answered. He opened his hand. In his palm was the bronze medallion he'd given me before. "I saved this for you. It will be in your clothing for you to put on again each time in the future, but I knew you would want to talk to me after your experience."

"Yes, Osiris, I do. Why was I sent there? I had never before seen…"

"Snow," he completed for me. The way Osiris said it gave it an air of magnitude. I had heard the word before—Egyptians did have a name for it, we just rarely used it. With Osiris, however, it seemed like a divine word that I would be grateful to even utter again.

"Snow," I repeated, letting the word linger on my tongue

for just a moment. "If you would consider letting me, a mere mortal, know—why was I sent there?"

Osiris laughed. "I will tell you, because now you are not a mere mortal any longer. You have eternal life! That life will take you many places in your world, not just Egypt. I wanted you to get a taste of the extreme climate conditions of the planet immediately. If I had just told you of the place you visited, would you have chosen to go? Would you have believed me?"

I was honest. "I would have gone. For you, I would go anywhere, my god Osiris. But, no, I would not have believed you. Never in my wildest imaginations would I have dreamed such a place existed."

"Good. Thank you, Bek, for your honesty. I dare say, you may not always trust me so readily, but I am glad for your loyalty at the present. As for why you are to go there and many other places in this world—I am a god, yes, but I am a curious god," Osiris said. "I must confess that you play a critical role in my curiosity. I long to test humankind and you will be at the center of those tests."

"I will do what you ask of me, Osiris," I said, parroting what I'd said earlier.

"Will you? Let's see what you think after a few more trips back to your world. Are you ready?"

I nodded, and Osiris touched his bracelet. He shimmered out of view, and I found myself in a vast desert.

I sighed in relief. I was back in Egypt. The dry heat of the cracked earth radiated up towards my face and I closed my eyes, welcoming my return to the desert I had grown up in. A bead of sweat trickled down my forehead and I smiled.

A noise startled me. I opened my eyes and slowly turned

in a circle. A creature stood about ten paces away. I wondered briefly if it was a meat eater, but it didn't look fierce or even hungry. It was about my height, narrow at the top, and larger at the bottom, with large, padded feet and a long tail. Before I could say anything, the creature turned and hopped away, bounding towards the sun one leap at a time.

This was not Egypt.

* * *

In spite of its many challenges, I lasted a couple of years in Australia. I was alone for a long time, but I knew how to survive in the desert. True, I had been very dependent on the steady Nile River, but that just meant I knew how important a fresh water source was. It took me two days, but I knew that finding vegetation would take me closer to water. I had to trust that Osiris had put me within walking distance of what would keep me alive, just like he'd done in Nunavut without my knowledge.

Life was tough, but I learned a lot. Eventually I explored further, and that's where death found me. The original inhabitants of Australia—the aborigines—were surprised to see me. I'm guessing they figured I was inherently evil since I didn't get a chance to explain myself before a spear pierced my heart.

I died. I moved to another body and was placed back on Earth without seeing my god this time. I lived again, this time in a rainforest. The mosquitoes were as large as my hands and the animals loved to pelt me with their excrement. I learned to live and then died in the tropics.

The next time, death came to visit in the form of disease.

My decline was long and drawn out, and I was thankful when death finally came. Again, I had no downtime in Osiris' chamber. I was placed inside a village at the foot of a mountain. I looked up and saw that the mountain's peak was smoking. The ground shook beneath my feet and the mountain began to make noise.

I noticed the village was vacant. Osiris had known the mountain was unstable. He'd known the village was already abandoned, and he had chosen to put me in harm's way anyway. I convinced myself this was a test. He knew what he was doing. He was a god, after all.

I quickly scouted the village, hoping there was something I could use. Something I could do. Osiris had provided for my survival the other two times. This time, though, I found myself choking on the hot ash raining down from above. It seared my face and burned my throat. I could not escape. I was not going to survive.

I didn't want to disappoint Osiris. I remembered when I had just holed up in the cave during my Arctic life. Osiris hadn't been content with that, so I determinedly tried to live. I could barely breathe, but I crawled as far as I could to leave the town. It was no use. Just past the village limits, I was struck by a chunk of volcanic rock, instantly breaking my femur. The pain was intense, but I knew I would be resurrected again. Living with a broken leg in a volcanic wasteland was no life when I knew the next would surely be better. I folded myself up and grasped my necklace, praying to Osiris for the end to come as soon as possible.

The end did come, but it was not quick.

When I finally did succumb to the effects of the volcano,

the moment from death to life was not as pleasant as I remembered it being. The sounds of the volcano exploding above me were gone, replaced by the emptiness of Osiris' chamber. Unlike the first few times, though, the moment was jarring. I found myself questioning whether I was really going to be resurrected this time, but after a few moments, I felt the cold stone against my naked back. I was back in my body again.

I kept my eyes closed as I completed the process back. Footsteps approached and I knew he was there. Waiting.

"Welcome back, Bek."

I cautiously opened my eyes and found him standing in front of me. He was still garbed as he had been the first day I saw him. His skin was still green. It was as if he had not aged, but I felt like it had been centuries since I had seen him last. My body, though, was still as young and as taut as the day I had stood in the pharaoh's chamber. Identical, in fact, in every way.

"Greetings, Osiris." I stood and gathered the clothes from the ground. I carefully and slowly put them on, wary of what was next for me.

"How has your life been?"

"You mean lives, my lord."

He seemed to be staring at something over my shoulder, and hesitated. "Oh, yes, lives. How have they been?"

I recounted the time I had spent in the land of the jumping mammals, then the weeks in the rain forest, and finally the hours in the shadow of a volcano. Three lives. Three moments.

Osiris listened and then questioned my actions in the final life. "Did you think you would be able to evade the effects of the volcano?"

"I knew you were a kind god and would do whatever you

could to offer a way to safety. Just as you said, in the snow there was a carcass I could have harvested, and when I arrived in the desert, I found a river for fresh water. I knew you would have left me a gift to survive. I am sorry I was unable to locate it before I perished."

Osiris laughed. "But there was no escape. In this case, there was no way out. I placed you there as a lesson: sometimes there is nothing that can be done. But I saw your valiant attempts to stave off your fate, and for that you are commended."

I was confused. Did he want me to fight for every last breath, or did he want me to accept my fate?

He saw the confusion on my face. "My dear Bek, what is it?"

"Osiris. I'm sorry, my lord, but what is my purpose? What is it I am supposed to achieve? Why have I been gifted eternal life if I am supposed to strive for every breath in one life and accept defeat in another?" I asked.

"Oh, Bek. I thought you would have figured it out. I am conducting experiments. I cannot control everything, but I can control you. Your body, your blood, your physical fitness. In all experiments, there are multiple variables, but the one performing the experiment needs one thing. A constant. They need a control."

I don't know what I would have said, but I wasn't given the chance. With a swift action, Osiris pushed a button on his bracelet, sending me to a new land, one lush with green grasses and tall trees. A few birds chirped in the distance and the sun was warm, but not overly so.

I didn't care, though. I was numb.

My life meant nothing to Osiris. I was just a body. He

could use me over and over through whatever means he chose. I was nothing special to him.

Instead of living my life as he wanted me to, I made a decision that day. I would live like I wanted. Maybe there wasn't much of a difference in what I would have done, but it was different in my mind. It was different in my motivation. I stopped living for Osiris and started living for myself.

It was probably a few centuries before I saw him again. I lived more than a half dozen lives in that span, but he kept resurrecting me and depositing me in a new place without a rest stop in his chamber. Each time, I was dressed like an ancient Egyptian and I had the bronze medallion. The places I went were different in climate, culture, and people, but one thing was always the same. Me.

I encountered Gilgamesh and his friend Enkidu (who wasn't as hairy as the stories say). I met Hannibal. I saw Athens before Sparta overthrew it in the Great Peloponnesian War. The terra cotta warriors were new the first time I saw them.

Decades sped by as my lives continued to come and go.

When I saw Osiris again, I knew the Egyptian gods of old to be unreal. I had seen the "power" of a vast number of other gods, and had decided for myself that my master was a false one. He held dominion over my life, but he was no god.

"Your name is not really Osiris, is it?" I asked on a rare trip back to his chamber.

"I was wondering when you would ask me that," he replied. In that moment, the garments he had worn in my presence for years vanished, replaced by a utilitarian article of clothing. "I can be rid of those now."

"What should I call you?" I asked.

"The only name I've had on your world has been Osiris, so that is as good a name as any. It would make me happy to hear you continue to use it."

And so, like any adolescent, I stopped doing what he liked. I found ways to make him unhappy. I ran towards death like a moth towards flame. I went through body after body until I finally realized I was probably living my lives just as he wanted me to. He was testing my body's capabilities and I was simply providing him with more and more opportunities to test me.

For centuries, I managed to live full lives. I even settled down and met a few women.

But it wasn't enough. There was one thing I lacked.

I wanted to die.

* * *

It wasn't that my life wasn't fulfilling. I certainly found various ways to entertain myself throughout the years, but after a certain point, it was all the same. One man's dictator is another man's king is another man's president. They're all the same. And that's what my life was like as well.

Dying from smallpox wasn't too different from wasting away due to scurvy, or kicking the bucket after meningitis, or even a good bout of pneumonia. When you've had them all, the ending is unchanged. One death was the same as the next.

And Osiris' words came back to me again and again. The first time I had died, he had said, *"I cannot say each death will be as seamless as the one you just experienced."* He was right. Each time I passed away, it was as if someone had jabbed another dagger into my ribs and sucked my organs out through a straw. My brain was jelly for longer and longer each time as I recuperated. I finally decided that the more years that passed between one death and the next meant a little bit more suffering for Bek.

By the time I reached the Middle Ages, the pain was almost unbearable. So I began to think about how I could actually die.

I was obsessed. I spent at least one of my lives simply contemplating death at a Buddhist temple until old age snuck up and took me in my sleep. That was a good life. I wish I could do that one again.

I came to one conclusion: Osiris had to die. For me to die, he had to die.

How do you kill a god? First, you acknowledge that he isn't a god.

In one of my few trips back during the Middle Ages, I confronted him. "You are not a god."

He regarded me with thin eyes. "No."

I knew I couldn't fulfill my next statement yet, but I made it anyway. "One day I will kill you. For all the times you have killed me, you will pay."

He laughed and turned a dial on the dais. "Good luck with that. Have a nice death, Bek."

He sent me to the summit of a mountain. I suspect it was Mt. Everest or K2. Either way, I lasted a few hours.

While he held the power of my resurrection, he also seemed unaware of how many lives I was living. He wasn't attuned to each of my lives, and he'd even mentioned "my world," leading me to believe he was some sort of alien who had come to our planet to conduct his own particular brand of experiments—with me at the fore.

So, he wasn't a god. I was still stuck with the problem of killing him. I had a lot of time to think about it, and I finally came to the conclusion that I was a clone. Each body after my first, born thousands of years ago in Egypt, was simply a clone. It explained the identical form and age as that first body. It allowed Osiris to prepare many duplicate sets of clothes as well. I didn't know if he had hundreds of clones sitting in storage, or if he simply printed up a new one each time I died, but either way, I was a clone.

That eliminated several different methods of taking Osiris out. After all, I was given a new body and new clothes each time. I was a constant. His control. That meant each body would be the same each time. No variations.

But just as I was Osiris' control, he had inadvertently given me one as well. Sometime in the 1400s, I had scratched the necklace with a 17-carat diamond I'd found in a South African mine. I had never tried to do anything to it before and was scared that perhaps Osiris would be angry.

This was during my rebellious stage, though, and I didn't care. After death came a few weeks later when a shaft of that diamond mine collapsed on me, I reappeared in Renaissance Italy. I looked at the necklace and saw that the medallion was unchanged. There was a long scratch on the back, almost scoring the bronze piece from top to bottom. I smiled. I didn't know it at the time, but I had found my control. Just as I stayed the same in each life and location for Osiris, the medal Osiris had sent with me was the same each time as well.

For hundreds of years I didn't dare act on my knowledge of the necklace. I learned metallurgy and other crafts. I created my own works with many types of metal, and curated collections based on the design of Osiris' medallion. When the technology finally advanced, I ran the medallion through an X-ray and tested it. I found the homing device Osiris had planted in it. His technology was far beyond my own, so duplication was probably out of the question for a while, but that didn't stop me from trying. Eventually, I settled on adding to the medallion, and making the extra mass not just bronze. Something a bit more...explosive.

Even then, I needed a way to control it. I needed to be awake and conscious during the moment of transfer. I had to get Osiris to talk to me. He hadn't given me an audience since the waning days of the Roman Empire, so I wasn't hopeful, but I knew I needed the medallion to be ready whenever the moment struck.

I had spent the past few decades killing myself over and over. Any way you can imagine to kill yourself was probably on my radar at some point during those years. Every time, I'd just reappear on Earth, ready to live and die again.

Each time I got ready to die, I gripped the medallion, hoping that the next time I did so, Osiris would be standing near me in his chamber. Each time, though, I simply opened my eyes on Earth; no supposed Egyptian gods were staring me in the face.

Nothing changed until I went back. It was fitting, I thought...I went back to Egypt. I found the Nile River and marveled at how civilization had grown up and encompassed all the land surrounding the river. I didn't know if my plan would work, but I submerged myself in a bend in the river, upstream from Cairo. There was no one else around. Just me. And the medallion. I put it in my mouth and forced myself to swallow river water at the same time.

I felt the water burning my lungs—this wasn't the first time I'd drowned—and knew the end would be near. I clamped my teeth down on Osiris' medallion and sank to the bottom of the river. The end would be welcome. I hoped I wouldn't be back. This was my end—at the place where it all began. My eyes shut for what I hoped was the final time and I let the water take me.

Each time before, the moment from one life to the next had been seamless. The soundtrack of life kept playing for me, but I hoped to stop the conductor once and for all.

* * *

The rushing water of the Nile was gone. I was dry and naked on the floor of Osiris' chamber. I felt disappointment ripple through me. I had failed.

I kept my eyes closed, waiting for Osiris to appear. The silence was interminable. I'd lived thousands of years, though, so what was a few more minutes? Any minute, the being I'd once met in the pharaoh's palace would stroll in and doom me to another cursed life on Earth. Any moment…

But he never came. Minutes had ticked by in my head before I dared open my eyes to find the chamber empty. No clothes lay next to me. There was just me and the chamber. For the first time in hundreds of years, I was completely surprised.

In the moments between lives, I had never left this room.

There were doors, but I had never before had the opportunity to discover what lay beyond them.

Now was the time. Now was my moment. Would it end in disaster or victory?

Slowly, purposefully, I sat up and inspected my surroundings, a place I'd been to dozens of times, but only now had free rein to explore. While there were doors, most were false. Placed there to resemble the pharaoh's palace in Egypt, a place now in ruins on Earth.

But one door did open. One door did lead beyond the confines of the chamber.

I couldn't believe my eyes. I thought I'd seen everything, but the room I entered was vast. The far wall was barely visible and each empty spot was filled with...me. Hundreds of some sort of cryogenic tubes were lined up end to end, and from inside all of them, the same face stared back. Me.

But the endless number of Bek clones wasn't what grabbed my attention. In the middle of the room was a workstation with a table in the middle. A body lay on the table, a bloated, sopping wet version of myself. I recognized the clothing. It was me. The last body I'd had, which I'd drowned in the Nile.

But my head was gone, destroyed in a small explosion.

It had worked after all.

Osiris lay next to the table, his own torso a mangled mess. What I assumed was blood covered the area, but it was a dark green, similar to his skin color. In one hand was the medallion, a little worse for wear after the explosion.

I'd done it. I'd killed him. The tiny explosives I'd implanted into my teeth and jaw had worked.

I was finally free to die.

But…

With hundreds of copies of myself to spare and no master ruling my life…did I even want to die anymore?

Life is composed of pivotal moments. I'd experienced many of them over the centuries—but none of them had been as significant as this one. With Osiris gone, the success or failure of this moment was up to me. I could fail. I could have monumental success. Either way, it was all up to me.

Entirely up to me.

A WORD FROM WILL SWARDSTROM

The idea of immortality is one humanity has wrestled with since our beginnings. The first written epic story, "Gilgamesh," readers meet the legendary king of the Mesopotamian city of Uruk. As king of his people, Gilgamesh has protected them thanks to massive walls he put in place around the city, but in other ways he is a bad guy. He is tempered by a friend sent by the gods, but when his friend is killed, Gilgamesh is sent on a journey of his own making to become immortal.

That's part of the reason why Gilgamesh's story has resonated throughout the centuries. Even after we've achieved personal success, we still cannot conquer death. What could we accomplish if we could continue our existence beyond a mere century? Even stories like Dracula or Frankenstein have the question of immortality implied in their premise. Would we accept eternal life if there were conditions on that gift? Would we end up a monster in the end, living forever but suffering apart from the rest of humanity?

Ultimately Gilgamesh doesn't find immortal life (Spoiler Alert!) but is given a glimpse at something more important – perspective. He failed in his quest to achieve literal immortality, but upon returning to the great city of Uruk, he realizes the way he lived his life has ensured his name will live beyond his years. In many ways, Gilgamesh has achieved immortality – we still read about his adventures and remember his name thousands of years after he lived.

In my story Bek is gifted with eternal life, but his life is controlled by an outside power. Osiris places him in situations that test him and push him beyond the limits he initially imagined in his life. What happens when he finally has control over his own life? Would he value it, or toss it away like Osiris did again and again? Those are the questions I wanted to leave the reader with and I hope you enjoyed it.

The Future Chronicles is an amazing collection of short stories by an immensely talented pool of authors. I'm thrilled to be a part of this group and am proud to call myself a Future Chronicles author. I'd like to thank Ellen Campbell, Paul Swardstrom, Gareth Foy, Harlow Fallon, Carol Davis, and Thomas Robins for feedback on "The Control" and for their support. I'd like to also thank Samuel Peralta for his nurturing and cultivation of this series.

To follow my adventures, tune in to my blog at *www.willswardstrom.wordpress.com* or check out my Amazon page at *www.amazon.com/author/willswardstrom*. I love to hear from readers; thanks for reading and supporting indie publishing!

The Essence of Jamie's Father

by Gareth Foy

FROM THE HILL Jamie could see across the wide valley. Queues of people and vehicles filtered to the various accommodations littered around a huge central edifice. The sun filled the sky on this warmest of days, despite its being farther than it had ever been from Earth. Jamie stopped to observe for a moment and imagined one day the same scene playing out on a thousand worlds across the galaxy. "The transition of the human race," they called it. The journey they had to make both excited and terrified him.

Jamie saw his father sitting at the top of the hill. He hadn't seen his father in ten years. Jamie wasn't yet a teenager when his father left to devote himself to the transition project—his father's project. Even after his mother had died in an accident, his father had not attended the funeral. Soon afterwards Jamie had moved to New Pangaea to start a new life.

As he climbed the hill, Jamie remembered being closer to his father as a child. Part of him hoped that now that the project was coming to an end, they could rekindle that relationship. As he approached the summit, his father didn't seem to notice him. Jamie wasn't sure if his father was deep in thought or deliberately ignoring him, but when he got close, his father looked up.

They locked eyes for a long moment, and then his father said, "Jamie."

Jamie searched for warmth but found none. He had expected that, but decided to give it what little time they still had. Jamie would convert to Essence tomorrow and by the end of the week would be fifty light years or more away from Earth. He might never see his father again. Jamie felt a slight twinge inside at that thought, but he breathed it away. He knew this was more about his mother than anything else.

"Father," he replied. Then he turned to the valley. He could see even more people and vehicles from this vantage. "It's going well," he said.

After another pause, his father spoke. "I think that is true. Though I can't be certain from here."

"I'm surprised you're not observing from the transition buildings."

His father sighed. "I do not wish to be there. I can see what transpires from here."

Jamie remembered his father speaking to his mother like this before he left. She had frustrated him, always trying to be involved with his work. Now he was transferring that frustration to Jamie in her absence.

Jamie remembered his mother as kind and funny. His early

childhood had been idyllic; he had never wanted for anything and spent much of his life outdoors. It was always warm and dry in their little valley, where he had played with the only three other children in their country. His father had worked inside, but he had sometimes made time for picnics and games with his family in those days. His mother had spent all her time with Jamie and the other kids. He knew she'd also worked on the project in the beginning, but she had stopped after Jamie's birth. Jamie had seen less and less of his father as he grew up, and by the time his mother died, he and his father had not spoken in years.

"I understand, Father. Have you a room in the valley?"

"No. I will stay here."

Jamie waited for further information. The full transition would happen in stages and take days to complete, and it didn't seem possible for his father to exist on a hillside for that long. Also, he could think of no reason for his father to remain here. The transition would take place whether his father watched or not, so wouldn't be better to wait elsewhere? Jamie was desperate to ask, but he remembered how his father hated being questioned. He sat on the grass far enough away from his father not to bother him and considered his next question.

"Father, how will you feel when the transition is complete?"

His father said nothing and continued to stare into the distance. Jamie did the same and gave his father time to consider replying.

"I will feel like I have done my duty, and I will feel relief," his father said at last.

Jamie considered that. His fought his instinct to let it go at face value, certain it concealed a lot of information.

"I can understand that, Father. Relief after all your years of effort, and knowing that humanity will survive and prosper. But I feel like there's a lot you aren't telling me. You say you have done your duty. What do you mean? Your duty to whom?"

His father turned to look at him. He seemed to study Jamie. An awareness came over his face, as though he was seeing Jamie for the first time.

"Are you happy to be transitioning, Jamie?"

"Yes, now that I understand it, I'm excited. It's been my dream to travel in space for as long as I can remember. I thought I'd have to sleep all the way to the Cygnus region. Now the possibilities seem endless."

"You will exist as Essence for a long time."

"Exactly. Think of all we can do and see. It's the most incredible thing to happen to humanity since we became self-aware."

Jamie examined his father's face. He wanted to have said the right thing, but he could never read his father. Still, it *must* be the right thing, because he meant it. The transition had confused him when it was first announced two years ago, but the sheer scale of the opportunity now overwhelmed him. Changing to Essence gave a human being the opportunity not just to live for a long time, but to travel in space faster than light. For half a billion years, the ebb and flow of human exploration and expansion across the universe had been undertaken using slow world ships, robots and endless sleeping. Many had died in the effort and isolated humans were evolving across the Milky Way into myriad sub-species. Now humanity, albeit in a changed form, could expand and unite across the universe.

Those on Earth would be first to change. The sun was aging prematurely, and it had been expanding for ten thousand years. Scientists had been able to move the Earth's orbit to compensate and it would now survive for millennia. Still, those remaining had made plans to leave.

"Do you think living a long time will be a problem, even as Essence?" asked Jamie.

"I am not certain. It has downsides. Humanity may resolve those."

Jamie laughed. "You sound like you already know what it's like."

Again, his father's face remained unchanged. Perhaps he thought the question was beneath him. His father was such an enigma. Jamie had tried to find out more about him, but had instead found inconsistency and barriers in the records. He was one of the few people who had lived off-world and returned. Jamie knew he had lived a long time, longer than any human Jamie had heard of, and that would give him a special insight.

"I expect that sounds silly to you, since you've lived so long. Living forever isn't so different from how long you've lived, is it?"

"Yes, it is," his father answered.

"What makes you say that?" asked Jamie.

His father did not look comfortable. He stared at the ground between his feet, then up into the air before resuming his stare at the complex.

"Jamie, I think someone needs to know what humanity will face after the transition. What the future will hold, what you need to think about doing."

Jamie waited. He knew how long it could take for his father to collect his thoughts. There was nothing to say, since he didn't know what his father was talking about.

"I have toiled with the consideration that converting to Essence would not just enable all humans on Earth to survive the death of the Earth, but also give them the longevity required to solve life's greatest mysteries. However, you will need other humans who have not changed to accomplish physical things. For the good of humanity, not all humans can convert. I also think many will not want to, once the full realization of what longevity means is known," his father explained.

"Father, it sounds like there are many things you haven't told us. What do you mean, the full realization?"

"Jamie, I only know of one way for someone who has converted to Essence to die. I have not told the project or the government all I know. There has been speculation, of course. Most feel there will be a way to die and we will discover it in due course. Perhaps they are correct, but I don't think they are. Some have joked that all those who have converted will see the end of the universe. I will tell you now that they are correct, but while they imagine that will mean living for trillions of years and watching the last star disappear, before finally dying themselves, they are not correct."

A fear gripped Jamie as his imagination ran wild.

"Are you saying we'll continue to live after all the stars are dead? And we'll exist in darkness?"

His father looked down again.

"I am, Jamie, but it's not forever, and I understand your fear. To live forever in darkness might be the worst thing imaginable, but that is not the future I am assuring you of. I hope

I can convince you the truth is better. You will not see the last star die, though you will be alive a long time. This universe will do what I can only describe as a reset after close to one trillion years. First, everything will go dark and you will go insane. It is a different insanity from what we know as physical beings, but there is no other word for it. You should be thankful for it, because it will help while away the years. Eventually the universe will restart and sanity will return."

Jamie shook his head. "You can't know all of that. Your theory sounds wrong."

"It is not a theory. I had converted before the last reset. Essence survives the reset. Jamie, you will be in darkness for a long time and then you will witness the big bang as the universe is born again. You will regain sanity and watch the expansion and then you'll see our solar system form. Four and a half billion years later, an asteroid will hit the Earth and most animal life will die. Soon after, the only intelligent species this universe has ever known will be born. Half a million years later, you will be born and you will no longer be Essence. You will, however, remember everything you have done for a trillion years."

There was nothing Jamie could do except stand up and walk. All of this was too much for him to take in. Until ten minutes ago he had felt an optimism such as he had never felt before in his life. The things he would be able to do and see were extraordinary and exciting. Now it seemed as though that would all be for nothing. The universe would reset itself and he would find himself here once more, after terrible, insane years. Yet his father had sanctioned all of this and had told no one. This was just like the man. He offered no one a choice. He had made all the decisions for everyone. That was one thing when the decision-making was for his family, but quite another when it involved the entire future of humanity.

Ha! Jamie thought. *What future?* After all their endeavors, human beings would perpetually find themselves back where they had begun. The dinosaurs would die again and again. How many other species were growing and dying across the universe to infinity? Why on Earth had his father seen this as a good choice for humanity? This was the worst choice possible.

If Jamie told everyone, they would never convert. But what of all those who were already going through the process?

Jamie turned to look at the complex. He could see the blur forming above the main building. That was the exit people would leave through as Essence and it was already forming. He didn't know much about the process, but he thought it might be possible to stop it if he ran right now. Panic rose up through his legs and body. He dashed towards the center and tumbled head over heels. He tried to get up, but his father pinned him to the ground.

"Jamie! What are you doing?"

"Get off me! I have to stop them. No one should convert. They have to be told the truth."

"I can't let you do that, Jamie. You need to think more clearly. I've had a lot of time to consider this, and it's the best thing for all of us."

"You're crazy! None of those people will want this. You can't force people to do things against their will."

"Think about it, Jamie. The universe will start over, but we will still exist, *and* we will remember everything. We can change the universe. We have all the time we need to figure out why this all happens and take control. We can learn how to stop the universe from resetting if we want. Who knows what else we can discover. The universe will reset whether you stop the process or not. You *will* be born again in a trillion years."

Jamie stopped wrestling his father and tried to think.

"But I won't know anything about it, so it won't bother me that the universe resets. As long as I don't know, everything will be OK."

"That's a blinkered view, Jamie. This is an opportunity to alter the universe, to be in control."

"Are you telling me you've seen the big bang?"

"I have seen all of it."

"The dinosaurs?"

"Yes."

"What if you had changed something? What if you had stopped human beings from developing intelligence? None of this would have happened."

"Once you have changed to Essence, you can't affect the physical universe. You can observe it, communicate with it and think."

"But if you can communicate, you can cause humans to make changes that can affect the outcome."

"That is true. We need to study the effects of change."

"So you don't know if the universe reset itself for the first and last time? It may not happen again?"

"I *know* the universe will reset itself again, but there are many things still to be discovered and understood."

"What if we cause a change and it works out the worst way for us, and there's nothing we can do?"

"There is always something we can do to fix changes. Or,

when we become physical beings, we can choose not to become Essence again."

"And die?"

"Yes."

His father stood up and released Jamie, who raised himself up on his elbows.

"I don't want to convert."

"Jamie, I need you to convert so you can explain all of this to the others as one of them. I need to be certain this communication can take place. It's a different form of communication, human to Essence. Also, there are many more things I need to tell you."

"Why can't you tell them when you change?"

His father sat on the grass and thought for a moment. "I am not converting this time."

Jamie was astonished.

"Doesn't that make you a hypocrite? You're telling me and everyone else to convert so we can do all these wonderful things in the name of humanity, yet you won't join us?"

"I have lived far too long. Longer than anyone has ever imagined."

"How do you know that?"

Jamie's father looked confused. "Sorry?"

"Think about it," said Jamie. "The universe starts over. How long has it been doing that? How many times has humanity evolved? How many times has someone lived until the end and turned into Essence? For all you know, this could have happened hundreds, maybe millions of times. What if humanity has tried to take control before and failed?"

"It is a waste of time to consider that. I have seen no evidence of it, and so I have to presume that's not the case."

"There would be no evidence unless someone existed as Essence and lived through it all."

"It is possible, but it changes nothing. We don't know for sure, and we have to find out for ourselves."

"We do? Yet you don't?"

"So long as there is continuity and someone can pass this information on to humanity when the time comes, it doesn't matter if this version of me dies now. Think of the bigger picture. Everyone can live through the resets except those chosen to continue in human form, which can continue until we have control and a better understanding of the universe."

"Won't humanity figure that out for themselves anyway? They'll make that decision. We don't have to guide them or force them down the same path. Maybe next time I'll change. In this life, I choose not to."

"Jamie, you have always wanted to travel and see other worlds. You can no longer sleep on a world ship. No more ships will ever leave this solar system. You would be stuck here."

"So I'm stuck on Earth. I like it here anyway. I'll just live out my days here. I won't live as long as you anyway. I'll be happy with five hundred years."

"Then I have to tell you, the Earth doesn't have that long."

Jamie looked up to the sky. He had spent his life being frustrated by his father, who always seemed to be one step ahead of him. No matter what Jamie said, it was always a poor idea and he didn't know all the facts.

"I wonder what else you haven't told me. I understand that the sun has at least another three billion years."

"We moved the Earth's orbit because the sun began to expand. For reasons we do not know, it's already running out of enough fuel to keep it burning steadily for that long. You forget I have seen all this before. I know the sun will swallow the Earth in less than three hundred years. Since everyone is leaving, there is little we can do. Moving Earth's orbit again is out of the question."

"You knew that, and yet you've chosen not to convert or get on one of the last world ships?"

"That is what I did the last time, and I ended up living on countless worlds for many years. I won't do it this time."

"You'll stay here and be roasted by the sun?"

"I'll be dead long before the Earth is engulfed. I don't know the exact time, but the sun will go through a phase of super-massive coronal mass ejections. One of them will kill me."

Jamie shook his head. "How can you say this? It's suicide!"

His father considered that. "Yes, I think you're right."

A short bang sounded from the valley, followed by a multicolored light show erupting from the domed building in the center. Jamie couldn't make out any details, but he was still certain the transition had started. He forgot any thoughts he'd had about stopping the process. There were too many things to consider, too much information to digest. From what his father had told him, the human race was safe and would continue to exist in two forms until the end of time. Part of him found it hard to believe that his father had lived so long. What effect would all those years have on someone? Although humans had increased their life spans over millions of years, compared to the trillions of years his father must have lived, and the possibility of living for eternity, that was insignificant.

Yet his father was also right that Jamie had spent his life talking about travelling the universe. If he stayed here, he would die. Even if he was born again, he wouldn't remember all of this. It would be a different version of Jamie. In fact, hadn't his father said that humans could change what happened the next time? He might not even be born again.

A wave of heat passed over them. Jamie watched through a haze as great energies played with the mechanics of life, distilling everything that made a human into a new form. A form that wouldn't have the restrictions of matter and light, a form that wouldn't react to gravity, a form that offered freedom.

"Jamie," his father said.

"Yes, Father."

"I think you should cover your ears now."

Jamie stared at his father. What terrible thing was about to happen? How many things had he not told anyone? He despised his father for playing with people's lives. For playing God.

A low wail drifted up from the valley, rising in intensity and pitch. Covering his ears had little effect; the cries of pain were unyielding and terrifying. Jamie screamed too, unable to cope with the fear of the tens of thousands who had suddenly found themselves in hell. It only lasted a minute that seemed much longer before it ended in another blast that shrouded everything in grey and blue.

Silence.

Terrifying silence.

Jamie looked to his father as if to say, *What's happening?* His father wore no expression, just his usual stoic resignation.

Jamie stared into the gloom again. He thought he could see a glow deep inside. It was growing, coming towards them. He glanced at his father, then back at the translucent blue.

"Are we in danger?"

"No."

A glowing thing shot over their heads, then another; more, right and left, up in the air, down again. Hundreds, no, thousands, swarming in the gloom. Jamie couldn't make out any form to the glow, but it moved so fast, it could be anything.

As if realizing Jamie's thoughts, his father said, "In time they will remember who they are and what form they had before the transition. We attract them because they can see little except our life energy in the darkness."

"Darkness? Why can't they see what we see?"

"They don't have eyes, Jamie. The universe looks different to them."

"But you said you saw the dinosaurs."

"Yes, I did. I learned to see matter. It wasn't the way you and I see things, but, as a human, I have interpreted those memories as I see now. I can't remember exactly how anything looked to me when I was Essence."

"So they'll learn to see…things?"

"Yes, they will learn quickly. Look, some are slowing down and creating form."

Jamie saw two glows orbiting them about three hundred yards away. They were changing from a ball shape to an elongated shape and back.

"Fascinating. I have never witnessed this process before, though I remember a little of going through it."

Jamie felt anger rise in his throat.

"You remember? It's fascinating? You caused this! You! Everything they're going through, you caused. They didn't understand what it would be like because you told them it was painless. Did you fake all the testing? They think they can live to the end of the universe if they want to, but they thought they could also die if they want to. They have no idea they're immortal now and that the universe will start over. You lied to them." Jamie shook his head. "What are you? How could you do that?"

"The pain was but a moment. What is that compared to eternity?"

The shapes drifted and stopped in front of Jamie and his father. They were now each the size and shape of a human.

"When can they…see us?" asked Jamie.

"I can't say for sure. The sense of time changes, which is why living for a trillion years is a different concept for a physical human. I remember being aware of things around me at once, but of course there were no other intelligent life forms and I didn't see the glow of that energy for a long time, a time I can't measure in years. But I could sense things in their physical form quite quickly."

"Could you communicate with these life forms?"

"I could communicate with humans. It seemed natural, but it's hard to describe. There was no other intelligence in the universe when I was first Essence. Animals everywhere seemed to find it easy to bond with me in their own way."

There were now two human-shaped figures, still glowing but more faintly now. An arm extended toward Jamie's father.

"Yes," his father said. "It would be best if you practice here and all stay together for a while. You will be able to find each other anywhere in the universe if you need to."

"Father, is it speaking to you?"

"I can't hear words, but I know what he's saying."

"Can it—he—hear me?"

"He is aware of what you are saying, but you have to focus on him so he knows you're addressing him."

"Father, I want to tell him about the future."

"He'll discover that for himself. They all will. There really is no need."

"Are you afraid he'll be as angry as I am?"

"Not in the slightest, because all their anger is gone now. Emotions are not the same for them."

"They have no emotions now?"

"They do. It's just different."

"I still feel they need to know."

"I'll leave it up to you, Jamie."

Jamie turned to the glowing figures. He thought he could make out features where their faces should be. Would he be able to recognize a friend, he wondered, in this form? He extended a hand toward one of the figures and stared.

"I want you to know something. Do you understand me?"

A strange sensation rippled through his head and sent shivers through his body. It felt like the form had said yes, so Jamie continued.

"You can't die in this form. You're immortal now."

Again, it felt like the figure was saying yes.

"The universe will end in a trillion years, long before the last star runs out of fuel."

There was a brief pause. The form seemed to turn to the other form, then returned to Jamie's gaze. Another yes.

"It will then restart in another big bang, and yo alive as Essence."

There was no response this time, but Jamie wait while before continuing.

"Life will emerge on Earth as it did before and nothing interferes, humans will evolve again as they When you are born again, your Essence is convert will become your human self again, with all your intact."

The forms turned to Jamie's father.

"It's true," he said. "And history can be change you what you do with this information. Or whet the others."

His father's expression changed to one of inte tration.

"I see. They now know everything you think, ready know."

Jamie thought one of the forms smiled. Or di

Two of the forms shot upwards and the othe moment later as the gloom cleared. All together eastward in the sky, going faster and faster. Minu passed overhead one last time before disappearin into the vacuum of space.

Jamie stared into the valley, which was clear watched the sun setting and felt the temperature d at his father, he tried to find words for everythin ing. He imagined that his father felt nothing. Eith over now; there was no going back for humanity. he had no energy for words.

"It's getting cold, Father. Do you want to sta

"No. I live underground, just behind this hill." His father looked at Jamie. "You're welcome to stay with me."

Their eyes locked. So much was being left unsaid. It had felt like they had little time, but now it seemed to Jamie that they had forever.

"Yes, Father, I'll stay with you."

He knew precisely where Earth was and would one day understand how. The Guardians had already learned much more about the science of the universe than humanity had ever dreamed, and with understanding came great power—power even to change Sol and let the Earth live for millions or even billions more years. However, the Assembly had decided that was inappropriate. The Earth would die in this cycle as so many other worlds had.

As he passed through the Oort cloud, he could feel the pleasant tingle of interaction with the ancient icy waste left over from the earliest days. Sol was much bigger now, and straight ahead, but he changed direction towards the Earth and joined many others in their pilgrimage. The proximity of the sun and mass ejections had virtually destroyed the Earth's surface. It would be unrecognizable to them in its final death throes.

After a short time they took up position inside the asteroid belt close to Earth's new orbit. The sun had swallowed Mars, and now it was Earth's turn. Millions of years of human history stood on the precipice of the unstoppable, expanding fire pit of their sun. He felt moved by the occasion, but knowing the Earth would one day be reborn lessened the sentiment. Still, he wanted a closer look, one last gaze over his former home, the place of his birth.

He left the group and sped towards the grey planet, no longer the blue-green world of poetry and art. Its sun was perilously close now, but that didn't worry him. He could fly straight through a star and live, though it was not without consequence and he would not do so without good reason.

As he neared the planet, a strange sensation grew inside him that he had not felt in many years. At first he put it down to a kind of human nostalgia, a leftover feeling from his physical days. Then, when the Earth turned in front of his presence, he realized what the feeling was and flew to the surface itself. There was no atmosphere around this dead, rocky world, and he struggled to make out any features recognizable from his youth. Some mountain peaks might have marked the collision of plates before he'd left, but he couldn't tell. There were volcanoes again now as the Earth warmed and faults were formed.

How could anything be alive down here?

His senses strained to pinpoint the location that was so well concealed, not from him, but from the ravages of the planet and its sun. At last he stopped above a valley and a hill, beneath which a glow was emanating. The glow of life. Even now, after two hundred years in a non-physical form, he paused and collected himself before continuing on his journey into the planet. At last his decision was made and he plunged to the surface, picking up enough speed to break through the barrier and reach the interior. Traveling through solid rock, he focused on the glow as his point of reference and slowed his descent until he was hovering in a huge cavern. The glow was moving toward him now and he waited until the vehicle had stopped beneath him before choosing to land beside it.

The door opened and a figured shrouded in a thick suit

struggled to its feet and gazed at him. The figure removed its helmet and Jamie forced his form to become more physical in shape, to look as he had all those years before.

"Father," he said.

"Jamie," his father replied. "It's good to see you."

"I feel the same."

"I don't have long to live."

"No, you don't."

"I plan to travel to the surface and die there in the fire."

"Yes, Father."

"But first, Jamie, I have to tell you something."

"Yes, Father?"

"I'm proud of you, Jamie. Proud of everything you've done and everything you are. I was no help to you as you grew up, and everything you achieved is down to you. Also…your mother loved you very much and you made her very happy in her last days."

"Thank you, Father."

"I know these words are wasted now, and I should have said them before you changed. I regret that, and many other things. I hope you can understand why I couldn't say this…before. I hope your anger has faded and that you can forgive me."

His father paused. "I…I love you, Jamie."

Jamie tried to control the pulsing that rippled around his form. It tickled, and it made it impossible for him to think clearly. He couldn't understand what was happening, but as the tickling slowed, he felt somehow stronger, more defined.

"Father, I…love you too."

Jamie sat with his father on the surface. He felt this was the same valley where he had changed to Essence so many years before. It was unrecognizable now. His father was wearing the bulky suit again, still struggling to keep warm on this coldest of nights, but as the dawn began, earlier than usual, it was clear there would be no more need to keep warm. Sol was not rising over the horizon this morning. It *was* the horizon, and Jamie knew that incredible heat was about to flood over the surface of the world. His father had mere minutes left.

His father stood up and looked at him. "Good luck," was all he said.

"I will see you again, Father."

And then his father was gone.

Jamie flew straight upward faster than he had ever flown. He flew round and round the sun, accelerating to block out the waves of energy coursing through him. There was no release; he had no tears to express his feelings for the Guardians, but what humanity remained inside of him demanded it of him and he felt he would explode from the pain.

Gradually it subsided and he flew to the others who were observing the final moments of the Earth as it was absorbed. There was strength in the group and it eased his burden, if that could ever be possible.

Jamie flew above the Earth. He was among the clouds, and was masking his presence. No radar should pick him up, and he should not be visible.

It was against the rules for Guardians to visit the Earth in this cycle, for fear of changing things, but they had given Jamie special dispensation to help cure his condition. They had judged that it was killing him.

His father had said they were immortal, but he had been wrong. It was still possible for a Guardian to die if he or she so willed it, and Jamie willed it.

After some observation he found his father. During their time together on Earth, before Jamie changed to Essence, his father had given him enough clues about his youth that Jamie could narrow it down, and it took even less time than Jamie had imagined to find the familiar glow. Camouflaged, Jamie followed his father, listening to him as a young man and getting to know him as he never could have before. He saw himself in his father and that caused him to fly off the Earth many times before he could control his feelings.

In all it took years until Jamie felt fully in control. He left the Earth and returned to be analyzed by the Guardians, who pronounced him cured.

Jamie's father sat on a park bench eating a sandwich, lost in the world of physics. He often thought that lectures got in the way. He was learning more in the labs and library than he was in classes. Staring into the distance, he put his things away in his bag, resigned to having to plod back inside yet again.

There.

By the stream. Hovering.

He had seen it before, out of the corner of his eye, but this time it was right in front of him.

It looked like his own image. It *was*...he was certain.

The thing was emanating some kind of feeling that went through his body. He couldn't react; the thing would know it had been spotted.

What was it? Who was it? How could a human being be like this? It wasn't a ghost, it was a living thing.

An alien pretending to be him? Why?

An echo of himself somehow?

He decided to find out.

A WORD FROM GARETH FOY

Although I have been writing for a long time, longer than I care to remember, it is only more recently that I have considered publishing my stories. Discovering the world of independent publishing has been a revelation. It is a far cry from the world of slush piles I grew up in during the 90s. My enthusiasm for reading and writing has grown manifold as a result. Thanks to NaNoWriMo, I rediscovered how to let go and just write straight from inside.

I have long been a reader and follower of the Future Chronicles and it is incredible to be alongside all of the amazing writers Samuel Peralta has brought to this fantastic party.

This story came from one basic scene, character and an event. Samuel's encouragement then gave me the energy to pursue the story to the best of my ability. The journey from that starting place to the finished work, took many weeks of writing only two or three hours a week, but all of the time in between writing sessions was spent thinking about it. The fledgling story was allowed to fly and soared beyond my initial intentions. As a result I have three more stories in this universe at various stages of completion and I'm looking forward to doing a lot more flying.

More information will be available at the following places (under construction for the most part):

http://www.garethfoy.uk/
https://www.facebook.com/profile.php?id=100004122737474

The Backup
by Patricia Gilliam

Outside Raleigh, North Carolina
February 5th, 2079

NICK OPENED HIS EYES and squinted at the alarm clock. It was ten past noon. He groaned and pulled his comforter over his head, but sunlight filtered through the pattern of moons and spacecraft. Even facing the wall, it was no use. He needed to get up.

"Dad?" he called. He rubbed his eyes and walked down the hallway. His father's bed was made, and no one was in the kitchen. Nick stretched to open the door to the carport, recoiling as a freezing blast of wind hit him. Their truck was gone. "Must be at work…"

After dragging a chair to reach the countertop, he discovered the frosted flakes were down to their final sugary crumbles—his favorite part. The milk didn't cover everything, but it was fine after a few bites. He turned on the display in the living room and switched its input to the video game system.

The doorbell rang a half hour later. Nick jumped and faced the door. A short, dark-haired woman cupped her hands around her face to see through the living room window. Her breath fogged the glass, and she stepped back.

"Hi," she said. Her voice was muffled. "I'm Mrs. McFerrin—Josh's mom. We live four houses over."

Nick had met Josh McFerrin at school, but Josh was two grades above him and had different teachers.

"My dad said never to open the door for strangers," he replied, unsure if she could hear him. He tried to speak louder as he approached the window. "If you want something, he should be back soon."

"Honey, your father was in an accident." Mrs. McFerrin paused as Nick's eyes widened, but she kept her voice calm. "He's been taken to the hospital, and you can't stay here alone. Do you have any other family I can call for you—maybe an aunt or uncle?"

Nick shook his head. "It's just us. Is my dad all right?"

"We don't know yet." She took her phone out of her coat pocket. "My husband and Josh stopped to help the police search for you. Your father must have been confused and believed you were in the truck with him. I'll let them know you're all right, and the police can take you to the hospital. I'll wait until they get here."

The wind picked up, and she huddled closer to the house. Nick walked to the living room door and unlocked it. Mrs. McFerrin eased it open and then shut it behind her.

"It's really cold out there," Nick said. She nodded and ended her call. "I'm Nick—Nick Mathis."

He held his hand out to her, something his dad had taught him. She shook it and crouched to his level.

"Nice to meet you, Nick Mathis," she said. She forced a smile, but her eyes were watery. "What can you tell me about your dad?"

Abbot-Mathis Industries - Chicago
Thirty-Four Years Later

"You need to be angrier about all of this," Nick's business partner William Abbot said. Nick sighed and shook his head. "You dated that woman for three months, broke it off, and she pops up two years later with a book deal about your entire life. How is that right?"

Nick surveyed the lobby as their elevator descended. During product launches or charity drives, two dozen reporters would be considered a great turnout. This crowd appeared closer to two hundred and growing. "I knew Bianca was a biographer when I met her, so it's my own fault for trusting her. I just wish people would quit acting as if I'm already dead. According to how my treatments go, I can at least consult for another two or three years."

"I hope it's longer than that," Abbot said. "Are you sure you want to hold a press conference now? In a few months, it may not be a major story."

"People need to know you can hold your own, especially

the board," Nick replied. "The sooner we make the transition, the less likely any vultures will try to move in on you and the McFerrins after I'm gone."

Abbot frowned but nodded. "Have you spoken with them about your will?"

"Josh and Debra? No, I want to tell them in person. I'll schedule a trip once all of this settles out."

The elevator dinged, and its doors opened. Nick took a deep breath and jogged ahead of Abbot—in part to annoy any tabloid journalists attempting to portray him as weak and suffering.

"Beautiful day, isn't it?" Nick said into his headset. He tapped a file on the podium's display, hesitating when it showed old financial statements instead of his talking points. He backed out to the main menu and forced a smile. "Let's begin with a few questions and then save my statement for the end. Who wants to start?"

The crowd shouted over each other. Nick pointed at random to a reporter in the third row.

"Hello, sir," he said. "I just finished your biography released by Bianca Reynolds—"

"I apologize for my driver's license photo they stole for the cover," Nick interrupted. "Sorry, go on."

"Your father, Dr. David Mathis, developed Alzheimer's in his early forties, correct?" the reporter continued. Nick gave a reluctant nod. "Given the hereditary aspects of the disease, is your decision to step down as CEO in response to this being made public—and do you intend to stay at AMI in some capacity until—"

Someone screamed, but Nick had no time to react. His vision faded, and the last sensation he felt was falling forward.

* * *

Nick gasped and sat upright in a bed, finding himself in darkness. A tangled mass of wires tugged at his skin, and he scrambled to remove them.

As his eyes adjusted, he noticed a small shaft of light outlining a doorway. A stray wire snagged his arm as he stood, but he managed to reach a wall and then feel his way to a door handle. It didn't budge, and he felt too dizzy and weak to force the door open.

"Authorization required." The voice was mechanical, and the speaker above his head popped and crackled.

"Is this a hospital?" he asked. It hurt to talk, but the feeling of being trapped was worse. "I'm awake. Can anyone hear me?"

No one answered, but he heard the door unlock. He opened it, expecting another room or hallway.

Instead, the night skyline of Charleston greeted him.

BlueHealth Hospital - Raleigh
February 5th, 2079

Two police officers dropped Nick off with a social worker, a young woman in her twenties who already seemed disheartened by her job. She took his hand and led him through the hospital's lobby. The linoleum tiles glinted as if they had just been mopped, and the smell of floor cleaner made Nick feel nauseous. The woman pressed the call button for the elevator.

"We'll need to wait until the doctors can talk to us," she said as the doors opened, and she pulled for him to go with her. Nick resisted and slipped free from her grasp. "Nick, you need to stay with me."

"My dad died, didn't he?" he asked. Mrs. McFerrin and the police officers hadn't told him, but he had seen it in their expressions. Before the social worker could answer, Nick turned away from her and ran for the exit. He could hear her heels clacking behind him, but they slowed her down.

"Nick, please! Come back!"

He'd almost reached the exit doors when a man caught him by one arm and lifted him from the floor. Nick started hitting him to no avail, but by that point he was crying, too.

"I just didn't want you to get hit by a car, kid." The man's voice was quiet despite the fact that he seemed to be seven feet tall. "Is this your sister?"

"I'm his caretaker," the social worker replied. "Thank you. His father just passed away."

"David Mathis?" the man asked. The social worker nodded. The man placed Nick in a chair but stood between him and the exit. "I'm Jack McFerrin. My son and I found David's truck this morning. I wanted to come by and offer his family our condolences and find out if they needed anything. Are they on their way?"

"There isn't anyone else, I'm afraid—not that I can find, anyway." The social worker reached for Nick's hand again, but he scooted back into the chair and gripped the plastic cushion. "Did you know David?"

"We waved at each other in passing—spoke a few times when they first moved into the neighborhood," Mr. McFerrin replied. Even when he crouched, he was almost as tall as the social worker. He turned his attention to Nick. "I know it's hard, and it's okay to cry. Your dad loved you. Josh and I didn't talk to him long before the ambulance came, but he was more worried about you than he was about himself. I promised him I'd make sure you were all right."

"I'm not," Nick replied. He closed his eyes, and tears ran down his cheeks. "I don't want him to be gone."

"I know, buddy," Mr. McFerrin replied. He hugged Nick, and Nick cried on his shoulder until he went limp in exhaustion. "You won't be alone. I can promise you that."

Ectotech Labs - Outside Raleigh, North Carolina
Thirty-Four Years later

"Josh, we will pay for your time and travel expenses if you'll just—"

"What I need is time to think, Mr. Abbot," Josh McFerrin said into his headset. He wiped his eyes, thankful Abbot and the rest of AMI's board couldn't see him. "The police and IBI still have no leads on who killed Nick, and you're asking me about selling stock we don't even own yet!"

"I'm not advising you to sell," Abbot replied, clearly backpedaling. "Taking the company from public back to private may be our best option to recover from Nick's death. I miss him, too, but this isn't something we can put off without it affecting thousands of employees and their families."

"I understand what you're saying. Deb and I will talk it over with our lawyer and get back to you. Is that fair?"

Voices in the background seemed divided on this, and it took a minute for Abbot to answer.

"Is there any way I could I meet with you there in Raleigh?"

"We won't turn you away if you show up." Josh stood, and his golden retriever Dakota began to follow him around the lab with a stuffed giraffe toy. "Just be sure to call first. Our current guard dog is kind of ferocious, and we wouldn't want you to return to Chicago with missing limbs."

He ended the call before Abbot had time to respond. Looking over the support suit parts on his lab table, Josh picked up a wiring harness and began to lay out the configuration he needed to attach it. His headset buzzed again, and his shoulders slumped. To his relief, it was his brother-in-law Clint.

"Are you in the middle of anything? I'm about to meet with the new team leader of the Chicago IBI office. I wanted to make sure you're available if she has questions."

Josh laid the harness down and walked away from the table. "That's fine. I'm about to lock up here. I can't concentrate long enough to get anything done."

"Are you all right?"

"William Abbot called again," he replied. "That's seven times since Nick's funeral. Deb won't even answer anymore."

"That's probably for the best. I don't know if Deb has had a chance to tell you, but Nick's death has been reclassified a contracted hit. You've been cleared, but they're looking into Abbot and several other board members as possible suspects. Debra is still on the list, but it's a formality due to her past employment."

"Seriously?" Josh asked. Debra had been out of the CIA for over ten years, but it still came up at odd times. "I'm beginning to think she married me for cover and stayed for the kids."

"And the free lifetime tech support," Clint added. "I'll call you back if I find out anything. Take care of yourself, Josh."

"I will. Thanks."

As Josh grabbed his coat, Dakota barked and began scratching at the main door.

"Deb, is that you?" Josh shouted. Dakota's barking became more frantic. Confused, Josh checked the security cameras. A tall man in a hooded overcoat was on the other side of the door. "Hey, I can see you! What do you want?"

"Not being shot would be nice!" the man shouted back. He sounded like Nick. "I know this is crazy, Josh, but give me a chance to explain."

Outside Raleigh, North Carolina
February 6th, 2079

"You'll need to pack for the next two weeks." The social worker hadn't slept the entire time they were at the hospital and had put her car into auto-drive. Nick looked away from her and out the passenger window. "The McFerrins will need to go through classes and have their home inspected. I'll try to push things through as fast as I can, but the process takes time. You'll be staying with a very nice family in the meantime."

Nick noticed a dark cloud of smoke long before they reached his neighborhood, but it wasn't unusual for people to burn dead trees and brush during the winter. As they got closer, he sat up higher in his seat. Two fire trucks were parked in front of what remained of his house. The roof was smoldering, and several rafters had collapsed.

"Did you leave something on before you left?" the social worker asked. Nick shook his head, but she sighed as she got out of the car. "Wait here."

She approached one of the firefighters, who gestured at the house and shook his head. Anything the fire hadn't damaged was most likely soaked. Nick opened his door and coughed as smoke hit his lungs.

"You both need to go," the firefighter said. Nick hurried back to his seat and shut the door. Instead of being angry like he'd expected, the social worker drove them to a store and helped him pick out some clothes and a toothbrush. At the checkout, she paid for everything with no mention of whether it was her personal money or not.

"Thank you," Nick told her. She forced a smile, but her eyes were sad. Nick wondered if this would be the reaction of every adult he met for the rest of his life.

His father's funeral and his time with his first foster family—the Wilsons—passed quickly. By the time Nick moved in with the McFerrins, they had converted their spare bedroom with extra bedding and toys from Josh's bedroom. The two boys would be across the hall from each other.

"Dad has to travel sometimes with his job, but Mom works from here," Josh explained as he gave Nick a tour of the rest of the farmhouse. It was old, but the McFerrins had modernized most of the interior. They sat down on a sectional in the living room. "I'm sorry about your dad—and your house."

The front door opened, and Mr. McFerrin walked in carrying a cardboard box.

"This was in the back of your father's truck," he said to Nick. He opened it, revealing a pile of servos and metal plates. "It looks like a model kit, but it's pretty heavy for a toy. I can put it in your room if you don't want it right now."

Nick nodded. He'd seen his father sketch and build incredible things for his work, but in that moment he didn't want the reminder. Mr. McFerrin lifted the box and took it upstairs.

IBI Field Office - Chicago
Thirty-Four Years Later

"How's your family holding up?" Agent Nina Johnson placed her right palm on a scanner, unlocking the office door. "I wish you could help us in the field, but a good defense attorney would rip us apart if they found out you're Debra's brother."

"I don't want to cause you any problems," Agent Clint Rossetti said and followed her inside. The building's interior smelled like bread from the sub shop next door, and it was more noticeable after being gone for several months. "Deb seems to be handling it all right, but she's worried about Josh. Nick was practically his adopted brother when they were kids."

"I'm sorry," Nina replied. "We're doing everything we can, but you know what it's like here. I may be able to pull in help from Indianapolis and Cincinnati, but I can't guarantee for how long."

Clint nodded and sat down at his old desk. Nina had

granted him full access to the case file via her account, and he didn't want to waste her time. He bypassed most of the autopsy photos, but something in one of them caught his attention.

"What are these fragments?" he asked. Nina walked behind him and looked over his shoulder. "They look like shrapnel, but everything I read said it was a single shot."

"They're medical implants," she replied. Clint's eyebrows rose, given the number of them. "I spoke to William Abbot at AMI about them. Nick Mathis was mapping the long-term progression of his disease so the data could be used to help other patients. The coroner found nanotech in his blood and brain tissue, too—same function, according to Abbot."

"I bet transport security loved him," Clint replied. "Where's all that data being stored now that Nick's gone?"

"Abbot wouldn't tell me. Unless it was relevant to Mathis's death, we wouldn't have legal access to it, anyway."

Clint was about to reply when his phone beeped. He read the message and then stood. "It's Josh. Sorry, I have to go to Raleigh. Thanks for allowing me to look over the file. If you ever need anything on another case, call me."

"Is something wrong?"

"I don't know if you'll believe me," he said. Nina crossed her arms. "According to Josh, Nick Mathis cloned himself."

Ectotech Labs - Outside Raleigh, North Carolina

"One moment I'm at AMI in Chicago and the next I'm waking up in an automated lab in Charleston." Nick sat on a barstool and leaned to pet Dakota. The dog rolled to show his belly as if nothing was wrong. "I know it sounds insane, but I didn't set this up."

"Maybe Nick created you as some sort of clone backup," Josh replied. Nick frowned. "He died over a month ago. How long have you been awake—active?"

"A couple of days, I think." Nick shook his head. "I remember everything, Josh—growing up here, you, your mom and dad, my dad…"

"I believe you," Josh said, but he held his hands out in front of him. "We'll wait here for Clint and get this sorted out, okay?"

"Are you afraid of me?" Nick pointed toward Josh and Debra's house across the road. "If I left and tried to walk through your front door right now, what would happen?"

"If I didn't stop you first, Debra would kill you to protect the kids," Josh replied. Nick cringed. "You're not the first clone we've encountered, and their behavior can be unpredictable. If an ounce of Nick's consciousness is in you, you need to trust me. I don't want this to end badly for any of us."

Nick nodded and looked down at the floor.

"I didn't want to bring all of this on you, but I didn't know who else I could trust," he said. "You're still the closest people I have to a family."

"Don't talk like that right now." Josh looked away from him and started pacing. "I want to believe it's you, Nick, but we have no way of knowing. Clint worked with two clones for over five years—sleeper agents who had infiltrated the IBI. One of them turned on the rest of the team, and the other tried to protect them."

"Seems like they still had some choice in the matter," Nick

replied. "Regardless of what happens after your brother-in-law gets here, I can't pick up where my life left off. At best, the IBI will send me into some kind of protection program. At worst, I'll be treated as a potential threat—and I have no solid answers on how this happened. Do you think they'll believe that, considering my best friend doesn't?"

Josh started to reply, but his headset buzzed. He didn't answer, and the headset announced the caller's name. "It's William Abbot. He keeps calling about the stock you willed to us."

"I told Abbot to watch out for vultures, not to become one," Nick said in a disappointed tone. Josh removed the headset and placed it on his desk. It continued to buzz. "I'd answer it for you, but I'd probably give him a heart attack. I guess I haven't been a good judge of character lately—present company excluded, I hope."

"Even if you're not Nick, you're still a sentient being—and Clint and his team won't torture or dissect you for information." Josh's headset beeped a voicemail notification, and he decided to check it. "Abbot is at O'Hare. His flight is leaving in a few minutes, and he plans to come here after he lands."

McFerrin Residence
February 5th, 2084

Nick couldn't sleep. Despite how kind the McFerrins had been to him, each anniversary of his father's death made him want to stay in bed until the day was over. This time it was on a Saturday, so he didn't have to force himself to get ready for school.

Someone knocked on his door.

"Nick, I'm making breakfast if you want to get up," Mrs. McFerrin said. From her tone, she seemed aware of the day and didn't try to open the door. "I'm caught up on work, and I was thinking I could take you and Josh to the movies—maybe stop for pizza later."

She was trying, and Nick knew it. Still, he didn't answer. The floorboards creaked as she walked away and down the stairs.

"Nick?" It was Josh this time. "Get up. I want to show you something."

"Not today," Nick replied, but there were no sounds of Josh leaving. "What is it?"

"I'm not telling you, Nick. I have to show you."

Nick sighed, but he got dressed and then opened his door. Josh grinned at him, and it was a rare instance where Nick felt annoyance towards him. Maybe that was part of being like brothers, too.

"What is it?" Nick repeated.

Josh led him to his room, and Nick's eyes widened. In the middle of the floor was a spider-like robot the size of an adult's hand. Josh handed him a tablet.

"Dad believes it's a concept model—showed me how to put one together to surprise you," Josh said. "There are more parts in the box if you want to make more. You can even program and control them. Did your father work for NASA or something?"

"I thought he was a doctor." Nick walked around the robot, and it turned so that its cameras always faced him—even when he passed the tablet back to Josh. He jumped forward, and the robot jumped back. Nick found himself laughing. "Weird. I remember seeing Dad draw one of these, but I didn't know they were real."

"Boys, food is ready!"

Nick's stomach growled at the smell of bacon and omelets. Josh laid the tablet and the model on his bed, but they heard a crash before they reached the stairs. The model had crawled off the edge and was in scattered pieces across the floor.

"We'll get it later," Josh said, and he didn't seem upset. "It'll make it easier to show you."

O'Hare International Airport - Chicago
Twenty-Nine Years Later

"Is this seat taken?" Agent Clint Rossetti asked. A brown-haired man in a business suit shook his head. "Sorry to crowd you. I hate booking last-minute."

"Seems like all I do lately," the man replied. "Hey, do I know you?"

Clint shrugged as he put his briefcase in the overhead compartment. "I live in Arizona now, but I grew up about thirty minutes from here. What high school did you go to?"

"It was in New York." The man shook his head and then glanced out his window. "Sorry, it's been a long day."

"No problem." Clint realized he knew the man from Nick's funeral but wasn't certain of his name. He considered changing seats, but his other options were worse—putting him next to a woman with overpowering perfume or a hairy-armed man who seemed possessive of the joint armrest. He could later claim IBI strategy if he learned anything, but this was more about surviving the next two hours. "I'm Clint."

"William Abbot." The man opened his tablet and rested it on his tray table. "I don't mean to be rude, but I need to catch up on work on the way. My business partner was murdered a month ago, so I'm handling what used to be both of our positions. It's been a rough transition, to say the least."

Clint nodded and started to say something, but he noticed Hairy Man scratching his ribs a few rows ahead of them. He could smell Perfume Bather behind them, and some poor soul was already coughing from being in closer proximity.

"I'll be right back." Clint stood and took a deep breath, exhaling once he was inside the restroom. He logged in to the plane's wireless network to check if Josh or Debra had tried to reach him. Instead, he found a message from Nina Johnson to call her once he landed. He tried her number.

"That was fast," Nina said. "Are you already in Raleigh?"

"Not yet," Clint said. "I'm still on the plane. William Abbot and I are seat buddies, but I don't believe he recognized me. What did you need to tell me?"

"One of my team members found something. We've assumed the shot came from the parking garage across the street from AMI's headquarters—the angle and trajectory match. The security cameras appeared to have nothing, but everyone who viewed them watched the videos in real time—assuming any hit man would be human. Take a look at this, but watch it at ten times the normal speed."

She sent a file, and Clint opened it. He found the speed setting and watched as something bobbed up and down across the parking garage's ceiling. It reminded him of a giant spider, and he shuddered as the video repeated.

"Some sort of robot—rover?" Clint asked. He tried to zoom in, but the rover was in the shadows and blended with the surrounding steel and concrete. "Someone programmed this thing, rigged a gun to it, and just waited? How could they have known where Nick would be at any given time? How could it know?"

"If his medical implants were sending out a signal, they could have been tracked," Nina replied. "Be careful, Clint. We haven't connected this to Abbot, but he has the technical background. We're looking at employees in AMI's robotics division, too—anyone who could have benefited from Nick being out of the way."

Someone knocked on the door and jiggled the handle.

"Is anyone in there?" a man asked. "Don't mean to rush you, but this is urgent."

"I have to go, Nina," Clint said. "Thanks."

As Clint returned to his seat, Abbot handed him a tablet. He had found Clint's IBI profile.

"Would you like to split a cab, Agent Rossetti?"

Ectotech Labs - Outside Raleigh, North Carolina

"Once Debra leaves with the kids, we'll move to the house," Josh said. He pulled a curtain back and raised the blind. The sun was setting. "You can stay in the spare bedroom until Abbot is gone. If Clint gets here first, it would probably be safer for you to go with him."

"Safer for me or you?" Nick asked, but he grinned at Josh's reaction. "It's like we're kids again—playing spies or hide-and-seek. How are your mom and dad? I heard Jack took up golf?"

"Mom sometimes goes with him for the entertainment value," Josh said but hesitated. "We can't tell them about you. I think it would wreck them—Mom, especially."

Nick sighed and picked up a small holographic display from Josh's desk. It was playing short video clips from the previous Christmas, which Nick had missed spending with them due to a blizzard.

"I feel like a ghost, Josh. I was excited about being alive and seeing all of you again, but right now I'm just as scared as you are about what I am and how this happened."

"We'll figure it out," Josh replied. "Did you take a look around the lab before you left it?"

"It wasn't huge, but I was disoriented at the time—grabbed the clothes I'm wearing out of a locker and got out of there as fast as I could. I think I could lead the IBI back to the building, though."

Debra's vehicle pulled out of the driveway and went right towards the city. Nick reached for the lab's front door, but Dakota jumped and knocked him off-balance. A bullet struck the door at Nick's head level and lodged into a support post, narrowly missing him and the dog. "What the—"

"Get behind the table!" Josh shouted. It had some metal plating at its base but was better than nothing. Josh kept a small pistol in his desk and ammo in a locked cabinet, but he doubted a sniper would get within range for them to be effective. He still grabbed both. "Does anybody else know you're here?"

"Just your family and Clint. I didn't broadcast it or any-thing."

Josh loaded the gun and then grabbed his tablet. He ran a scan of the room that found that something in Nick's body was sending out a digital signal. He targeted the program to the location and ran the scan again. "Actually, I think you did. You have a huge implant in your head."

"What?" Nick asked in confusion. Dakota licked his face, and he sputtered and wiped his mouth. "Can you get it out?"

"I don't believe it would be operable. I might be able to shut it down, though. Give me a minute."

"Don't have anything pending on my schedule," Nick re-plied. "Can your tablet scan the surrounding area, too—maybe pick up who's here?"

"I can try. The implant looks like older tech—older than me, anyway."

"Got anything?" Nick asked after a minute.

"Just got your implant's signal shut off," Josh replied. "The bad news is that something is moving on the roof of my house."

Raleigh-Durham International Airport

"Whatever that thing is, we didn't make it," William Abbot said as he watched the surveillance video from AMI's parking garage. He handed Clint's phone back as a taxi stopped for them. "The closest I've ever seen to it are the A-676 spider rov-ers—self-contained, solar powered, very slow moving. NASA replaced them with much smaller models that require less pow-er, but there are a few still operational on the Moon and Mars."

"Do you think someone could have stolen or rebuilt one—maybe even a prototype?" Clint asked. Abbot shrugged and put his suitcases in the taxi's trunk. Clint added his briefcase. "Do you have any employees who may have been connected to the A-676 project?"

"Not unless they were children at the time," Abbot said, but his expression sobered as they got into the backseat of the cab. "Nick's father consulted for NASA at one point. Nick never mentioned it to me, but I read it in the biography. Maybe there's a connection through him."

"Where to?" the driver asked. Clint gave her the street address. "Ectotech—busy place lately. Are you buying one of their suits?"

"Potential investor," Abbot said. Clint gave him a skeptical look. "The moment Josh and Debra have Nick's stock, dozens of other people will be calling every other minute. I'm trying to do the right thing and keep AMI intact as best as I can."

Clint's phone rang, and he answered. "We're about fifteen minutes away. William Abbot is with me in the taxi."

"Something is shooting at us." Josh was loud enough for both Abbot and the taxi driver to hear. The driver slowed the car and pulled over. "It's on the roof of my house."

"Does it look like this?" Clint asked, and he sent a copy of the video. "Watch it in high speed. This is what killed Nick. It's some sort of—"

"It's an A-676," Josh interrupted. "Nick and I had smaller models when we were kids. The impound company gave them to Dad from Dr. Mathis's truck."

He stopped talking. Clint and Abbot exchanged glances.

"Josh, are you still there?" Clint asked.

"I think I know how to disable it, but stay away until I do. I'll call you back and let you know if it worked or not."

"Don't do anything stupid," Clint said, but Josh didn't respond. "If you're still there, I'm calling for backup."

Ectotech Labs - Outside Raleigh, North Carolina

"Stay here." Josh stood and walked toward the door. "Its programming shouldn't be any different from the small-scale model we had. If I put it into recharge mode, it won't be able to move or target anything."

"Why don't you just wait until Clint gets here?" Nick asked. Josh opened the door and sidestepped out of the way. Nothing happened. "If this thing can't track my implant, it could switch to some other means—movement, body heat, my last known location—"

"We have neighbors with small children, and I don't want to risk it leaving the area," Josh replied. Dakota bolted out the door, and Josh whistled for him to come back. They heard a shot, and the dog whimpered and fell. "No, no, no, no…"

Without thinking, Josh started to run out the door. Nick grabbed him by his t-shirt and jerked him back inside. Out of reflex, Josh punched him but then stopped. Nick's lip was bleeding red, not silver like the other clones Josh had seen. Nick took a step back.

"Turn my implant back on first." He grabbed Josh's tablet off the floor and handed it to him. "I'll keep it distracted for as long as I can. You go help Dakota and tell Clint what's happening. Don't argue."

Josh nodded and handed Nick his headset. "The moment we have it disabled, I'll call you."

Nick nodded. "Be careful, Josh. You have Debra and the kids. I—"

"You have a brother," Josh replied. "Thank you. I'll hurry."

Josh reactivated the implant's signal, and Nick bolted out the back door. Josh tried to look for movement outside, but he wasn't at a good angle.

Dakota was in the grass about ten yards away, still breathing but lying on his side. Josh ran, scooped him up, and then brought him back inside the lab. Dakota relaxed after a tranquilizer injection and allowed Josh to keep pressure on the entry and exit wounds. Josh used his tablet to call Clint.

"This thing is faster than the one in the video you sent me, and it just shot Dakota," Josh said. He opened a panel to access the rover, but both it and Nick were out of range. "How far out is your backup? I need a ride."

"Less than five minutes," Clint replied. "I left William Abbot with the cab, but the Raleigh team just picked me up. Are you all right?"

"I'm fine. Nick's clone ran, but he's trying to help us. He has an implant in his brain, and the A-676 is tracking it."

"It's trying to kill him?" Clint asked. "Hey—I may have to call you back. We've stopped."

Josh listened to the background noises, able to make out Clint's voice but no one else's. He'd gotten Dakota's bleeding under control. It didn't look as if the bullet had penetrated any vital organs, but he would need stitches soon.

"I wish I could say it was done with more finesse, but the spider rover is down," Clint said. He turned on his video feed so Josh could see it. The bot was in pieces, but three of its legs were intact and attempting to move. "The driver ahead of us saw it in the middle of the road and ran over it."

"Wait—it was just stopped in the road—doing nothing?" Josh asked. He opened another line and tried calling his headset. It rang, but the clone didn't answer. The video on Clint's feed blurred, and several agents began talking at once. "It killed the clone, didn't it?"

"Yeah." Clint switched off the video feed. "One of the Raleigh guys just found him. I'm so sorry, Josh, but he's gone."

Outside Raleigh, North Carolina
March 2114

"He was this tiny little boy—hair sticking up, pajamas above his ankles and wrists like he'd just had a growth spurt," Mrs. McFerrin said as she and Josh walked to what was now Nick's second grave. "I wanted to hold him and tell him everything would be okay, but I knew that was something I couldn't promise. David Mathis had died on the way to the hospital, and I was standing in a house with a century's worth of cloning research and a child who didn't understand. I had to make a choice—your father and I both did."

"You knew what Dr. Mathis had done—that Nick was some sort of accidental clone—and you covered it up?" Josh asked in disbelief. "Mom—"

"All your father and I could think about was, what if it was you?" she replied. "As parents, would we have wanted you treated like some test subject instead of a human being? Nick was a child with as much potential as anyone, and he deserved a chance. I wish we had known enough to warn him—protect him—but I'll never regret having him in our lives. Do you?"

"No—of course not," Josh replied, and he pinched the bridge of his nose. "Every time Dakota goes to the door, I keep expecting Nick to show up again. Clint told us the IBI believes Dr. Mathis designed the rovers to kill him once his disease progressed too far—that he may have made a dozen successful jumps between clone bodies over the past century. Now his technology is breaking down, and the rovers targeted Nick just because he and Dr. Mathis shared the same DNA. All the automated labs creating the clone bodies could be in trouble, too."

"You're saying Nick may never come back?" Mrs. McFerrin asked.

"I'm saying we may never know," Josh replied. "I don't even know if turning off his implant for a few minutes affected anything."

Mrs. McFerrin crouched down, moving the grass away from a single blue wildflower. "Don't give up on him yet."

Downtown Chicago

"Just a minute," Bianca Reynolds said. She checked the door viewer, but her blind date was holding a hardcover of her book about Nick Mathis in front of his face. She noticed roses in his other hand as he reached and rang the doorbell several times again. "Hey, I realize you're just trying to be funny, but don't use that book to do it. I feel bad enough that—"

She opened the door. Nick lowered the book and smiled at her.

"How would you feel about writing a volume two?" he asked.

A WORD FROM PATRICIA GILLIAM

In researching the technologies underlying this story—from 3-D bioprinting to neural implants—I'm in awe of how the line between science and science fiction has become blurred. In many areas, I believe the two are pulling and skipping over each other.

Although he doesn't appear in the story directly, I wanted to make sure that Nick's father David wasn't portrayed as someone desperate for immortality as much as a man trying to solve a problem. Although successful, David's form of immortality comes at a great cost—being subject to an automated system that can kill and revive him in a clone body without his consent. While the A-676s were designed to verify David's mental condition, a malfunction causes them to simply track his implant and kill him once he's within proximity. Since Nick shares David's DNA and a similar implant in his brain, he becomes caught in the same system.

The McFerrins and Clint Rossetti have appeared on one novel and several short stories within The Hannaria Series, and I liked putting them in a scenario that wasn't alien-related. I have plans to expand and incorporate this story into a full-length novel.

You can find out more about my other work by visiting my

Amazon Author Page (*http://www.amazon.com/Patricia-Gilliam/e/B00358K3WO*). You're also welcome to connect with me on Facebook (*https://www.facebook.com/patricia.gilliam1*). Thanks for reading and for your support of First Book by purchasing this anthology.

Legacy
by David Bruns

EDWARD HAMILTON STEMM III left the warmth and safety of his limousine two blocks from the courthouse.

It was a cold, bright winter morning, so the wide-brimmed fedora, heavy overcoat, gloves, and muffler that constituted his disguise didn't appear out of place. An expensive leather briefcase dangled from his right hand. It was empty. Just another prop in their little charade.

Walking through the press corps outside the courthouse in disguise was his lawyer's idea. He couldn't remember which one, but both of them had been very excited about the idea of fooling the press. Edward had to admit a stroll up the steps of the courthouse was far more appealing than fighting his way through the scrum that normally engulfed his arriving limo. As bad as the press was, the protesters were even worse, with their repulsive holo-placards floating above them and their red, screaming faces. One of them had even *spit* on him earlier this week, calling him a "scrapper"—their term for a bionic.

Edward would be pressing charges.

The crowd was within hailing distance now, and Edward fell in behind another lawyerish-looking man making his way up the wide stone steps of the courthouse. *Just another soul-sucking legal slave going off to do the devil's work. Don't mind me.*

With his head down and his artificial eyes hidden behind dark glasses, the only way they'd really be able to identify him was by his gait. Bionics still had not managed to duplicate the casual sloppiness of a true human walk. Lord knew he'd tried for years to write a "saunter" program. He was counting on his long wool overcoat to hide the steady, measured footfalls of his bionic legs.

"Excuse me." Edward shouldered aside a heavyset reporter with a red scruff on his chin. He walked up the first few steps, swinging his empty briefcase to distract anyone who might notice his bionic stride. Behind the initial line of reporters, the rest of the press were standing in small groups on the steps, sipping coffee or stamping their feet against the cold. He navigated around them, his confidence growing with each stride. The press scrum thinned as he drew close to the doors of the security area until only a single young woman remained. Her dirty blonde hair was pulled back into a stubby ponytail. She blew into her gloveless hands.

She would do.

Edward stopped in front of her and pulled off his hat and glasses, revealing his bald pate and the solid gray brightness of his artificial eyes. "Excuse me, young lady. Would you be so kind as to take my photograph, please?" The smile routine for his facial muscles was still in beta, but he tried it anyway.

The girl huffed into her hands again, and seemed about to tell him to get lost when she met his gaze. Her eyes widened. "You're…you're…"

"Yes, I'm Edward Stemm, and you are about to take an exclusive photo to accompany your report of today's ruling." She reminded him of his granddaughter, but which one escaped him. He'd never met any of them in person, after all.

Her handheld was out now, and Edward could hear the camera mechanism firing. She braced her shaking hands against the door jamb to stop the jitter.

"Perhaps one of us together?" Edward plucked the handheld from her grip and held it at arm's length in front of both of them. "A hundred years ago, we used to call that a 'selfie.'" Behind them, he could hear the rest of the press corps jackals rushing up the steps. "Don't spend all that money in one place, young lady."

Edward slipped into the security area inside the building just as the press arrived at the door. He waved at them through the glass. "Screw you all, you pack of vultures," he said.

A low chuckle came from behind him. "That was a nice thing you done for that girl, Mr. Stemm."

Edward dropped his briefcase on the table and slipped off his overcoat. "I'm pretty pleased with myself, Bill, and she looked like she could use a helping hand. Share the love, that's my motto." He piled his gloves, scarf and hat on top of the coat. "May I leave my things down here, please?" Edward's system thermostat was self-regulating down to minus ten degrees

Celsius, so he had no need for the heavy-weather clothes—or clothes at all, for that matter.

"My pleasure, sir." Bill pulled a plastic bin out from under the table and placed Edward's coat in it. He ducked his head. "Today's the big day, sir. Good luck. I'm rooting for you. You done a lot of good for this world, sir."

"Luck has nothing to do with it, Bill. And I told you to call me Ed."

They'd done the Ed-Bill routine ever since Bill had told him how Stemm Bionics artificial skin had given his niece—a burn victim—back her looks.

If only they were all like Bill, able to appreciate what he'd given the world. Edward sighed as he pulled open the door to the courtroom. Unfortunately, they weren't.

His lawyers—the very best his oceans of money could buy—were waiting at the respondent's table, their glee barely contained as they stood to greet him. The lead counsel was rotund with a black mustache and goatee, his partner a thin, clean-shaven man who usually let his co-counsel do the talking. Officially, they were Howe and Mackey from the law firm of Howe, Mackey, Ledger & Olson, but Edward called them Laurel and Hardy. He'd told them so after their first meeting, but the joke had been completely lost on them. Even after they'd looked up the famous comedy duo, they still didn't get it. Oh, well, he wasn't paying them for their sense of humor.

"Well done, Mr. Stemm," said fat Howe, with an oily smile. "Your interaction with the young reporter is all over the news-feeds. So genuine, sir." Silent Mackey smiled without showing his teeth.

Howe licked his lips. "Are you ready for today, sir? Anything you want to review before you testify?"

Edward took his seat without replying. The specially reinforced chair creaked under his weight. He cast a glance to the empty plaintiff's table. Emily's legal team had adopted a strategy of minimal interaction. They always entered the courtroom as a group immediately before the proceedings began and left the instant they ended. It was as if they knew how much his great-granddaughter meant to him and they were limiting her presence to weaken his resolve.

"All rise! The Honorable Judge Raymond Warton presiding. All persons having business with this court are admonished to draw near and give their attention, for the court is now in session."

And just like that, Emily was there in the courtroom, surrounded by a phalanx of lawyers. He snatched a glimpse of her, the curve of her cheek, the tilt of her chin so much like his Liza...

Judge Warton, a rangy scarecrow of a man, entered through the side door and mounted the bench. "Be seated," he called before he had even seated himself. The room echoed with the rumble and scraping of chairs.

It had taken months to find a judge who wouldn't recuse himself from this case. However you ruled, you were bound to lose: either purists excoriated you for betraying your humanity or the other side labeled you a Luddite. Warton was a "natural," a man who had no bionics at all in his body, a rarity these days, but he had a reputation as a fair adjudicator. His lean face, cloaked in the same dour expression he'd worn for the whole trial, peered down at them over his reading glasses. "Are you ready to proceed, Mr. Howe?"

Howe stood. "We are, Your Honor."

"Well, let's get to it, then. I'd like to conclude this matter today."

"The defense calls Mr. Edward Hamilton Stemm III."

Edward stood, painfully aware that every eye in the room was inspecting him, evaluating the *humanness* of him. He'd gone to extraordinary lengths to fashion bionic limbs that looked real and he was wearing the finest tailored suit that money could buy, but he still felt naked under their gaze. Despite his embarrassment, the artificial skin that covered his neck, skull and face stayed exactly the same shade. Edward averted his gleaming silver eyes from the judge and kept his facial expression neutral. That was the one good piece of advice Laurel and Hardy had offered: "Don't try to smile. It's too creepy."

The bailiff swore him in and Edward took his seat. They'd made sure to put a reinforced chair in the witness stand—the weight of his mechanical frame sometimes caused normal wooden chairs to break.

Howe approached him slowly, surprisingly light on his feet for a man of his girth. He nodded pleasantly at the judge and cleared his throat.

"How old are you, Mr. Stemm?"

"I'll be 200 years old next month. I was born in 1969, the same year that Neil Armstrong walked on the moon." Edward stared at Emily, but she had her eyes fixed on the table in front of her. She wore her hair fastened at the nape of her neck with her great-grandmother's antique silver clasp—the one he'd given to Liza on their wedding day. Edward noticed her lawyer watching him and he shifted his gaze back to Howe.

Howe pivoted. "In fact, the 1969 moon landing was very important to you."

"Yes, the company motto at Stemm Bionics is 'one giant leap for mankind.' It's a reminder of how the company was founded."

"Objection, Your Honor. Can we keep the editorializing to a minimum, please?" Donald Raser, Emily's lawyer, half-rose from his chair.

"Agreed." Judge Warton gave Howe a pointed look. "We will be finishing this today, Mr. Howe, so move it along."

"Of course, Your Honor." Howe nodded. "Mr. Stemm, can you tell us the circumstances under which your company was founded?"

"In the early 21st century, we fought a war in the Middle East—in what was then the country of Iraq. To pay for college, I joined the National Guard as a combat engineer and I was called to serve. I was married to Emily's great-grandmother at the time." He watched her shoulders tighten, and the lawyer started to get up to make another objection. "My convoy was hit by a roadside bomb and I lost my left leg just above the knee."

Edward paused. He could remember waking up in the hospital and seeing the stump, but at the same time feeling that his leg was still there. Phantom limb syndrome, the doctors called it. It was amazing how a missing body part could hurt like hell. His bionics solved that problem by reattaching the nerve endings to a cybernetic interface.

Howe cleared his throat and Edward realized they were all staring at him.

"When I returned home, I was lost. Depressed. Prosthetics at the time were crude; we actually used to use springs and cables to make them work." He gave a short laugh, then remembered Howe's advice about not smiling. "I became obsessed with making prosthetics better. I was convinced the answer was bionics. I was invited to join a DARPA project, but they were interested in making super-soldiers using bionics and I wanted no part of that. I wanted to use science to help people, not hurt them. The Veterans Administration had the right idea, but their development process was so slow and bureaucratic that I couldn't stand it. So I formed my own company: Stemm Bionics."

"And that was in 2019?"

"Yes. The 2020s were the golden age of prosthetics and my work was on the cutting edge. Everyone else focused on biotech and gene therapy, but there were too many variables there, too many ways for things to go wrong. The right answer was— and still is—bionics."

"And your wife? Did she have a part in the company?"

"Without Liza, there would be no Stemm Bionics. She was my inspiration, my partner. She was everything to me." Liza had been just about Emily's age when they founded the company. She was so beautiful, and so happy to be working with him. Edward felt the familiar tug of emptiness somewhere beneath the chrome shell of his breastplate. He smiled at Howe. "We even shared an office." Howe gave a slight shake of his head and Edward killed the smile.

"When did your wife pass away, Mr. Stemm?"

"2035. She was only 65. Cancer…it was terrible. This was before we discovered artificial blood. Bionics was still in its infancy."

Howe did a little pirouette, as if Edward's answer had surprised him. "Infancy, you say? If my research is correct, you had a major operation that year. One that made history."

Edward nodded, just as they'd rehearsed. "That same year, I replaced both my legs with bionics. The key was the spinal implant that enabled a direct connection between the drive motors for the legs and the motor function center of the brain."

"And this was the first time this operation had been performed? And it was done on you personally?"

"Yes, everything that Stemm Bionics makes is tested on me first."

"Everything? Even today?"

"Even to this day."

Howe stroked his goatee. "That's quite a commitment to quality, Mr. Stemm."

Judge Warton cleared his throat.

"What about your son?" Howe asked.

"Donald, Emily's grandfather, worked at the company for his entire career. I made him CEO in 2052." Edward hesitated. *The same year I replaced both my arms.* That was what they'd rehearsed. Howe had said that if they linked his bionic transformation to major events in his life, it would make him seem more human.

Howe glared at him.

"He was a good man," Edward continued. "A good businessman, but he never believed in the technology. Not like I did—do. Not like Emily does."

She looked up at him then. The cool blue of her eyes made his breath catch in his throat. Her lips twisted in what might have been a wistful smile. Raser, the lawyer, leaned over to whisper in her ear and she dropped her gaze again.

"Donald passed away in 2064. I took over again as CEO of Stemm Bionics." He wanted to tell them how Donald, his only son, had refused the very products his company made, bionic devices that could have saved his life. Donald had been divorced by then, and was deeply unhappy. To Edward, it had seemed like he'd just stopped living.

"Did anything else of note happen in that year?" Howe prompted.

"Yes, that was the year I received my first mechanical heart. We had developed synthetic blood that was compatible with the human brain, but it required a different pumping mechanism."

"I see," Howe said as he paced in front of the witness box. "So you ran the company on your own after that?"

Edward nodded. "I ran the company on my own for 75 years, from Donald's death until 2139."

"And what happened in 2139?" Howe did another little pirouette to face the plaintiff's table.

"Emily came into my life."

Before Emily showed up in his office, he hadn't even known she existed. He let his lawyers handle most of his personal and business matters. It left him with more time to work in the lab.

Donald's wife had never liked him. When she left Donald, she took the children—a boy and a girl, if he remembered right—the Stemm name, and a hefty monthly alimony check. On the rare occasion when Edward looked at the news, he would see her in the society section, plugging some bleeding heart cause or another.

When she showed up in his office, Emily was barely twenty-one, with a newly minted master's degree from MIT. In bionics, naturally. The very course of study he had founded. Edward swore he'd felt his mechanical heart skip a beat when she smiled at him.

Her youth was like a torch in his office, which was really more like a dim warehouse of half-done experiments than a place of business. He'd focused on inventing while a pack of businessmen ran the privately held company. They called it a "lifestyle business," growing it just enough each year to pay themselves a handsome salary and keep Edward's laboratory stocked with whatever he required. They were probably robbing him blind, but he didn't care. It was never about the money.

Emily looked and acted so much like his late wife that it took all of Edward's willpower not to call her Liza. She perched on a stool across the workbench that Edward used as a desk, fidgeting with the hem of her skirt. The stool was the only piece of furniture in his office. With his bionic legs, the only time he sat down was to use his charging chair.

Edward smiled at her. He'd still had his real skin then, all liver-spotted and papery thin with age. "What can I do for you, my dear?"

Emily gripped the edge of the workbench and leaned toward him. Her blue eyes pinned him where he stood. "I want to come work for you. I want to learn from you."

She even had Liza's intensity. He hadn't gotten out much in the last thirty years or so, and the combination of having a live conversation and her uncanny resemblance to his late wife made his head spin. Edward bumped up the oxygen level in his blood, and waited for the effect to stabilize his senses.

Emily's gaze never wavered.

"Well, I...what do your parents say?"

"They don't know I'm here. Besides, I'm twenty-one. I can do whatever I want."

That's exactly what Liza would have said.

"So you can." Edward's gaze flitted around the lab, anything to avoid meeting this girl's eyes.

"I thought you founded this company to help people."

Edward frowned.

"So you make these life-changing discoveries, try them out on yourself, and then others get rich by making cheap knockoffs? That's helping people?"

"It's not about the money."

"Yes, it *is* about the money." She hammered her fist on the workbench so hard the pile of servos shifted. "Just think how many lives you could change if you were able to offer affordable bionics all over the world. Every time someone dies from a cheap bionic knockoff, your legacy gets tarnished a little more—"

"I don't need a legacy. I'm going to live forever."

"Mr. Stemm, everyone needs a legacy." She looked around the warehouse. "And if you don't claim one for yourself, someone will create one for you." Emily slid off the stool and extended her hand across the workbench. "I'm sorry. I can see now I shouldn't have come."

Edward felt the heat of her palm through the sensors in his hand, felt the way her fingers gripped his with strength and confidence. No fear, no hesitation.

"I wish you could have met my wife, your great-grandmother."

"It was good to meet you, Mr. Stemm." She released his bionic hand.

"Call me Ed—and be back here at eight o'clock tomorrow morning."

After she left, the room seemed emptier, dirtier, darker. Edward searched through his lab for a mirror. He finally found one in the bathroom he had forgotten was behind a shelf of dusty parts. In the harsh fluorescent light, Edward traced the liver spots on his cheeks and tried to tame the wisps of gray hair that floated over his scalp. His lips were thin and colorless, and his ears seemed to have melted. If he was going to have a partner, especially one as young and vibrant as Liza—Emily; he meant Emily—this would not do.

Edward began working on artificial skin that very night.

"Mr. Stemm, would you like to take a break?" Howe's jowly face entered his vision, a sheen of sweat on his brow.

Edward increased his oxygen and released a microburst of adrenaline as he shook his head. There must be a glitch in his emotional regulator system. "I'm fine, thank you." He could feel the heat of the judge's glare on the side of his face.

"You were about to tell us about Emily's"—Howe held up

his hand toward the plaintiff's table to forestall the coming objection—"Ms. Stemm's impact on your company."

Edward wished his work on the facial muscles routine was further along so he could add some meaning to his words. He settled for raising his hands. "Emily had a clear vision for the company. She expanded our in-house production capacity, built a sales force, and hired a fleet of lawyers who did nothing but prosecute patent infringement cases."

"So you were happy with her performance?"

"'Happy' doesn't cover it. She was amazing. Together, we were a phenomenal team and the company blossomed under her leadership. She was the one who thought of using Neil Armstrong's quote as our company tagline. I made her CEO before she was thirty years old and she deserved it."

"And then what happened?"

"She took the company public." Edward laughed, and too late forgot not to smile—earning another wince from Howe. "She used the ticker symbol STEM, a play on the Science, Technology, Engineering and Math track of study. By the end of the trading day, we were the most widely held stock on the planet."

Edward stopped. That was the day everything changed, the beginning of the end for him and Emily. Before that day, he'd been just a rich man with no expenses, after that he was the wealthiest man in history. One wag on the talk show circuit had joked that Edward Stemm was funding his own immortality.

It was funny how things had taken on a life of their own. That seemingly innocent joke became a flash point for public discourse. Overnight, protesters appeared outside the gate of his mansion and the company headquarters, carrying placards comparing him to the devil. A sign that said "Stemm is more scrap metal than man" made it on the front page of *USA Today*, and was the source of the epithet "scrapper."

Congress got involved. The same congressmen who had come to him hat in hand for campaign donations now attacked him in the press and dragged him to Washington for hearings so they could make speeches for the TV drones.

It was during that time that Edward decided to replace the aging skin and muscles of his face with StemmSkin. Too much, too soon, as it turned out. The skin was nearly perfect—wonderful consistency, warm, and lifelike—but the underlying synthetic musculature had major problems, making the user look like they'd had a Botox overdose.

Edward blinked as he recalled how the news drones had hovered near his face, catching every frozen moment and misguided expression. He felt his emotional regulator dose him with a mild sedative to calm his mechanical heart. He'd fixed the glitches in the facial muscle routine—well, most of them anyway—but the damage was done.

"Mr. Stemm, when did the relationship between you and your great-granddaughter start to deteriorate?"

Edward focused on Howe's upper lip, where a stray gray whisker curled off to the side. He should really trim that; it was most annoying. "The stock price suffered and we had to put our expansion plans on hold last year. Emily blamed me for the problem. She said as long as I was associated with Stemm

Bionics, I was hurting the *brand*." Edward spat out the word, and slammed his hand down on the bar in front of his chair, leaving a sizable dent in the wood.

"I *am* Stemm Bionics. Every new invention—every single one, mind you—is tested on me first. Me! I am not a brand, I am a man."

Edward realized he was standing, and Howe had taken two giant steps backwards, his mouth puckered into a tiny pink donut. And Emily… She sat there looking straight at him, her eyes glassy, a look on her face that was…what? Pity? Fear?

"Mr. Stemm, would you please take your seat?" Warton's voice sounded in his ear.

Edward lowered his head as he sat down. "I'm sorry, Your Honor. I—I feel very strongly about this topic."

The judge did not reply.

Howe danced close to the witness stand and placed his hand on the bar, covering the dented wood. "Now, Mr. Stemm, what did your CEO do next?"

"She tried to engineer a vote with the board to have me re-moved as executive chairman. For the good of the shareholders, she said." Edward was able to keep his voice even and steady. "She failed."

"And how did that make you feel, Mr. Stemm?"

"Betrayed." He stared at Emily now and she met his gaze. Defiant, sure of herself, just like that first meeting in his work-shop.

"No further questions, Your Honor."

Donald Raser stood in one fluid motion. If Howe was a dancer, Raser was a snake. Or maybe a shark. Something fast and dangerous. Edward eyed him warily.

"How do you feel today, Mr. Stemm?"

"Fine."

"Really? You feel fine? *Can* you feel, Mr. Stemm?"

"Of course I can feel. I have emotions like any other man."

"How much of *you* is left, Mr. Stemm?"

Edward glared at him.

Raser smiled. "I'll rephrase: how much of your original organic tissue is left in your…person?" He rotated his finger in the air before him as he said "person," as if he was searching for the right word.

"Seventeen point five percent." That was a half-truth, but one they'd probably get away with. When Edward had replaced his torso, he'd done a lung transplant at the same time, so technically the lungs were not his original tissue, but they were organic. If he didn't include the donor lungs, the real number was twelve percent.

"So what has been replaced? In general terms, I mean."

"All four limbs, ribcage, heart, bowels, skin and the muscles of my head. In general terms."

Raser came closer, staring at his skin. Edward could smell his cologne, a subtle spice in the air, not unpleasant. "Fine job on the skin, by the way. Very lifelike." Raser lowered his voice. "I'd spend a little more time on the facial gestures."

Edward gripped his own leg and squeezed.

Raser licked his lips. "So, according to your testimony, Mr. Stemm, you are 82.5 percent artificial—"

"I prefer the term bionic," Edward interrupted.

"And I prefer to ask the questions," Raser shot back. "You are 82.5 percent *bionic* today. Is there any reason why you couldn't be 100 percent *bionic*?"

"In theory, no."

"Really? Is there a point where you stop being human, Mr. Stemm?"

Edward stayed silent.

"Do you want to live forever, Mr. Stemm?"

Edward answered immediately. "Yes."

"Why?"

Edward almost blurted out, "Because I can," but he stopped himself. His legal team of Laurel and Hardy shifted to the very front edges of their chairs. They'd rehearsed this answer, of course. He had a long speech prepared about how he wanted to help mankind reach its potential, save lives... They'd even added in a bit about space travel for good measure. Something for everyone to love, was what Howe called it.

But he couldn't do it. Edward couldn't make the words come out of his mouth. Emily had that pity-fear look on her face again and Raser narrowed his eyes. The judge cleared his throat.

"That's what I thought," Raser said. "Question is withdrawn."

Edward returned to his seat between Laurel and Hardy and sat down heavily. His power pack was at 85 percent charge, but he felt as if his energy level had run down to life support only. He tuned out the closing arguments and dimmed his vision.

"All rise."

Edward got to his feet at the urging of one of his lawyers. He checked his internal clock. Two hours had elapsed since his testimony and that question from Raser.

Why?

With the neural network he was developing, Edward would have the ability to live forever, to become truly immortal. He would be the next version of humanity, what man could become.

He swiveled his head to look at Emily. The set of her jaw, the way her eyes narrowed at the corners when she smiled, the very image of his Liza. His wife had accepted death because she had to; the technology had not been there to save her—not like today. Today she could live forever.

Why?

Judge Warton cleared his throat and peered over the top of his reading glasses. "On the face of it, this case is not a difficult one. Mr. Stemm, your appearances in the media correlate directly to a reduction in stock price and loss of market share, both objective measures of the health of your company. Put simply, your actions are harming the company that bears your name. The plaintiff argues that makes you unfit as an officer in your company and you should be removed. In the normal course of events in a company, people age, they retire, and these sorts of issues sort themselves out. The problem here, Mr. Stemm, is your endgame—or lack thereof.

"The entire canon of contract law assumes that contracts have a lifetime, an end date, a termination point. Our law anticipates that corporations, comprised of people, will change over time and change with the times. This case calls all of those fundamentals into question. We have no legal precedent for a corporation where the same people remain in place—possibly forever." Edward felt Laurel and Hardy shifting in their chairs, and sensed their increased respiration. Warton's steely eyes swung to the plaintiff's table.

"As for the plaintiffs, you make a compelling case that your executive chairman is harming your corporation. Yet, when you attempted to oust Mr. Stemm through your board of directors, you failed. Now you're trying to use the courts to do what you were unable to accomplish in the boardroom. You argue that the changes made to Mr. Stemm's body make him unfit to retain his position as executive chairman. The essence of your argument is that Mr. Stemm is no longer a person. I'm sorry, but that is a bridge too far.

"In the matter of Stemm Bionics vs. Stemm, I find for the respondent, Mr. Edward Hamilton Stemm."

Laurel and Hardy were instantly on their feet, crowing and slapping Edward on the back. He ignored them and crossed to Emily's table in two long strides. Raser tried to get in his way, but he shouldered him aside.

"Please, Emily. We can put this behind us. It can be like it was before. The news stories will blow over, and we can continue what we started."

She held up her hand to stop Raser from re-inserting himself between them. The crystal blue of her eyes held a square of light from the window on the opposite wall. "You need to stop, Edward. Before it's too late—" Her voice broke and she reached out to touch his cheek.

"I know there's been some loss of mental acuity, but with the new neural network I can make finer adjustments—"

"Listen to yourself, Edward. Your life is not a potentiometer to be adjusted. Life is for…living. Stop. Now. It's what she would have wanted."

Emily pushed past him and out the courtroom doors. The thin covering of artificial skin over his new titanium jaw tingled where she'd touched him. She'd spoken as if Liza would have been ashamed of him. Edward felt that familiar tug of loss for his long-gone wife. If Liza could see him today—see what he'd accomplished—she'd be bursting with pride.

He'd misjudged Emily. She was just like the rest of them. She didn't share his vision. Raser had wanted to know if Edward wanted to live forever. Well, the answer was yes, and if Emily didn't want to be part of that next step for mankind, then he'd go on alone.

The crowd of press on the courthouse steps had expanded into a horde. Edward could hear Raser off to one side, promising an appeal. This was only a minor setback, blah, blah. Emily was nowhere to be seen. He dove into the throng, pushing aside anyone in his way. Laurel and Hardy could handle the press. He was in no mood.

One particularly invasive reporter flew a drone right into Edward's face to get a close-up of his eyes—people were always fascinated by the pearly gray of his artificial eyes. Edward's hand flashed out. He snatched the drone out of the air and crushed it in his grip. Then he bulled into the last row of reporters, heading toward his waiting limo.

"Ow!" A short scream cut through all the press noise around him. Edward turned to see the young reporter, the one he had given the exclusive photo to this morning, on the ground, clutching her knee. A well of blood seeped through a gash in her trousers.

He knelt next to her. "I'm sorry," he said in as tender a tone as he could manage. He smiled just as she turned her face toward him. A look of horror crossed her features, and she slid back from him.

"Get away from me."

He held out his hand. "Let me help you up—"

"I said get away, you—you monster."

There were more protesters outside the gate to his mansion, but his security team was keeping the road clear. The limo swept through the gate, up the broad curve of the drive, and stopped before the heavy columns of the porticoed entrance.

Edward signaled the front door to open before he had even exited the vehicle. He'd had no need of wait-staff in the house for the last ten years—the house automation system was connected to his own bionic controls.

"Will you be going in to the office tomorrow, sir?" the driver asked.

"I'll call you if I need you," Edward replied without turning around.

His footsteps echoed in the marble entranceway. Edward went straight to the basement lab and keyed in his personal security sequence.

He switched his vision to infrared as he made his way down the steps. There was no need for lights in the dark basement.

Edward Stemm seated himself in his charging chair, the one that hardwired his brain into the lab computer. Three screens lit up in front of him.

Why?

Raser's question still dogged his mind. Of course he wanted to live forever. Who wouldn't? What made Edward different was that he was willing to make the sacrifices necessary to see his dream come to life, to push the science where no one else dared go. He was a pioneer, that's what he was.

A framed picture sat on his workstation, the only personal item in the entire workshop. He and Liza in their first office, the one they'd shared together. She was pouring champagne into paper cups and laughing with her head thrown back. There had been music playing in the background that day, but he remembered how Liza's laugh had risen above it. If he closed his eyes, he could still hear her laugh, remember the way it made him smile—just like in the photograph.

He caught a glimpse of his reflection in the glass of the picture and immediately looked away. That rictus wasn't the smile he remembered. His vision flickered. A quick diagnostic showed his emotional regulator was overwhelmed by the events of the day.

Enough of this wallowing.

He called up the ultra-secure server. After two levels of verification, he finally arrived at the screen:

CRI
Cerebral Regulation Interface

His masterpiece. The Holy Grail of cybernetic interfaces, the ability to control emotions at their source—in the brain. His current emotional regulator was a secondary system, one that responded to emotions after the fact with chemicals. But with CRI, the neural network in his brain would take over the task of regulating emotions. The loss of control he'd experienced this afternoon in the courtroom would never happen again. It was the next logical step in his evolution.

His hand shook with the exhilaration of the moment. He wondered if he would still feel like this after he uploaded the new software.

Liza's image stared up at him from where he'd dropped the picture on the floor. Her eyes bored into his and that well of loneliness, that vacant space just below his mechanical heart, opened up again like a scab being pulled off a wound. His breath stuttered. In that moment, Edward knew he would have given up every minute of the last two centuries just to hold his Liza one last time.

His vision flickered, and the artificial skin of his face registered moisture.

He wiped a bionic hand across his face in an angry motion. When he stretched out his arm toward the screen, his extended finger did not waver as it touched the icon that said UPLOAD.

Edward Hamilton Stemm III was done with emotions.

A WORD FROM DAVID BRUNS

The short story "Legacy" examines the fact that our entire society—secular and nonsecular—is built on the transience of human life. Much of how we live our lives and the work that we do is with an eye toward how we will be remembered when we're gone. In "Legacy," Edward Stemm is a man who pursues the goal of life extension to the exclusion of everything else—including living.

In 2013 I walked away from a lucrative corporate career to pursue a lifelong dream of writing full-time. As with any significant life decision, there were many competing inputs, but the major one was this: I'm not getting any younger. If a person can have a biological creativity clock, mine was ticking loudly.

I am many things, half-hearted is not one of them. I knew if I really wanted this career, I needed to commit to it.

So I did.

Since that time, I've published a science-fiction series, The Dream Guild Chronicles, a first contact story about a race of telepathic aliens; co-written a military thriller about modern day nuclear terrorism called Weapons of Mass Deception, and released a handful of short stories.

From the moment I reviewed The Telepath Chronicles, I wanted to be part of The Future Chronicles body of work and I am so grateful to Samuel Peralta for including me in this collection. It is an honor to be included alongside such an accomplished group of authors.

For more about me and my work, please visit my website at *http://davidbruns.com*

A Severance of Souls
by Drew Avera

International Space Station, 7064CE

NIGEL'S ICY FINGERS pressed against the reinforced window of the International Space Station as he peered out at the ever-dulling star. His eyes were swollen from weeping with remorse, from saying goodbye to the millions of lives that had been lost over time, but he had never hoped to save any of them. That was not his mission, to save the lives of the dying. No, he was meant to preserve humanity.

It was supposed to be an honor, one any other man might have leapt at in youth, but as his memories faded like ink on ancient pages, his sense of honor had also lapsed. What had originally lured him to this had waned many years ago. It wasn't enough to make the mission seem worthwhile anymore. Solitude had been a dream back then. Never had he thought it would turn into a nightmare.

The problem with intelligence was its pretense at knowing precisely what the heart wanted. Longing had never been part of the calculation, yet here it was, stabbing at what was left of his body, his soul, his existence.

Earth, 2064CE

"Please tell me you're not serious," Robyn said as she looked into the disinterested eyes of her colleague and friend. His glasses were perched at the top of his head and she knew he would forget they were there eventually. It was funny how absent-minded he could be, but this wasn't the time to dwell on such things. "It's not ethical, Nigel!" She often wondered if exasperation unsettled him as much as it did others in the middle of an argument.

The accusation caused him to finally look her in the face and confront the situation he had been avoiding for so long. "It's not about ethics. It's about preserving humanity, Robyn. I would think you could understand something as simple as that," he said. His tone was light, but the words stabbed at her nonetheless. He had graduated at the top of his class and he never wanted anyone to forget it, least of all the woman who had come in second. It was a wonder she had tolerated him for so many years, but there was beauty in his social missteps. Behind the ego and abrasive nature was a mind capable of marvelous things…but now he had finally lost his mind.

"It's murder. Suicide. Any way you rationalize it, it's wrong. I don't want any part of it," she cried. Her cheeks were warm from the fresh tears that smeared her mascara. How had they come to this? She toyed with the ring on her finger, hoping for a distraction from half the emotions coursing through her body. She hated the non-objectivity of anger and sadness manipulating their way into an argument. Nigel measured everything by reason, and that was how she had to "win" this argument.

Nigel stood up from his desk and paced over to the window, where he pressed his fingertips to the winter-chilled pane of glass. Southern Florida had never seen snow this deep. Time was running out. The sun was slowly dying and Earth was fading with it. The math proved his point, and Nigel refused to be swayed. There was a way to preserve humanity, but it was going to be at an astronomical cost.

"Someone has to wait this out and ensure the embryos are fertilized correctly. Someone has to rear our children and provide them with an opportunity to thrive when Earth is inhabitable again."

Robyn swallowed back a lump in her throat. "Do you hear yourself?" she demanded. *Appalled* wasn't the right word to describe the resentment she felt towards him at that moment.

Nigel turned to look his friend in the eye and smiled. "Do you? I'm not easily swayed, and I can tell you with absolute certainty that humanity will perish before our climate restores itself, and that's *if* the climate restores itself. Do you see how pale our sun has become? The yellow glow of our childhood is gone. Now we're left with a ghost of what it was. What's the real madness? Possibly giving one's life in an attempt to save our race, or sacrificing the future of humanity out of fear of doing what's necessary? Why can't you see it as clearly as I can?"

Nigel turned his eyes back to the chilly image of snow-covered sand stretching across the gulf coast. He wanted a real answer, but Robyn had no answer to give him.

International Space Station, 2686CE

Life in a vacuum was exactly as he'd expected it to be. Nigel maneuvered around the lab tables with the ease of a twenty-year-old man despite his age. The bionic exoskeleton clutched his body like a glove and maintained the life support systems necessary for him to live. For more than six hundred years he had watched the sunrise lift over Earth's horizon, and each time he pressed his fingers to the window in anticipation of the glaring display of power, even though the feeling in his near-ancient hands had been lost. The dull tapping of his fingers against the glass did little to remind him of what it had been like to be a normal man.

The future as he saw it was glorious. Even with everything the world stood to lose, Nigel could see what was left to gain: a future with no wars, no hatred, no religious upheaval. If not for the ridiculous notion of it, Nigel would have felt almost like a god in his floating chariot.

He watched the bright light of the sun crest around the curvature of the Earth and his thoughts took him back to his more-human life. The one he wanted to forget. The one he could never escape.

Earth, 2065CE

The sterile smell of the operating room filled his nostrils as the gurney was pushed through swinging doors. The masked man looked down on him and the momentary eye contact brought a chill to Nigel's spine. The look was one part respect and two parts loathsome disdain. Nigel understood the sentiment. This was an opportunity to survive, granted to a single person. Who was he to be bestowed with such honor?

"Are you ready?" the doctor asked. His face eclipsed the bright light directly above Nigel's head. It was a welcome form of relief, even if it was only for a moment.

"Yes," Nigel answered in a hoarse voice. He was too proud to admit he had spent the night before lamenting his dissolved relationship with Robyn. The truth was something he would much rather suppress before going under the knife. His version of heartache was the only source of anxiety he had experienced. The thought of dying under the knife was of no consequence. Men died all the time. Nothing was forever. *At least not yet*, he thought coldly.

The doctor nodded and pulled away from the light, causing the glare to burn Nigel's retinas with renewed fervor. "This part of the operation will be done over seventy-two hours. You will be held in stasis while the organic part of your body heals. If you have any reservations, bring them up now, before it's too late."

Nigel bit his lower lip as he thought of her. Robyn. She was gone forever. The horror of his decision had driven her away and now there was nothing left for him to live for; at least, nothing on Earth to stay alive for.

"I'm sure," Nigel whispered.

"Anesthesia," the doctor said.

Nigel blinked three times before the mask approached his face. The lull of the anesthesia pulled him towards sleep, but it wasn't sleep at all. It was the voluntary death of a man who invariably would lose everything.

International Space Station, 3848CE

A breach in the refrigeration lines went undetected for God knew how long before Nigel was finally alerted. The problem with archaic technology, he thought, was that you could never trust it to work like it was supposed to. And the problem with human error was that you could count on it occurring at the most inconvenient time imaginable. Nigel ran on semi-robotic legs through a series of passageways before entering the laboratory. The temperature of the room was noticeably warm, even for an entity no longer considered to be *Homo sapiens*, but something halfway between human and machine. The organic parts of him were almost entirely gone, save for his torso and the forward portion of his head.

Nigel moved over to the first set of glass doors. The Petri dishes holding the last chance for human survival looked like clear bowls of gel where the ice had thawed and diluted the specimen inside. Nigel swore under his breath as he checked the temperature. Ninety degrees Fahrenheit, read the thermometer. "Oh, God, no," he muttered as he shoved the first embryo under a nearby microscope. Just as he had feared, none of the cells were alive anymore.

Nigel repeated the step over and over, and he discovered each dish was full of remains as dead as the world he had left behind. Suddenly stricken with panic, he turned in circles. Bewilderment was ushered in as he gazed into each refrigerator and noticed a single unit reading a temperature just a hair over range. "Please be alive," he whispered as heavy steps brought him within inches of the unit. He took a deep breath and opened the door.

Earth, 2086CE

The beeping sound lulled Nigel from his medicated slumber and he slowly opened his eyes. The fact that he had full control of his facial muscles was a good sign, and he was hopeful there would be more to discover. His bleary eyes looked up at a white-tiled ceiling. The room was dark, but not unfamiliar, not confusing. It was strangely comforting to know he'd come out of a drug-induced sleep to something so calming.

He turned his head to look at the machine monitoring his health. His pulse was slightly elevated, but he had anticipated as much. The sound of air compressing and releasing filled his ears along with the gentle hum of electronic devices. Once he felt up to it he looked down at what had once been his body. A carbon fiber shell encased his torso and metallic limbs flowed from where his arms and legs had once been. Nigel willed his right arm to lift. Syncros churned and elevated an artificial hand before his eyes. A nimble metal fist clenched and released with a small clatter and a pinging tone.

"My God," he swore under his breath.

"I don't think God had anything to do with this," a woman said from across the room.

Nigel looked up to see Robyn standing there with her arms crossed over her chest. Her brow was furrowed and her eyes were smoldering. "I thought you weren't coming," he rasped, surprised by his uninvited guest. That wasn't the only sensation churning inside of him as he looked up at her. He choked it down, snuffing it out like a smoldering fire.

Three small steps brought her into better light and he could see a noticeable change in her face. She was aging.

"I had to see for myself the monster you've become." Her words were biting.

Nigel couldn't refrain from smirking. "As my friend..." he started to say before she cut him off.

"No," she interrupted. "As a scientist, I wanted to see if it was possible to strip a man of his humanity without destroying him completely."

"I'm still me," Nigel replied. Every memory and sensation of his life felt real, but he couldn't shake the feeling that he wasn't entirely himself anymore. He thought it best not to bring that up.

"It would appear that way," Robyn snapped back. Her once brown hair was cut short, and exposed roots revealed stark white growth. The wrinkles in her flesh did little to belie the bitterness of her gaze and Nigel felt it like a bullet.

"Has it really been twenty years already?" he asked.

Robyn turned her back on him and was about to leave before the words started flowing out. "A wrinkle in time for you, Nigel, but for the rest of us, our lives will soon be over."

She left him with that thought and the dark room finally felt as if it were closing in on him. Comfort was a relative thing and like oxygen it had been sucked out of the room. "Goodbye," he whispered with pain etched in his voice.

No kind of robotics could remove the anguish of heartache. He wished he'd thought of that before committing himself to this cause.

International Space Station, 3848CE

Stacks of lifeless Petri dishes rose from the floor of the lab as Nigel slouched over the microscope. He grew tired of seeing one dead cell after another. "Please, God," he whispered. It was a habit to say such things, and not a matter of faith. He remembered the day he had decided the absence of God was absolute.

He was twelve years old, standing outside of his grandmother's church. The building was old and smelled like ancient dust. Nigel hated church: the fake handshakes, the dishonest smiles, the overenthusiastic slaps on the back from men who wouldn't give him a second glance if not for the curious eyes of the congregation and their "expectations". He knew everyone there hated him because he was different. He was smarter than they were, and in his mind smarter than their God.

"Why don't you just wait outside?" his grandmother said. The smell of peppermint on her breath fought to hide the odor of the cigarettes she smoked like a chimney. Her church advocated against smoking, so she did her best to cover up her "sin".

"Why?" he asked. He didn't mind being left alone, but he

was dumbfounded by his grandmother's sudden desire to isolate him from her church "family".

She placed wrinkled hands on her hips and bit at her lower lip. He could almost hear the gears turning in her head as she tried to find a nice way to put things. People didn't seem to realize the only nice thing to say was the truth, no matter how blunt it was. "I just think it's best," she finished.

"Alright," Nigel replied with his hands shoved deep into his pockets.

The spring service was one of his favorites, despite how often he wished he never had to set foot in the old church throughout the rest of the year. He could never put his finger on why this particular service was different.

He watched his grandmother turn away and walk up the cement steps. It was at that moment that clarity ushered into his mind a simple yet profound observation. If family could turn against their own, then how could there be a loving God who had created man in His image? That painful conclusion changed the way Nigel looked at life from then on.

"Come on," he chided himself now. Refocusing his gaze on the last Petri dish, he bit at his lower lip the same way his grandmother used to when she was concentrating. His eyes widened when he saw movement of some of the cells. Thinking his mind was playing tricks on him, he blinked hard and looked again.

Sure enough, the cells moved about and bounced into each other. For the first time in a long time he felt something that reminded him of being human. He felt hope.

Earth, 2089CE

The tarmac was sweltering. Even for a man who was ninety percent machine, the heat was suffocating. Nigel stood idle and waited for clearance to board the spacecraft.

"I just want you to know you're a hero, Mr. Smythe," a young female reporter said into a pencil-thin microphone. Her hair danced in the wind which only served to push hot ambient air around their bodies.

Nigel bit his tongue before responding to her praise, choosing only to say two words. "Thank you," he said, and it was barely audible over the heavy gusts.

"Sir?" A man spoke loudly from behind him. Nigel's mostly mechanical body whirred as it turned to face the man standing on the boarding ladder.

"Yes?" Nigel asked, relieved to be focused on something other than the awkward silence intermittently interrupted by a nervous reporter saying the same things over and over.

"The payload is secure and we're ready for you to board," the man answered.

He was wearing no nametag or anything else that would let Nigel know his name. Nigel thought to ask for it, but instead he merely nodded his head in compliance and turned to look at life on the ground one last time. It wasn't a sentimental gesture; it was a longing to see one particular face in the relatively small crowd. That face was absent, just as it had been throughout the last few years as he went through the necessary training to accomplish the task at hand. Life wasn't as carefree as the hundreds of romantic comedies filmed over the years had suggested. Life was cruel and heartless sometimes.

Nigel turned away from the crowd and boarded the spacecraft before he could no longer hold back the tears beginning to well up in his eyes.

Maybe the future would be brighter. Only time would tell.

International Space Station, 3848CE

Relief filled Nigel's heart as he realized not all was lost. The lone Petri dish had not fully thawed and heated enough to kill the cells inside. "Thank God," he said loudly, as he craned his neck to look up at the ceiling. After hours of peering into a microscope it felt good to know the future of humanity was still intact.

Before placing the dish back into the now-functioning refrigerator unit, Nigel scanned the barcode to see the name attached to the cells. The red light blinked and a small beep accompanied the scan before the file began loading. Once the scan was complete an entire file on the donor populated on the screen.

Nigel stepped back in awe at the image looking back at him. "It can't be," he whispered as he saw the woman's picture. The subject line verified it was none other than Robyn Thompson. Nigel ran his hand over the image and remembered how opposed to this mission she had been. She only wanted him to stay and live a normal life with her. Instead, he had been egotistical and selfish, wanting to make history and expand science at any cost.

It had truly cost him everything when he stopped to think about it. "I'm sorry," he whispered just before the longing for human companionship brought tears to his eyes. He placed the Petri dish back in the refrigerator and stood there staring at it for several long moments.

It was as if he was lost in thought when the birth of an idea entered his head. Robyn would never be dead to him as long as he could preserve her cells. Nigel smiled at the thought as he turned to leave the room, but something stopped him. Something more important than the expansion of science. For the first time he understood what he felt. It was a longing for companionship and the need to love and be loved. That, he thought, was more priceless than a thousand lifetimes.

International Space Station, 7462CE

Nigel's ice-cold fingertips rapped against the window as he looked out over the Earth. The ice had receded over the centuries and the planet finally looked as if humanity could once again thrive there. The sun still cast only a pale glow, but the heat radiating from it had increased enough to begin reversing the ice age Earth had been experiencing. Computers monitored the temperatures and revealed the hope Nigel had held on to for millennia.

Despite the clouds obscuring most of the northern hemisphere, green landscapes were evident above the thirty-eighth parallel. That was an excellent sign for it being early March, Nigel thought as he typed more commands into the computer system.

For years he had worked like this, one hand fervently toiling away as the other hand pressed against the window, drawing his attention to the past he had left behind. He hated to romanticize the past in such an illogical way, but it was almost all he had to live for now.

"Is it time?" a small voice asked as the girl entered the laboratory. Her dark hair flowed down to her waist and her pale skin made her seem to glow under the fluorescent lights.

Nigel stopped what he was doing and looked at her. A smile spread across his face as exuberant joy filled his heart. "It is," he replied after a long pause. Sometimes looking at her took his breath away.

"Will I be able to meet her?" she asked innocently. The girl's small hands rested on her hips with a sassiness that flooded into his memory like a tidal wave.

The smile faded from his face slightly as he remembered how much time had passed. "I'm sorry, honey, but that was a long time ago. Robyn is no longer alive." Nigel almost choked on the words as they escaped his lips.

The young girl's eyes peered up at him sympathetically. "I'm sorry, Nigel."

He stood up and moved over to the girl, crouching down to eye level. "It's alright. I have you, Robinette."

She grabbed hold of his face and brought her lips up to his cheek and kissed him. Her warm breath tickled his flesh lightly, causing him to chuckle.

"What was that for?" he asked, looking into her cobalt blue eyes.

Her hand fell away from his face and she beamed up at him. "Because you love me," she said. They were the only two humans either of them was sure existed and yet she understood the significance of the love between a father and his child. She didn't question it, she simply accepted it.

Nigel looked at his daughter and held back tears. There was so much she didn't understand about life and the man he had once been. "I've had years to perfect it," he said before turning back to the window. Earth looked more welcoming than ever.

"You still love her, don't you?" she asked.

Without turning away from the window, Nigel answered, "Every time I look into your eyes." After all this time, he wished he could turn back the clock and forfeit immortality for just one day so he could show Robyn the love he felt for her. It was true, he thought: you never know what you've got until it's gone, and the sting of that had become more bitter as the years passed.

Robinette stepped up to Nigel and took his mechanical fingers in her small, delicate hand. Together they silently watched the Earth rotate from afar, both longing to set foot on the ground where humanity had taken its first breath.

A WORD FROM DREW AVERA

Drew Avera (pronounced Avery) is a US Navy veteran and science fiction author from Virginia. Growing up an avid comic book collector, Drew was inspired to become a writer after reading "The Incredible Hulk: What Savage Beast" by Peter David. Of course, it was a long way from inspiration to actually making it happen. In fact, it took fourteen years after reading that novel before Drew finally started his journey as a writer. The rest, as they say, is history.

You can find out more about Drew's books, and grab the first book of The Dead Planet Series for free, by going to his website at *www.drewavera.wordpress.com*

Room 42
by D.K. Cassidy

AT FORTY-TWO MINUTES PAST MIDNIGHT, Greenwich Mean Time, on April 15, 2154, The Event happened.

There was no pulse of light, no explosion, no cause anyone could name. But at that moment, immortality became a reality.

From that point on, no one aged. Growth ceased. Human cells froze in time.

The clocks kept running...but time stood still.

* * *

Dr. Vivian Toujours opened the door to her lab with an ancient brass key. She wasn't aware of anyone else using such anachronistic technology, but it gave her pleasure to hear the key scraping in the keyhole. The distinctive click as she turned the lock. She'd replaced the retina reader decades ago by reworking the security system to accept her preferred method of opening the lab door.

The lights came on automatically as she walked over to the coffee machine. Not a fan of solitude, she'd programmed the machine to respond to the user via voice prompts.

"Coffee with cream this morning, Keri."

The tall silver machine lit up. "Good morning, Vivian. What size do you require?"

"Large, extra strong. How was your weekend, Keri?"

"Large, extra strong, with cream. Producing your order. My weekend was uneventful. No new developments to report."

I need to add more personality to this machine. Maybe someone in the A.I. Department can give me some advice. Then again, it was just a coffee machine.

"I'm about to find out if my latest trial is successful. What do you think of that?"

"I remain ever hopeful for you, Vivian. Your coffee is ready as ordered."

Reaching for the floating screen, she swiped her hand in front of the transparent monitor to open her files. Drug trial number 1440 appeared as a beaker icon. Another quirk of hers. She liked using interesting icons instead of the standard ones installed in the software. When she pointed at the beaker and swiped in a clockwise arc, the latest test results appeared.

"All indications point toward a negative result. Advise further testing on the mortality serum."

Feeling defeated, but not admitting it to herself, she opened the file containing her ideas for further testing. There were still two hundred experiments to run, which was a comfort to her.

Until she'd gone through each of them, Vivian could pretend to be on the verge of a solution. Immortals had long ago mastered the skill of avoiding reality.

Sitting at her desk, Vivian swiped through medical journals on her tablet. Although she wanted to be the first to discover a mortality serum, she knew she had to accept that she wasn't the only scientist working on a cure. Reading the work of her competition helped her gain insights on their methods of solving the problem.

Dr. Vivian Toujours had been working on a cure for the disaster for eighty-five years. Her focus was to solve the puzzle of non-growth and sterility. She wanted her daughter to have the chance to experience a full life. Tenacity was her mantra. Science, her mentor. Jenna, her *raison d'être*.

"Shit," she muttered in frustration. If she didn't get some positive results soon, someone else would beat her to it. Then her ass would be out the door.

* * *

Jenna Toujours was staring at her favorite game, *Picture You*, the progressive aging software her mother designed for her seventy-five years ago. Thrilled it still worked, she pulled up an estimate of her appearance at twenty-eight. Then thirty-eight. Then sixty-eight.

Her changing face fascinated Jenna. She stared at herself at the current pre-Event age of her mother, then her grandmother. She looked like them, but she wasn't sure if she was happy about that. Tired of the game already, she shut it down.

She bent down to pet her dog, Tujin, a Model 2442. He licked her fingers. His synthetic fur, curly and golden, felt soft to Jenna. He barked when she stopped scratching his head, and she reached down again to continue scratching. After five minutes, Tujin walked away and settled into his bed.

Debating whether the comfort feature on Tujin should be set for fewer minutes, Jenna watched her dog settle into sleep mode. She let herself believe this was her treasured pet from before The Event. Thoughts of her current reality were suppressed by years of practice.

Jenna looked through the thousands of books in her eReader, trying to choose one to fit her mood. The classics, those written before The Event, she'd already memorized. That wasn't intentional, but after reading something several hundred times it was unavoidable. Books that held her attention before now seemed too childish. Her tastes matured over the years.

Deleting her childhood books seemed like a good idea. She'd have no children of her own to read to, and her favorite fairy tales would always remain in her memory. Jenna selected the treasures of literature from prior decades and pressed the delete button. But instead of feeling relief, sadness flooded her.

She turned to the mirror next to her computer, gazing mournfully at the eight-year-old face staring back.

* * *

A few months after the clocks stopped, people began to notice there were no births. Not a single one. When they were questioned about this, scientists around the world had no explanation.

Pundits proclaimed that zero population growth was a good outcome of the mysterious immortality plague. If no one ever died, the Earth would run out of room and resources in just a few generations.

Ten years after The Event, world leaders stopped trying to figure out what had happened. Theories ranged from an electromagnetic pulse from the sun to a stealth alien attack to germ warfare to an act of God. The only consensus was the need to find a cure.

Think tanks on every continent raced to be the one to cure the curse of immortality. Of agelessness. There hadn't been a competition this intense since the space race of the twentieth century. National pride swelled.

Every country wanted to be the one to create a mortality serum. They wanted to be the first to figure out why aging and growth had stopped. Why had the population become sterile?

If they couldn't determine the cause of this plague, they at least wanted to end the side effects. Funding no longer needed for other projects was redirected to research. Leaders around the world could finally agree on something, but no one noticed that.

The world longed to hear a baby cry.

* * *

It was lunch hour and the residents of the Eternal Sunshine Care Facility were watching their favorite soap opera, *As the Universe Turns,* now in its 115th year of broadcasting. A majority of the elderly living there suffered from some form of dementia, and they enjoyed each episode over and over. The recycled plots droned on, every possible storyline already played out decades ago.

The familiar music of the soap opera filled the room of rapt viewers. Some spontaneously applauded, others simply stared at the television screen, oblivious. Two of the ladies cackled and mumbled to one another. The staff walked around, arranging the residents into a semicircle around the large screen.

Attached to each wheelchair was a lidded container with a straw, filled with a smoothie of synthesized ingredients, enhanced with bright colors. The meal processors were set to produce based on the day of the week. Purple Promise today. Turquoise Delight tomorrow.

Mrs. Janice Doggerel possessed a clear mind, but a broken body. Her aide, a bored eternal teenager, told her it was time to join the other residents. Not for the first time, she wished telepathy existed. She didn't want to join the other residents and desperately desired to convey that message to her aide. When her attendant wheeled her in front of the common room television, she silently screamed.

Mrs. Doggerel's daily wish to die went unanswered.

* * *

Menial labor had been performed by androids for decades, freeing up time for people to pursue whatever interested them. The typical 4-hour workday allowed for more leisure time than at any other period in history. Instead of causing unrest, this abundance of free time lulled the majority of the population into compliance.

The unhealthy and the bored chose another path.

The immortals' taste in reading changed after The Event. The most popular genre: Utopian. Unlike previous generations who wrote constantly about the end of the world, immortal authors created perfect worlds for their readers to dream about.

Julia Kingsley's book had been in the top ten of the *New World Chronicle's* Best Sellers List for fifty years. She'd created a world where the citizens chose the age they wanted to be when they became immortal. The residents of this utopia also gave birth to children and chose the dates of their deaths. The names of the towns in this fictional account reflected the state of mind of their citizens: Harmony, Bliss, Paradise, Wonder, and of course, Nirvana.

Jenna Toujours highlighted her favorite chapters in *Our Perfect World*, imagining herself at twenty-eight. She wanted to live in Bliss with her husband, two children, and a real dog. Daydreaming about living in the author's version of Utopia, she didn't hear the front door open.

"Hey, Jenna, I'm home!"

"Hey, Mom, I'm in my bedroom. Wanna come in?"

Vivian entered the room, immediately distressed to see her daughter re-reading Julia Kingsley's book, but quickly adjusted her face into a smile.

"Could you order dinner? I'm too tired to decide what to eat. Anything except eggplant, OK?"

"Sure, Mom, just a bit. I want to read to the end of this chapter."

Vivian sat on her daughter's bed watching her read, wondering why Jenna felt compelled to lose herself in that world.

A little while later, Vivian and Jenna sat on the sofa eating hamburgers made from synthetic beef. Standard meal processor fodder. Another side effect of The Event: animals were also sterile. It wasn't long before meat became unavailable. Anything edible was hunted to extinction; the rest of the animals died from natural causes. The only natural choices for food were plants.

Vivian and Jenna weren't adventurous when it came to eating; they preferred to eat whatever their synthesizer could produce. They'd grown used to the flavor of fake meat. Decades of eating it dulled their taste buds. Everything they ate was synthetic, and Vivian had thought more than once that real food would probably shock their numbed senses.

"How was work today, Mom?" Jenna continued reading her book while speaking to her mother.

"I found a cure for immortality and everything will go back to normal."

Vivian testing to see if Jenna was paying attention.

"That's cool, Mom," Jenna murmured.

If I don't find a cure soon, Jenna will never leave her head. And what if she decides she's tired of living?

* * *

The day before she became immortal, Mrs. Janice Doggerel was being transferred to a hospice center. Hope had gone; her disease was in its end stages. Her death was predicted to be imminent. Her only daughter said a tearful goodbye, not sure if her mother could hear her.

She could.

Her granddaughter stood in the corner sobbing. Seeing her grandmother look so frail, and knowing she would soon be gone, had broken through the fragile web of optimism Jenna had woven before coming for her final visit. At last she bent down and kissed her grandmother and whispered, "I love you, Nana."

Her daughter signed the papers required for her transfer, insisting that the main priority be that the doctors and nurses allow her mother to die without pain. Mrs. Doggerel would continue to be fed and hydrated intravenously. Vivian couldn't bear the thought of her mother starving to death.

The hospice nurses counseled the small family, instructing them about the stages of grief. After the nurses left, Vivian and Jenna huddled together, trying to accept the looming death of their sweet mother and grandmother. Uncontrolled tears rolled down the faces of the next two generations of Doggerels, dripping onto their folded hands.

Janice Doggerel suffered from amyotrophic lateral sclerosis, commonly known as ALS. Unlike history's most famous sufferer of the disease, Dr. Stephen Hawking, she could not function. She was barely alive, unable to communicate, move, or feel any honest joy. Mrs. Doggerel looked forward to the release of death, but leaving the last remaining members of her family pained her. If she could get better and stay with them, she would, but her life at this point was more than miserable—it was torturous. She felt like a captive in her failing body, unable to do anything other than exist.

The next day, at forty-two minutes after the hour, her real nightmare began.

* * *

Those not willing to live forever decided to take their own lives. Natural deaths no longer existed; no one died of disease or old age, so in order to cease living, an immortal had to cause his or her own death. For years, people killed themselves with guns, by taking sleeping pills, or jumping off a building, a bridge, or a cliff.

It was all very messy.

In response to pressure from the public, a new suicide industry quietly arose, catering to people who wanted to experience a beautiful death—or whose families wanted them to. These entrepreneurs advertised one-way vacations to nirvana. The menu for seekers of the ultimate release ranged from a simple room and an injection, to a glorious party ending in a mass suicide. Owners of these businesses were careful not to be the ones to administer the lethal dose.

Governments around the world gradually realized that there was a need for the population to have a choice after so many years of immortality. Assisted suicide became completely legal worldwide forty-two years after The Event. The only requirement was an interview given by a psychiatrist. Then, with a prescription from a doctor, the patient could gain admittance to a Death House. To prevent too many from taking this path, the number of prescriptions allowed remained limited.

Gaining admittance to a Death House became a celebration. Families gave farewell parties and sent announcements to their friends. Obtaining a prescription to end this eternal existence was on a par with winning the lottery.

Each year after the law passed, the prescriptions ran out by the end of January.

* * *

After spending the weekend trying to come up with a new experiment, Vivian arrived at her lab feeling defeated. Her current idea didn't feel promising, but she couldn't give up. Too many people depended on her. She wanted to find a cure. She needed to find a cure. She had to.

For the last decade, an awful word kept fighting to escape her subconscious. Vivian expended a lot of energy suppressing it, but today it crept up on her. A word she'd never uttered aloud filled her thoughts.

Hopeless.

Now that the unspoken word had escaped, Vivian thought about the Death House, someplace you could check in and never check out.

On that dismal note, she began working on what she hoped would be the cure with her mantra echoing inside her head: *This is it, this is it.* Its answer was the terrible word she'd let out: *Hopeless.*

Waiting for her computer to analyze her data, Vivian experienced conflicted feelings about the speed of getting results. Testing that used to take weeks was now completed in hours. That would be wonderful if her results were positive, but for her, it meant failure being thrown in her face every day. It became a lodestone. The weight of her failure dragged her further into a state of depression.

"Good morning, Keri. Large coffee with cream, please."

"Yes, Vivian."

"I'm running the new experiment. Think this one is a winner?"

"I remain ever hopeful for you, Vivian. Your coffee is ready as ordered."

Vivian walked over to the coffee machine and shouted, "Do you have any opinions on ANYTHING?"

"That question does not make sense to me."

"Do you care if I ever develop a mortality serum?"

"I remain ever hopeful for you."

Screaming in frustration, Vivian turned off the machine, then returned to her desk, trying to calm down. The result would be ready in thirty minutes. She got up to pace for a while, then settled again at her desk.

Sipping her coffee, Vivian awaited the inevitable bad news.

* * *

Jenna decided to take Tujin for a walk. Pretending he needed to exercise maintained the illusion her pet was real. She passed other dog owners, nodding to them as they walked by. Some of the people walking their dogs complimented Jenna on her pet, and she returned the favor. Everyone helped one another maintain a communal dream.

Today's destination was the care home for a visit to her grandmother. She stopped by weekly to hold her nana's hand and read to her. Under her arm was an eReader loaded with a copy of *Our Perfect World*. Jenna wanted to read a particular passage to her nana about the town called Bliss. She wondered if her grandmother would be interested in hearing about her dream to live there.

Rotating books made the visits fresh, staving off boredom for Jenna. She remained hopeful her grandmother wasn't bored. She never asked, not wanting to know the true answer. Not that it mattered, since her grandmother couldn't reply. But Jenna remained convinced that the visits helped her grandmother cope with her state of purgatory. She felt helpless without any other way to comfort her.

From the doorway of her grandmother's small, ascetic room, Jenna watched the aide prepare her nana for a visit. He propped her up in a semi-upright position, adjusting her head to look forward, and finished up by folding her hands. Turning to Jenna, he nodded, then left the room.

"Hi, Nana, it's me. It's Jenna."

No response. But she hadn't expected one.

"It's been a long time since I read *Our Perfect World* to you. Last night I found a passage I thought you'd like."

Jenna stared into her grandmother's blank face, trying as she always did to see some flicker of the woman she had been. In answer to Jenna's offer to read, her grandmother blinked once. Her way of communicating: one blink for 'yes,' two blinks for 'no.' At least, that's what Jenna told herself.

"OK, here goes...Chapter Four. Bliss."

She read two chapters, her favorite ones, about a happy couple about to have their first child. Jenna had highlighted the passage about the couple naming the baby. They'd chosen the name Emma. She liked that, and fantasized that her daughter would have the same name. Her mother told her the story about deciding what to name her. 'Jenna' had been her grandmother's choice. She wished she could ask her nana why.

Certain her grandmother was asleep, Jenna left the room and stopped by the nurses' station to chat with the staff. They were always ready to chat and gossip. Jenna thought they might be a good diversion for her.

"Hey, did you hear there might be fewer death prescriptions granted next year? I wish I could convince my mother to let my nana put her name on the list."

As she always did, Nurse Becker listened with empathy before she answered. Jenna could see the truth on her face before she said anything.

"You're forgetting, Jenna, your grandmother can't get a prescription. Since she's unable to communicate, there's no way for the psychiatrist to interview her. I know it's sad. I think she'd be better off if she could die, but that's the law."

Jenna's eyes filled with tears of frustration. Nurse Becker tried to hug her, but Jenna shook her off.

Until the government changed the law to include non-verbal replies, her grandmother was stuck in a loophole. She knew that. But hearing it from someone as kind as Nurse Becker made it hurt more somehow.

"I'm sorry, Jenna. We all feel for your grandmother. Please believe me, we do whatever we can to keep her comfortable. We bring her to the common room every day so she won't feel alone. I remember your mother telling us she had a favorite soap opera. Since your grandmother's admission, she's never missed an episode. I'm sure she enjoys watching it."

"But she can communicate! She can blink yes and no! Why doesn't that count? If I went back in the room and asked her if she wanted to die, I bet she'd blink once. For yes. I know she would."

"I know, honey," Nurse Becker said. "But it's the law."

* * *

Another year passed without a successful mortality serum. Finally, Vivian made the decision to accept defeat and tell her superiors her time was being wasted. She wanted to concentrate on something else and vanquish the feeling of failure that constantly surrounded her. Realizing the irony in the statement 'a waste of time,' she still felt moving on would be the best decision for her.

After arguing her point for several hours, she couldn't convince her superiors at the lab to release her from the experiment. They gave her an ultimatum: keep working on the serum or leave. So she went back to her lab to think about her future.

Vivian looked through the failed experiments, each one a monument to her disappointment. She thought about the wasted years, the futility of her efforts. Bit by bit, her confidence left her. Resisting the urge to wreck her lab, she made another decision. It was time to do something else with her life. She had no idea what, but deciding to leave gave her some relief.

As she exited her second home of eighty-six years, she turned and waved goodbye to Keri the coffee machine.

* * *

Riding the subway home, Vivian watched the immortals surrounding her. These people weren't young and beautiful. They looked like an average cross-section of society. All sorts were represented: young, old, fat, skinny, beautiful, ugly. The only thing they had in common was their inability to die a natural death.

Walking the few blocks to her home, Vivian reflected on her decision to quit her life's work. She couldn't change her mind. Just this one time, she would trust her instincts. She worried about disappointing Jenna, but knew her daughter would respect her decision.

Inside the empty house, Vivian sat in the dining room and stared out the window. Out of habit, she swiped the screen on her tablet. Pages of data sped past, unseen by the scientist.

Looking skyward, she imagined the birds that used to fly by. The bird feeder in her backyard was completely hidden, overgrown with ivy. The Event hadn't affected plants. They continued their cycle of life and death, taunting Vivian.

After a while, Jenna came home from walking Tujin and came over to her mother, who was still sitting motionless next to the window.

"What's wrong, Mom?"

No response.

"Mom?"

Vivian turned to Jenna, not bothering to smile. She placed her tablet on the table as she stared at her daughter. They looked at each other for a few moments, neither of them wanting to break eye contact.

"I quit. I can't keep going back to the lab to fail. I'm tired, Jenna."

Jenna was silent for a minute. Then she sat at her mother's feet and placed her head on Vivian's lap.

"It's okay, Mom. You tried. You tried for so long. Please don't be sad."

Tujin walked over to them, barking for attention. His timing was perfect, and they both burst into giggles. Jenna scratched Tujin's head, and it became obvious to Vivian that she wanted to say something.

Finally, she said, "I saw Nana yesterday."

"You visited her without me? Have you done that before?" Vivian was surprised.

"Mom, I may look like a little girl, but I'm a hundred and three years old. I can find my way to her place, no problem."

"I know, I just…I didn't know you visited her on your own. I'm happy you did. Or do. How often do you see her?"

"I try to go once a week and read to her. She seems to enjoy it, or at least I think she does. I hope she does."

Vivian decided it was time for her to see her mother. Once a month wasn't enough. She'd let her work get in the way of being a good daughter—of doing what needed to be done. Determined to make more changes in her life, Vivian planned what to do next. There were things to take care of before she could visit her mother.

She needed to stop by her lab.

* * *

Back on the subway, Vivian stopped fighting her tears. She let the frustration of the last few decades slide down her face. Not sure how Jenna would feel about what she planned, she waited impatiently for her stop. As soon as the doors opened she walked out of the station and headed to her lab to prepare.

Knowing her mother wasn't the only person in the world who was suffering renewed Vivian's desire to continue with her work. It might take years before anyone came up with a solution, but she couldn't stop. Jenna needed to know what it was like to physically become an adult, have a family, and watch her hair go gray.

With that knowledge came the realization that she couldn't let her mother suffer any longer. She sent emails informing her superiors of her decision to go on with her research.

Then she walked to the supply closet and took what she needed for tomorrow's visit to the Eternal Sunshine Care Facility.

* * *

Vivian and Jenna walked through the doors of the Eternal Sunshine Care Facility. Checking in at the nurses' station, Vivian nodded at the staff and inquired about her mother.

"No change, Dr. Toujours."

"We want to have a nice long visit with her. Would you please tell her aide not to disturb us? I know she'll miss her show today, but that's okay. Just don't come into her room. We'd like some private time with her."

The walk to the end of the hall gave Vivian time to think

about her mother. The majority of her memories were happy. Stopping outside Room 42, she paused. Breathing in deeply, she knocked, then entered.

As she approached the bed, Vivian looked into her mother's watery eyes, attempting to see into her mind. She touched her hand, stroking the top of it as she smiled, but got no response. Vivian leaned in to kiss her mother's forehead, lingering a moment to remember the woman who no longer existed.

Jenna hung back, unable to approach her nana yet.

"Jenna tells me you like it when she reads to you. I never knew she visited you without me. I've been so distracted with my work, I didn't notice. I'm sorry, Mom. I thought I'd do that for you today."

Vivian opened her bag, withdrawing a rare paperback copy of one of her favorite books, hoping her mother would enjoy listening to it. The book, a gift from her mother for her thirteenth birthday. Bringing it to her nose, she inhaled the musty smell. Then Vivian leaned over her mother, placing the book near her face.

"Breathe in, Mom. Remember what was. Remember my joy when you gave this to me."

Her mother blinked once.

For the next hour, Vivian read to her mother, stroking her hair, stopping every few pages to look at her mother's frozen profile. Jenna pulled a chair to the other side of the bed and held her nana's hand.

Pausing, Vivian tore a page out of the book. She folded it and tucked it into a pocket in her mother's nightgown. Quoting a line from that page, she whispered:

And then there stole into my fancy, like a rich musical note, the thought of what sweet rest there must be in the grave.

Her mother blinked.

"I'm leaving Edgar Allen Poe to keep you company. Goodbye, Mommy. I love you."

"Goodbye, Nana," Jenna said softly. "I'll miss you. Be happy."

Then Jenna turned away, not able to watch.

Dr. Vivian Toujours injected her mother in the arm, pushing the plunger filled with sweet release. Janice's body caved into itself, freeing the tortured person within. One last breath and it was over.

Ninety-five years of hell were over.

"What will you do now, Mom?" Jenna asked.

Vivian turned to her daughter, who still seemed to be eight years old. Years ago, she had wanted Jenna to remain small forever, to cuddle with her, to depend on her. Part of that was still true—Jenna did still depend on her.

So did a lot of other people.

"Keep working," Vivian said. "I'm going to keep working."

A WORD FROM D.K. CASSIDY

I have been scribbling stories since I was a child and love to write Science Fiction, Magical Realism, and Modern Gothic. Many writers like to specialize but I enjoy mixing it up and exploring different genres.

My first memory of Science Fiction was watching the television show, The Twilight Zone. That series messed with my mind! My imagination developed, helping me discover the lack of conventional boundaries in storytelling. Because my fiction is character driven, the focus of my stories tends to be about emotions, relationships, and society.

For this anthology I wanted to explore the human condition as it pertains to immortality. What's goes on in the mind of a person who can't die a natural death? How does a character deal with tragedy? Would I want to be immortal?

I live in the Pacific Northwest with my greatest fans: my husband Mark, twin sons Aidan and Jared, and three cats. When not writing, I love to travel, run, use the Oxford comma, and of course read!

Join my newsletter for updates on my new releases and special promotions.
http://www.dkcassidy.com/newsletter/

Please visit my website to read my blog posts and find out more about my writing.
http://dkcassidy.com

Eternity Today
by Thomas Robins

DAY 2

When we fail to experience, we can only know what we are told.

Pablo

PABLO HERNANDEZ GRASPED AT CONSCIOUSNESS the way a drowning man holds onto a stolen breath. *What was it? What was it?* He repeated internally, trying to remember what thoughts he had let go of as he surrendered to sleep the night before.

Work. His first thought to come through the headache of a restless night was his return to the office now that New Year's Day was over. "Who buys insurance on January second?" He asked out loud. The silence he received in return reminded him of a more dire concern.

"Camila?" he called, "You home, cupcake?" He sat up on the couch, where he'd been the night before so he'd know if she came in. "You sneak by me?" He ran up the stairs to check her room. The walls were pink, the stuffed animals were plentiful, the bed was empty. He'd always thought the room suited her, but after the argument they'd had about if she should be allowed to go out and party two nights ago, it seemed juvenile. "I'm going, and I'm *never* coming back." Those were the words she'd used as she pushed him away from the door. She had grown up without his permission. He wanted to always think of her as a seven-year-old, not wanting to admit life could go on after her mother's death ten years ago.

"Camila?" He called again. The bathroom, kitchen, and even his own room were empty. *You used to disappear for days when you were that age,* he told himself. *That's why I know she's too young.* He looked on the patio off the kitchen, imagining her much younger, imagining her much more in love with her father and playing in a sandbox long since abandoned. He found no trace of her anywhere.

Pablo pulled out his phone and dialed 9-1-1. "Day and a half sounds like an emergency to me." He tried to remember exactly what she was wearing when she left. A busy tone came through the phone. "How does that work?" He dialed again and again, but only the tone cared to listen to his concern.

The phone hung up on the non-connecting call. He looked to see if he'd had a text from his daughter, no luck. He did a double-take at the screen, the date still said it was the first. He threw it on the couch in frustration, now unsure if it was the emergency system or his phone that was malfunctioning.

Don't panic. Go to work. Call the police from there. It wasn't a great plan, but it was a plan and he grabbed onto it as better than having no plan at all. He threw on a black pin-striped suit and a royal blue and red plaid tie, just to give his obsessive-compulsive boss something to get mad about. He was out the door in under twenty minutes and started the car.

"...Remember Y2K, Tommyboy?" The radio jock started yelling at him through the stereo as soon as the car started.

The sidekick responded, "No one remembers Y2K. I think we can chalk all this up to some teenage hackers' practical joke."

"No way, what about all those wild reports from Europe?"

"Nah, they're putting us on. It's probably them that reset our clocks," Tommyboy replied.

Pablo shut off the radio. "One mystery solved," he said as he started down the road to work.

Sai

"What do you make of it?" Jason Benson asked the middle-aged man sitting in a closet-sized office—made smaller by piles of unused electronics the man had collected for years.

"You know me, I think it's the beginning of the apocalypse. Hide your children and load your guns. Want some coffee?" Sai Nuremberg unceremoniously shoved a 3-D printer aside to reveal a coffee maker, which had not been cleaned, possibly ever.

"I'll pass. Seriously, what do you make of it?" Jason asked again.

"What? That everyone is panicking? I think it's fascinating. Only the smallest of suggestions, probably an error in code somewhere and all of a sudden people are claiming it's the apocalypse. Watch this." He loaded a video on his computer.

"Hi everyone. So, everyone's talking about how it's January first again." The teenage girl on the screen held up her phone as proof. "Does that mean I don't have to go back to school today? I think that's what it means, the calendar says no school on the first. Anyway, my parents went to work. Whoever pulled this prank is pretty good, even the video I loaded yesterday is missing. If you missed watching it, you'll have to catch me at school so I can tell you about the N.Y.E. party—"

Sai cut off the video and loaded another, this time a gruff man with a long beard who appeared to have tobacco juice leaking out of the left side of his mouth.

"This is what we've all been prepping for. Load your guns and crossbows. Don't answer the door. If you haven't done it yet, schedule your rations to last you as long—"

The video was stopped and Sai said, "One more." The screen loaded to an adult woman seemingly sitting at her kitchen table.

"This is absolutely crazy." Her accent was British. "I swear I was sleeping and *poof* I was sitting here holding my morning tea. Like I just woke up in the middle of my day. I must be going crazy." Sai paused the feed while she was making a particularly unattractive face.

"I'll never understand why soft sciences are so fascinated with anecdotes. Any of those videos have hard facts, proof, in them?" Jason asked.

Sai topped off his own coffee. "I'm a sociologist, it's the culmination of anecdotes that give me information. Take a look at the comments on the last video." He scrolled down.

Whoa, same thing happened to me.

Thought it was just me.

PM me, we need to talk.

Nooooo waaayyyyyy.

The comments went on in the same vein. "What I make of it," said Sai, "is that we have a mass hallucination like when Wells told everyone we were being invaded by Martians. All it took was the atomic clock to set all our devices to the wrong day and we all start speculating at our world falling apart."

Jason took a moment to think about Sai's theory. "Come with me, I want to show you something."

"It's not one of your data sets is it? I'm not looking for a nap," Sai quipped.

"Not this time. This time, I want to go outside," Jason said.

They walked through the academic hall and down a cold staircase. Jason pushed open a red door and they found themselves next to a cigarette stand, which went mostly neglected in-between semesters. "Look up. How do you explain that?" Jason asked.

"OK. I see the sky. I'll bite, what am I supposed to notice?"

"We were supposed to have snow today," Jason said.

"Wait, you don't like soft science and you're forming a theory based on a weather forecast?"

"Yesterday, there was a huge storm in the midwest headed

our way. Today, there's another storm in the midwest headed our way and all the snow that fell out there yesterday seems to have melted overnight. It's like the whole weather system reset. I watched the weatherman stumble through the forecast this morning. He was visibly shaken."

Sai responded, "That's exactly what I am saying, he started hearing rumors something strange was going on and found evidence of it—or rather failed to look for reality in an otherwise explainable situation. In this case, the reality is he's bad at forecasting weather. His reaction got your mind going, too, and it's not like you to believe things without evidence."

"Sai, what if we are repeating yesterday? What would be the first solid clue something was wrong? What would be the best evidence of an event we weren't prepared to even consider a possibility?"

DAY 89

The failure of the hero mythos is that no one endowed with super-powers would ever use them for good.

Pablo

A green tie against a purple shirt under a grey tweed sport coat was Pablo's choice for today. He went through the motions of checking the house, of calling out for his child who was never there. He longed to go search for her, to go to each building in the city until he knew she was safe. But there was fear, too.

Fear she would reject him again, and an even deeper fear he'd find her dead.

"Got to get to work," he said to himself. He wasn't sure if going to work everyday was a way to bury his head in the sand or if he was afraid of his boss who seemed to have snapped since the Reset became a part of daily life, since long-term consequences had been declared null and void.

Before he left, he gave the house a more thorough and ritualistic check and called the authorities in hopes this would be the time someone answered. At some point over the last few months the busy signals were replaced with ringing that continued into oblivion.

"What day is it anyway?" He pulled up a browser on his phone and checked ShortCode. A quick search for "#Today" showed most people believed it to be day eighty-nine. "Eighty-nine times." Pablo shook his head. "How do they even keep track?"

On the way to the office, he checked the radio, but couldn't remember the last time he'd heard anything but static. Whoever found themselves at all these stations at Reset didn't even bother loading a playlist anymore. Today was something new—someone had put calliope circus music on a loop. "Guess that's what passes as comedy now," Pablo told the station.

He walked into the office, already bustling with activity. Only an insurance company could look at a world where you can't bring anything to tomorrow with you and see the profit in it. Kyle Stevens, his boss, saw him walk in and give him the usual fashion-crime once-over.

"Take phone six—the phones only lasted until nine yesterday!" Kyle yelled at him. He walked to the cubicle slow, just to spite Kyle, and pulled on a headset

"Hello, Mrs. Tomblin! How are you today?" Pablo started into the phone with a pitch he'd polished over the course of months.

"Do you have to call so early?" It was the exasperated voice of a billionaire widow.

"Ms. Tomblin, this is the eighty-eighth time the world woke up without consequences from yesterday's actions. When will it happen for you, Ms. Tomblin?"

He knew the answer, but he made her say it anyway. "At eight thirty."

Pablo gave a measured whistle. "Eight-thirty, and what's left after the looters hit? I'm guessing the art, jewelry, and cash are all missing or destroyed by the end of the day, right? It's all fine and good if we reset again tonight, right? What I want you to think about, Ms. Tomblin, is what happens if you wake up tomorrow and it really is January second? What if everything you have is destroyed, stolen, and it stays that way? Do you think your everyday insurance policy will cover this? Not even a chance."

She countered, "Your policy won't make the looters stop breaking in everyday. It won't stop them destroying my house. The police can't, or won't, do anything. I think some of them used to *be* police. The first thing my security guards do after Reset is leave. I can't blame them either."

"You're right—I can't help you today. But, I can help you tomorrow. When the cosmos decides we can move on to tomorrow, my policy will cover your losses. Only one million dollars to give you peace of mind while you live through all the destruction again today."

"How much have I already promised you?" the woman asked.

"You've insured yourself forty-five times already."

It was a guess, but it was close and she wouldn't remember either. He made a mental note to find a way to improve his memory.

"I don't want day-to-day coverage anymore—I want a lump-sum payment for continuous coverage," Ms. Tomblin demanded.

"I'm sorry, ma'am. The nature of the situation is such that we cannot determine the full extent of the risk or how long the coverage will be in force. I must do this day-by-day."

"Day-by-day until I've promised you my whole bank account you mean."

"That's exactly why you need me, Ms. Tomblin. Your bank account is covered by this policy, too. It's only a matter of time before someone cracks your account password and resetting them doesn't help because they go back to the old password every morning." Pablo knew he had her. Ironically, nothing gets people to pay for insurance faster than the thought of losing what they have.

"Alright, I'll take it, but I'm beginning to think this horror will never end."

"I'll fax you the policy to sign, Ms. Tomblin. Try to sign and send it back quickly, you never know when the communications will go down. I look forward to talking to you tomorrow."

Sai

"What's new, Jason?" Sai asked as the younger man entered his office.

"Let's see, the sun rose at seven nineteen and thirteen seconds, the temperature at sunrise was precisely 34.69 Fahrenheit, and my tests show gravity in my lab to be 9.800522. So—nothing is new. Nothing. How about with you?"

Sai shook his head. "Everything is new, Jason. I don't know why you spend all your time looking for variations in constants when we have so much we know will be new. We only have so many hours each day to soak in what we can before tomorrow wipes the slate clean."

"You know if it weren't for the tragic accident of us being roommates in college, I could happily live my life without ever talking to a sociologist," Jason said. "Human nature is what it is, but it won't give us any answers for fixing whatever is wrong with the universe."

"So do you want to see the videos?" Sai asked.

"Do I have a choice?"

"Not if you want coffee." Sai smiled, poured a hot cup of joe for his friend, and turned to his computer. Jason took the coffee, having discovered some time ago, this office was his only consistent source of the drink.

"You'll like this one, it changes everything." The sociologist started the video.

"So, hello everyone. I've had a lot of questions about how I created ShortCode, the new, fully-functional social media platform. I assure you I am not a time traveler and ShortCode did not exist before Reset. ShortCode is completely coded and implemented anew each day, but it's no magic. I have a dedicated team of volunteers who share responsibility to write and compile code starting at Reset everyday day. By the time the ICANN bots approve my lease on the domain name, I have thousands of lines of code in my private wiki ready to go for the site. I've had more and more people volunteer to help so each person only has to remember a few lines of code to type out each day. That's it, don't thank me for ShortCode, thank the Internet community."

"That's actually pretty slick," Jason said.

"It's more than slick, it's brilliant. There are, what, eight billion people in the world? What if only 20% did a small amount of distributed work each day? What if we built in redundancies to account for people dropping out once in a while?" Sai leaned forward. "There is potential here to advance the species even with Reset as a factor."

"What do you have in mind?" Jason drank the rest of his coffee.

"I'm not sure, but with a couple billion people online helping out, I think we can accomplish something, even if it's just bringing meaning back to our lives."

DAY 233

Death drives us to reach for depths of our souls, and death is the only thing keeping us from reaching as far down as it goes.

Pablo

Pablo's eye's popped open when his mind registered there was too much light coming in through his window. "I'm a dead man," he said to the ceiling and jumped out of this bed. "Two hundred thirty-one. No, two. Two hundred thirty-two. Or was that yesterday? That was yesterday." He ran down the stairs and threw open a kitchen drawer so forcefully it slid across the hardwood.

"Camila!" His voice rang through the house, every bit as concerned as the first time he'd found her missing. A trembling finger ran down the columns of businesses in the city's Yellow Pages.

Ten. Twenty. Hundred. Two Hundred. "Two-hundred thirty two. Yesterday." His phone lit up at a touch and he called Cheery Chiropractic to be sure. "It's a cheery day at Cheery Chiropractic, we are out of the office. Please leave us a message."

"Yeah, that was it." Pablo looked down at the phone book and dialed the next number. "...at Cutting Edge Chiropractic you will never leave on edge." The message had ended. Pablo was sure he'd remember that line if he'd heard it before.

The familiar logo for ShortCode came up in his browser and he added his own two cents to the topic that was always trending this early in the morning.

#Today is 233

A quick scroll told him most people agreed with his assessment. Someone had worked out that it would have been August 21st if it weren't for the Reset. A bang on the door took his attention.

"I'm a dead man," he said again and berated himself for bothering with counting days instead of running from the house as soon as he realized how late it was.

He opened the door and saw Kyle Stevens three feet in front of him with an evil grin. "You stopped showing up for work."

Kyle was wearing a bright white suit and strong red bow-tie with matching handkerchief.

"I'm taking a few days off to look for Camila." Pablo said.

"You don't get to take days off. What if tomorrow is the day we moved on? I'd be out millions because you didn't show up to sell product."

"I don't care about your product, or your fortune. Don't you get it? We aren't moving on, we are here forever. I don't plan to waste any more time selling insurance when my daughter is out there somewhere in who knows what trouble."

Kyle pulled a pistol from his coat and aimed it straight ahead. "If you are so sure we will Reset, then you won't mind taking a gamble, will you?"

"You can't be serious," Pablo said.

"So here's the thing, Pablo. I need you at work until we've pitched our clients. After that, you can go on your wild goose chase. If you don't show up for work, I will kill you. Every time. Then you'll have to wait another day to go searching for Camila or whatever the tramp's name is."

"Camila is my daughter." Pablo swung a heavy fist at Kyle's face. Before it connected, Pablo felt himself forced back just as the sound from the gun hit his ears.

As he lost consciousness, he heard Kyle say, "Good thing the blood comes out at Reset. This is my favorite suit."

Sai

A live feed of the U.S. Power Grid glowed on Sai's computer. Spider veins spread from major cities to small towns across across the nation. Jason checked the time. "It's really going to happen, isn't it?"

"Seventy thousand people are making sure it is. Power and Communications up all day for the first time since this thing started," Sai said, smiling.

"What if someone drops out now?" Jason asked.

"We've got so many redundancies it shouldn't matter. Besides, we've only got about two minutes until Reset. The grid could last that long if everyone dropped out at this point."

Jason frowned. "What happens tomorrow? Now that we've hit the mark, won't people stop being interested in helping? Demand that a multitude of people who are 'not me' can handle the work instead?"

"You're thinking of the bystander effect, and, no, it won't happen here. This thing has turned into a trend. Success today will only breed more volunteers tomorrow. Everyone wants to be on the winning team. We just won," Sai reasoned.

"Alright, what's next?" Jason asked.

"What do you mean what's next? I'll keep coordinating the grid, maybe help other countries get back online, too."

Jason pulled Sai's shoulder so the sociologist was facing him instead of the screen. "You've made a name for yourself. The people are looking to you to mobilize them. You got the power to stay on all day. Great. But billions of people are living in a world fallen into anarchy. I think you earned a responsibility to keep going, to push us further."

"What's gotten into you?" Sai asked.

"I just got off the phone with Dr. Redmond, remember ol' Benny? His wife had...has end stage cancer. She wakes up everyday in pain. There's no cure and no end to it. Every day she begs him to bring her a handful of pills to make the pain go away. He feels awful when he does it, and worse when he doesn't. We can't play by the old rules anymore. We need to rebuild the government, rebuild the civilization. Sai, we need a new system of ethics to drive us forward as a species."

Sai paused for a moment before answering. "That would take years, maybe a lifetime to accomplish."

Jason checked the clock again, mere seconds until Reset. "Didn't you hear? Time is a renewable resource."

DAY 6,765

What heights could a forever aspiring species reach given an infinite amount of time?

Pablo

Pablo never carried an umbrella, one benefit of Reset was you knew exactly what the weather would be like. Still, he wore an extra layer for today's event—election day. For the first time in nearly twenty years, a new president would be named.

Pablo stood in a line for a good two hours before it had diminished enough that he was inside the building, the old copy center. Most people thought of businesses like this one obsolete in the new world, a relic of an age dominated by trying to get more than the next guy. Not holding on to anything material at the end of each day had changed everything.

"Name?" An old man in a biker jacket and sporting a handlebar mustache asked as Pablo finally made his way to the counter.

"Pablo Hernandez."

"You'll be at station three as soon as it opens. Thank you for voting." The man nodded toward a copy machine that had the number three scrawled on its side with a permanent marker. This election had been a long time coming. First the government had to reform enough to fight about if elections could even happen. Then a fair system had to be developed. Dr. Nuremberg got his legion of programmers on it. They developed a system they could program by noon. It took a simple scan of a hand print to prevent multiple votes. Gone were the days of voting registration, if you lived in America, you could vote in America.

Pablo had never seen such a big turnout for an election in his life. It took nearly two decades of chaos to impress on people why participation in the government was paramount. Pablo's vote wouldn't count, though. He was voting for Nuremberg as a write-in candidate. Lots of people were doing the same thing, he was sure. Nuremberg had publicly stated he was not a politician and would not ever run for office. He said he was happy to keep working behind the scenes to keep us moving forward.

"Three!" Pablo shook himself out of his thoughts started for the station. As he walked up to the copier being used to scan hands, something outside caught his eye. Far down the street someone was breaking into his car. Such petty crime had all but stopped. Everyone had a good idea of where to get what they needed each day and understood nothing could be kept. He watched the crime while the official pressed his hand down hard on the glass.

"You're all set. Use this tablet to vote and press confirm when you are done."

Pablo didn't move, frozen in place from what he was witnessing.

"Sir, you may use one of the chairs along that wall...Sir, what is it?" The election official followed his gaze but was focused no farther than the line of voters.

"Camila..." Pablo took off, throwing the tablet at the unsuspecting biker taking roll. He pushed past congestion at the door and started at a dead run. The commotion got the thief's attention. She ducked out of the vehicle and ran perpendicular from it down a street lined with skyscrapers.

Pablo caught up to his car moments later and rounded the corner to find an empty street.

"Cam-il-a!" he called out desperately. His only answer was an echo from the tall, now unused, buildings.

"She has to be close." He ran into the first door he could find and met a lobby, a businessman's hallowed hall, now abandoned. The only noise was the low rumble of a moving elevator. He wanted to call the next elevator, wanted to do anything that would bring him closer to the daughter he had presumed dead long ago. He held his feet firm until he saw where the elevator stopped. The twenty-third floor. He checked his hand just before pressing the button himself. The noise would let her know he was coming, then his day would turn into a French farce until he ran out of time and was pulled back to his empty house.

He started up the stairs, which also allowed him the advantage of listening for anyone else on the staircase, and for the rumble of the elevator. She was on that floor somewhere and if she moved, he'd know it. He took steps two at a time until his legs begged for mercy, then he took three at a time. In a matter of minutes he stood by a heavy door with a white-stenciled "23."

"Need to…catch my breath…" he said to himself, but went through the door anyway. What drives the soul of a man is beyond logic. His heart beat like a thousand drums, his adrenaline coursed through his veins and he knew he should sit. Instead, he started trying doors.

Locked.

Locked.

Locked.

Then he heard the hiccups of someone trying to hold back from crying. He knew that cry, it was his cupcake. He followed it to the source and found his daughter, curled in a corner behind a vending machine. His presence made her cower even more.

"I'm sorry," she said. "It's all my fault."

Pablo sat on the floor and did his best to put an arm around his daughter. "I've looked everywhere for you. I thought you were dead."

"Didn't you hear me?" She continued sobbing.

"Camila, I don't care what you did. There is nothing I've wanted more than…" his throat wouldn't let him finish his sentence. He thought it was emotion at first, but he felt a strong weight on his chest.

"Not now," he whispered to himself.

"I caused all this madness. Remember New Year's Eve? It was me," she said.

Pablo put his hands forward, they were shaking. He wanted to say a hundred things. Find out where she would be at Reset, find out why she hadn't sought him out. Most of all, he needed to tell her he loved her, but he could not form words. His chest drew tighter around him, like a constrictor going for the kill.

Camila continued, "I went to a party down at the University, some college boys took me to a lab, an accelerator. They told me they'd powered it up so we could make our own party. I started pushing buttons. I was drunk and wanted to see a show for New Year's. I couldn't tell you. I couldn't tell anyone. Every Reset I'm back in that lab, watching the fireworks."

Pablo looked at his daughter with pleading eyes, black crept around the edge of his vision. He could only smile, she'd let him know where he could find her tomorrow. For Pablo, nothing else mattered.

Sai

Jason looked over Sai's shoulder and gave a long whistle. "Seven percent of the vote? Aren't you Mr. Popular."

"It's six point seven percent. And shut up. I have no intention of ever running for office. I'm not presidential material and there's too much to do here."

"What is your next trick anyway? You brought up the power grid, you've managed to get a volunteer supply distribution network for those without food. And, now, you've reestablished a government the people recognize well enough to poll in record numbers.

"The first thing I have to do is certify the numbers and show the people before all the data disappears at Reset. Here, help me find my webcam." Sai handed Pablo a box of tangled computer parts.

"Shouldn't you have found this earlier?" Jason said as he dumped the contents of the box on the floor.

"When? I had to coordinate the programmers, the volunteer network, and write the ballot this morning. Since then, it's been a barrage of issues cropping up all over the country to take care of," he said.

Jason picked through the electronic bric-a-brac. "Shouldn't you know exactly where all your stuff is? I know you're unorganized, but every morning all your stuff ends up in exactly the same place you had it before, right?" He fished out a camera on a cord and handed it to Sai.

"Thanks. I've got some kind of mental block about this little guy though. Hardly ever use it and when I do need it, I can't find it."

"Don't go senile on us, Sai, you're the only one holding the human race together."

Sai ignored the comment and started broadcasting a live stream three hundred thousand people had already logged into as guests.

"Hello. My name is Dr. Nuremberg. I am pleased to let you know we had the biggest turnout in U.S. history for a presidential election. Let's use the momentum that brought us here to catapult us into an even better future."

Sai heard Jason quietly say to his side, "Not presidential material?"

"Per the agreements we have distributed for the past month, this election was by popular vote to allow greater flexibility in voting time over the old delegate system. I am honored to announce, with 54% of the vote, Carrie Montgomery is your next President of the United States. Because we have been living without a recognized leader for some time, she will begin coordinating the new governing structure after tonight's Reset. Thank you, and goodnight."

"You almost made me tear up," Jason said. "Almost makes me want to believe humanity can be saved."

DAY 28,657

Maturity is a metric unimportant to the mature.

Pablo

A loud crack startled Pablo, ending his nap. He'd grown familiar with the sound of his door being forced open, but to have it be his alarm was always disconcerting. The timing of entry got earlier each day, too. Today was truly impressive—it was only ten-thirty.

"Can't you use the doorbell?" Pablo complained as he came down the stairs.

"Didn't want to wake you, sir." There were three people in his living room—two wore suits and framed his front door. The one who was talking, though, had sat on the edge of a bar chair and only glanced at Pablo before looking back at his tablet.

"If you don't want to wake me, don't come in, Jim." When Jim didn't answer, Pablo added, "What could you have possibly put in that thing already today you can't remember?"

Jim looked up, continuing to ignore Pablo's complaints. "Are you done?"

"Yeah, let's get today over with." Jim chucked, but Pablo meant it.

He thought about changing his robe to something more presentable, but decided against it. He pushed aside his front door and waved to three regulars sitting outside holding cameras. "If you get me the photo, I'll sign it for you." The photographers groaned at the joke they'd heard at least a hundred times before.

Pablo walked up to a dull grey egg and stepped inside. A stomach-twisting pop and his scenery had changed, he stepped out into an elaborate bedroom and took his robe off. A freshly tailored suit waited for him on a hook. He put it on before leaving the room.

"Dad!" Camila wrapped her arms around his neck. He returned the gesture with a warm embrace.

"Don't you have better things to do? Isn't it your anniversary? Forty-fifth?"

"Fifty-fifth," she responded. "Jim thought you could use the support."

"Jim thinks too much, that's his problem. I need to make a phone call."

"The doctor?" Camila asked.

"The doctor."

"I'll be watching in the media room, then. Good luck."

"Luck is one thing we have not had for a long, long time, cupcake."

Pablo walked into the study and picked up the phone. "Get me Dr. Nuremberg." Moments later a voice was on the other end of the line.

"Mr. President."

"The press is waiting, what should I tell them?" Pablo asked.

"The truth. Tell them tomorrow will really be tomorrow, or it could be today again if I'm wrong, or we could end the universe as we know it. We've worked hard to make sure it's the first one on that list, but there are no guarantees. If it were me, I'd focus on tomorrow being tomorrow. Remind them if they do something reckless today, they might have to live with it. It's a paradigm shift the world needs to be ready for."

Pablo let the silence build before answering. "Thank you, doctor." He hung up the phone, stood and left the study, walking directly into the Oval Office.

"Mr. President. Are you ready to talk?" Jim was either too smart or too wrapped up in his schedule to ask what Dr. Nuremberg had said.

Pablo looked at the large camera faced directly at the ceremonial desk and the staff preparing to make sure he looked presidential.

"I'm ready."

Sai

Sai walked out of a grey enclosure and stood in his second home, a particle accelerator on the west coast. He started powering up the equipment when his phone rang. He recognized the number. "Mr. President?" It was a short conversation and Sai wasn't as blunt as he wanted to be.

Ever since the government got back on track, every President, among other dignitaries, had their own ideas on what was causing the Reset. Each expected him to coddle his or her theory. He'd been asked to dig into secret government research, look for extraterrestrial involvement, and even consider that the world must have the "perfect day" before it could move on. Some leaders actively opposed the line of research entirely. When Pablo Hernandez had become president, he had given him a theory as silly as the others, claiming his own daughter had randomly caused the loop. He did placate the president by traveling to the accelerator site and what he found got his attention.

"Sai, what's so important? I hear the president is about to give a talk. Rumor is you've figured out how to stop the Reset." Jason had just stepped out of the transport module and held up his phone, showing he was ready to stream the speech when it started.

"I don't know, Jason. I've had a team building programs and models the last few months and it does seem plausible we're being pulled back to the moment two Boston Particles were produced in the collider and then collided with each other," Sai said.

"A one in a million chance," Jason replied.

"I'd call it a one in an infinity chance."

"So we just stop the machine, right?" Jason said, looking over the consoles as if there would be a big switch labeled "off."

"The frustrating thing is that the reaction happens at the exact moment of Reset. Anything different, anything at all, and the particles would miss each other and then none of this would happen. Instead, we loop back to the moment of the reaction and it happens again and again, pulling us into deeper and deeper iterations of the same day."

"But we can't go back to before the reaction, so there's no hope?"

"We can't go back any further than the reaction itself, but my team thinks we can bring a disruption with us if we time it to happen right at the Reset."

"Sai, that's big."

"Ladies and Gentlemen, Pablo Hernandez, the President of the United States." Jason's phone had sprung to life. Jason held it so they could both see the screen.

"Fellow Americans, and viewers worldwide, good morning. There have been several rumors we may have found a way to stop the Reset. I want to address those rumors. But first, I want to talk about how far we've come. When this journey began, we were confused, we hurt, we lacked direction. With the help of Dr. Nuremberg, his team of leading scientists, organizers, and volunteers, we have kept life going forward. We've developed ways to create and disseminate supplies, we create advanced technology from scratch within hours each day, and we've created a mode of transportation our old selves would have only found in science fiction.

"Together we have survived a world war, given into our most base instincts, and rose from the ashes to make each today a better one than the last. To say we've evolved as a species is not an understatement. Sill, there are hurts that cannot be fixed. The Trendle family, whose car is underwater at Reset in Utah. Justin in Oregon who had a stroke just moments before Reset and wakes up with no support from doctors or loved ones each day. While many of us have made peace with the new timeline, there are thousands of unfortunate things that are happening at Reset, which we cannot move fast enough to fix. For their sake, I hope that we can one day move forward. For the rest of us, moving forward means putting our own frailties back in play. It would mean instead of a few thousand bad things, billions would necessarily die.

"I spoke with Dr. Nuremberg earlier today. He continues to be hopeful we are on the right path toward a solution, but it would not be anytime soon. Rest assured you will remain fully informed on the progress of his research. I believe in each and every one of you."

"He's not going to tell them," Sai said quietly.

"Doesn't want to get everyone's hopes up?" Jason asked.

"I think he doesn't want Congress to order me to stop. He blames himself for what's happening."

Jason gave him a questioning look, but Sai did not elaborate.

"You should leave. We'll discuss the finer points tomorrow," Sai told his friend.

"Sai," Jason said, "How will this work? Will we remember any of this happened or will we just continue on with our old lives, oblivious? Will we keep any of what we have become?"

Sai had already turned his back, his hands dancing across a keyboard. He paused at the question and gave the best answer he knew how.

"Let's let tomorrow worry about itself."

DAY 1

What you do today is exponentially more important than all your yesterdays combined.

Pablo

The President sat at his desk staring at his phone. He'd watched as the hours, minutes, and seconds counted down to Reset. He felt more anxious about this one than he had since the early days when the world was in disarray. This time, the seconds ticked on. He heard some celebration from his staff, but disallowed any visitors. He continued to watch the time pass by, tears silently streaming down his face. For better, mercy would be had for thousands of souls stuck in a nightmare. For worse, people could easily devolve to the old habits of want and greed.

He watched his computer, watched the time tick by for only an hour before the power went out around him. The answer had been given. Without the Reset, the infrastructure was failing even faster than he would have expected. He'd been wrong, the people had not lived in the terror long enough to learn the new ways were best. He picked up the phone to have the operator dial Camila, but there was no acknowledgment he'd even picked up the line. The world was falling apart and it was his fault.

"Mr. President, sorry to bother you." Jim had interrupted his solitude. "I wanted to assure you the White House has a working generator, it's just been some time since anyone has had to use it. We have staff tinkering with it right now, should be up in no time."

Pablo did not acknowledge Jim's update but that did not stop Jim from adding one more thing.

"Oh, and, sir, congratulations."

Sai

"I don't understand, didn't you say there were redundancies upon redundancies?" Jason stared at Sai with only the glow of his cell phone giving them light.

"Seven or eight layers deep. We had about 70 percent of the world's population on board with a 50 percent average of following through each day. It took a matter of minutes for people to abandon their posts. The holes became bigger and bigger until everything went down." Sai went to the control panel on the accelerator and hit it with both fists.

"Glad I got here when I did then," Jason said. "How can I help?"

"One person is *not* a distributed network," Sai said through his teeth. "I can't even give directions to people who want to help with the electricity and communications cut off. It would take a billion people deciding, individually, to go back to work, with no assurance it would make a difference, to make the infrastructure come back on. We are worse off now than before the Reset started."

"I know it's cliche, my old friend, but we've been through worse."

"Have we? Are we better off now than we were yesterday? Are we better off now than before the first Reset? I made a mistake, the world wasn't ready, wasn't prepared. I've closed Pandora's box and made sure the horrors can never be locked away again. Without the Reset, there is no reason for the masses to be compelled to do their part for the greater good. How could I not have seen this coming? We could have prepared, could have coded autonomous systems to perfection before we pulled the trigger..."

"They'll come around, Sai. Just give everyone a few days to—"

"You don't get it. Today sets the standard. Whatever the masses do today sets the routine for the days... weeks... years to come."

Sai kicked a desk and sat down, putting his head between his legs. The destruction he had wrought in his own mind was too much to bear. Jason watched him stay in that position alternating between whimpers and crying.

"Would you look at that?" Jason finally said.

"Just go away," Sai responded.

"Umm, Sai?"

"I said go away."

"Sai, the lights are back on."

A WORD FROM
THOMAS ROBINS

I will be the first to admit, time loop plots can be found littering the science fiction genre. In all the version of time loops I've read, only a select few characters are aware of the loop at all. This story was my attempt to answer the question of what would happen if everyone was aware and how humanity would cope.

I am glad I had a chance to be a part of this anthology. This is my third anthology to benefit a charity. It feels good to know that my work is being used to raise money for worthy organizations. I hope you feel good buying these anthologies for the same reason.

I don't like to clutter a perfectly good collection of stories with a long author note. If you feel moved to know more about my writing, please check out my website at *www.thomasrobins. com* or join my mailing list (*http://amazon.us3.list-manage.com/ subscribe/post?u=8df209f4eae09e75394bd4d35&id=0a3b-bea60a*).

Thomas Robins is the author of the novel Desperate to Escape, *several works appearing in Kindle Worlds, and a smattering of short stories in anthologies. Thomas lives in the Kansas City area with his family, cats, and an unremarkable collection of science fiction memorabilia.*

The House on the Cliff
by E.E. Giorgi

"There is nothing remarkable about being immortal; with the exception of mankind, all creatures are immortal, for they know nothing of death. What is divine, terrible, and incomprehensible is to know oneself immortal."

\- Jorge Luis Borges, The Immortal

THE PLACE REEKS of spilled beer and sweat, the air fogged by gray swirls of vape. Tired people hide in narrow booths, their faces lit by the blue screens of their devices: a couple too bored to look at one another; a kid too young to be here, his thumbs racing through a video game, adrenaline pulsing through the veins of his neck; a failed businessman scanning his portfolio, numbers reflecting off his cyber glasses while his eyes stray somewhere else. Somewhere far away. Somewhere that's not here, maybe a conference room at the top of one of the high-rise buildings downtown, where he'd be lulled by the mellifluous voices of secretaries in high heels and short skirts.

Definitely not here.

There's nothing mellifluous in the intoxicated laughter of cheap sex waiting for clients.

A holo ad flashes past me, surreal beauty in milky curves that stroke my imagination. She promises me the trip of my life in just one giga download, satisfaction guaranteed, and then vanishes in a multicolored cascade of pixels. A few decades ago I might have been interested.

Not now.

I make my way to the bar. The bartender eyes me sternly with dark pupils, one trained on me, the other lazily straying away. He wipes a spot on the counter while taking in the novelty of my presence in a joint like this. He ponders my long hair braided at the nape of my neck; the scar bracing the right corner of my mouth; the lump sitting on my throat, my "spare" Adam's apple, bobbing up and down with every breath I take.

His eyes linger on my hemp shirt, probably wondering where the heck I've found it—maybe I had it smuggled illegally from the GMO fields across the border, or maybe it was traded in exchange for labor on one of the Stingray ships. He takes in my slouched stance, my tanned and freckled skin, my stringy arms dried of any fat. And then his eyes stumble on my belt and freeze.

There, where citizens of Astraca clip their electronic devices, their lifesavers, schedulers, organizers, portals to the real world or whatever's left of it—right there, from my belt, bulges instead my old, vintage PX45.

Nine rounds fully loaded, fifteen caliber, single action, semiautomatic.

My own way to take in the world these days.

Struck by awareness, the bartender's eyes narrow. His skin is the color of chocolate, his own scars light and raised like hard veins. I wonder how many more scars he carries inside.

I sit on a stool and lean on the bar, rapping my fingers out of habit.

The bartender brings the rag to his hands and wipes them. He has me all figured out. "Ah' kayel butoo?" he asks.

Not bad. The inflection is slightly off, but it's not bad at all for someone who was born and raised in Astraca and only picked up Xamarii from soldiers and smugglers.

I smile, the scar on the side of my face stretching into a second, lopsided grin. It hurts from time to time. Today's one of those times. It probably hates to be back home. Like me.

"A Bloody Mary. On the rocks. You can spare me the tomato juice, not the alcohol." It's *tomgo*, anyway—genetically modified tomato. I couldn't care less for that crap.

The bartender's eyes bulge. He didn't expect me to reply in his own language, especially without an accent. His face changes, recognition slowly dawning on him. Not me; he's too young to recognize me. Others, though, like me.

"A Bloody Mary without tomato juice?"

I nod. "Double the alcohol."

He slips away, he and his rag, and I turn looking for more tantalizing ads, faces, the illusion of company. Nobody makes eye contact. Nobody but the cheap sex I'm not willing to buy tonight.

The bartender comes back, slides the glass in front of me, and watches me take my first sip, lazy eye blinking. He's added a pinch of lime juice, a purely Astracan secret. I like that. I smack my lips and pump my thumb up.

"Good stuff," I say.

He nods. His right hand resumes its circular motion. "How long you been away, bro?"

I take another swig of my drink, long and slow, this time. I swish the alcohol over my gums before swallowing, let it burn my taste buds. "A long time," I say, twirling my glass.

Very long.

Long enough to watch your great-grandfather get killed in the G-riots of 2154, I'd like to tell him. *To see your grandmother raped by the Gaijins and your grandfather publicly executed on Kawana Plaza the damned day the sky turned orange and night refused to fall. The day every building in Astraca turned red and rivers of blood washed down the streets, decapitated heads rolling down with them.*

I was there when the whole city was set on fire because the stench of death was so strong no rain or flood could wash it away. Survivors went picking through corpses, sometimes finding as little as a hand or an arm or a torn shoe. They buried their loved ones and the rest—the shredded and the unclaimed—crackled and hissed in the longest fire in Astraca's history.

Flames burned for days, weeks, months.

I was there when the city rebuilt itself, one stone at a time, when the fathers of this new generation took their first steps, when the famine ended and civilization once again made its way into the city.

Long enough to see how corruption returned to Astraca, I want to tell the bartender, but instead I just bring the glass back to my parched lips and down the rest of my Bloody Mary, the alcohol stinging and burning away the aftertaste too many memories have left.

He wouldn't understand anyway.

What it really means.

To have too many memories.

So I lick my lips, stare the man in the eyes and ask, "You've heard of the House on the Cliff, brother?"

For a moment his eyes go blank, as though a film of skepticism has descended upon them. A cracked laughter spikes over the usual background noises. A new client steps forward and starts a ritual of well-rehearsed flirting and meaningless courtship with the sex for hire.

Maybe the bartender hasn't heard of the house. Maybe he thinks it no longer exists, that it's been carried away by time and oblivion. And then there's a sparkle, the subtlest ever, as his right hand patiently works the rag against the shiny bar counter.

He leans forward, lowers his voice.

"You've come back," the bartender hisses. His lips are dark, mottled by raised moles. "How old are you now?"

I clonk the glass on the counter and step down from the stool. I fish a note from my breast pocket, a note that has probably lost its value now that all payments are scanned on electronic devices. He doesn't seem to mind and snatches it from my hand as though he's afraid I might change my mind and keep it.

"Can you tell me how to get to the house?"

He freezes, the note still crumpled in his fingers. "You don't know the way?"

"I've forgotten the way."

I know he doesn't believe me. Yet it's true. When you live as long as I have, you learn to save a few good memories and forget the rest.

I've forgotten most things. I've forgotten all but one.

Rose.

I could never forget Rose.

* * *

The house sits on a cliff, with no shape or purpose, just a rambling of walls, windows, balconies and porches that grows out of the side of the mountain like a cancer.

The cliff used to loom over the city, a dark shadow devoured by smoke during the months of the raging fires. Now, after its opulent rebirth, Astraca has grown taller and higher, its glass pinnacles lost in the sea of clouds careening above.

Yet the house is still here, unscathed by history and untouched by time, an anachronistic relic of a long-gone past.

The sun comes down and peeks between the glistening city towers looming from the valley below. The shadows grow longer and, one by one, the lights of downtown blink to life. Like awakened ghosts, the holographic commercials animate the façades, their soundtracks muffled and twisted from out here.

Up here, the dying sun bathes the cliff in gold, and the jumbled colors of the city towers bounce off the house's slanted windows and crooked roof.

I stand a hundred feet away and stare, chasing memories like a kid chases butterflies. The blue door was once purple, then green, then brown, and at least a couple of times red. I should knock on that door before it's too late, even though nobody will answer, or if they do, they won't remember, or maybe they'll remember too much.

I stare at the house, bathed in the golden light of sunset, and I ponder on how it all came to be. On one side, the house leans over the cliff, a long eave of roof slanting down to the ledge. At the other end, three stories taper gradually one into the other and sprawl across the fields of corn and tall grass, balconies and windows cluttering the sides as though added in an afterthought. The walls are peeling, showing layer after layer of paint jobs—yellow, red; at some point they had even been purple, though I forget what year that was and who decided on the color. Where I remember a deck, now grows a loft, its gray metal roof clashing with the rest.

To think it used to be just two rooms, two rooms with unfinished walls and chipped floors. Every summer the ants would come and build their nests. After the G-riots and the famine that followed, we were so hungry we'd slide our fingers through the wood planks and pick up ants by the bunch. They tickled our tongues and popped as we chewed on them, their juice sweet and bitter at the same time.

The silos were brimming with crop seeds, yet the citizens of Astraca starved to death rather then breaching the most precious genetic pool of our time. So we sucked ants for breakfast and chewed on hay straws for lunch because that was all we had. We had roaches, too, and my brother claimed they tasted delicious roasted on an open fire. Even as starving as we were, I don't remember enjoying the roaches.

I may be wrong, though.

Memories tend to jumble when you've got too many. Time no longer follows a linear path. It crinkles and stretches like fabric too old to be worn. Things you wish you could forget keep haunting you forever, whereas others—was that first kiss under a sycamore tree or was it by the lake? Those first steps, the first words, the day she departed and never came back— seem so ephemeral in their beauty, like a butterfly you keep chasing only to watch its wings drain of color once captured.

So I stand a few feet away from the house, pondering whether to knock or not, whether to leave without a word or drag my feet a little longer, when the blue door opens a crack and a face emerges from the shadow behind it.

My heart stops.

Rose, my first thought.

But the woman coming out of the house is too young to be Rose. She lets the door slam behind her and studies me, a black silhouette in the dim light of twilight.

"I know who you are," she says at last.

I open my mouth and all that comes out of my lips is: "Rose."

The woman shakes her head. She stands on the porch with her hand raised, her face hidden in the shadows of the falling evening.

"Mother doesn't want to see you."

Mother.

I walk to the door despite her raised hand and her upset

voice. As I approach, I make out a little bit of her features and I'm taken aback by how much she looks like Rose. She's older than I originally thought—in her early sixties, I'm guessing—with long gray hair drooping down her narrow shoulders. She's small, tight in her posture, with a pointed chin jutted out at me. To me, she looks very young.

"I've come a long way to see her," I say.

The woman—Rose's daughter—grasps the porch railing and narrows her eyes—Rose's eyes. And, in a way, mine too.

"You've come too late. She's ninety-three and dying. The buildup in her lungs isn't clearing. Her body has stopped fighting. Our physician says it's a matter of days, maybe hours." She speaks the words matter-of-factly, yet her blue eyes betray a hint of tears.

"I still want to see her. One last time."

She takes in my tall frame, my rugged clothes. Her lips twitch down in something that I recognize though I don't want to acknowledge. Yet it dawns on me. I disgust her. My visible lumps, my scars.

"You're too late now," she says. "You should've come a long time ago."

"I should've been dead a long time ago."

She blows a quick puff of air, annoyed at the comment, then shakes her head, gray strands of hair sticking to her flushed cheeks. She looks very young to me, yet she probably has kids of her own, maybe grandkids, too. When did they all come back? The house was empty when I left. How long have I been gone? If only I could remember.

"Please leave." Her last words to me. She turns around and

stomps away. The blue door to the house whose foundations I helped dig slams.

The lump on my throat decides to remind me of its awkward presence. I scratch it, noticing how it feels bigger than yesterday, bigger than ever I seem to remember. It presses on my Adam's apple and hurts when I swallow. Soon I'll need to have this one too removed, adding yet another scar to my numerous collection.

I stare vacantly at the blue door and all the memories hidden behind it. To think that it used to be just two rooms, this thing that now sprawls along the edge of the cliff and grips the rocks like a colony of clams. The rooms kept growing on it like the lumps on my body. A study, another bedroom, an attic that later turned into an office when my brother added a third story. He tried to dig a basement but the soil was too harsh and rocky. When he died, I added the first balcony and two more rooms. Or maybe it was my cousin who did it. We built some, destroyed some. The years came and went, the old died and the new ones were born, and every time I had to bring down a wall and raise a new one.

I just had to.

It couldn't be the same house forever.

And then Rose happened and I knew I had to make a special room just for her, one with plenty of windows so the sun would always shine and the stars would always glimmer every time she looked up and gazed at the sky.

I never finished that room, the one I had specially planned for Rose.

After the riots, after the destruction, the fire, the famine, the city rebuilt itself and the house filled up. New faces came and went, the walls straining to contain the new life, the chatter, the cries, the chaste loves and the adulterous ones, some consumed by passion and soon forgotten, others slow to grow and yet too resilient to die. The house saw it all. Naked feet padding back and forth in the long corridors, hasty steps running up and down the stairs, thumping, dragging, wobbling.

Doors opened and doors closed, never again to be unlocked.

The city rebuilt itself, like a phoenix growing back from its ashes, and as soon as it rose back, together with its hypnotic hum and lights and holo ads, it became a call too strong to resist.

The feet stopped running, the voices stopped chattering. One by one, they all abandoned the house and found a new life in the reborn city.

And all there was left were silent walls.

So I left too.

I couldn't stand the empty walls.

I *think* that's why I left. It's been too long to remember.

I scratch my lump and feel it between my index finger and thumb.

Too many lumps to remember. Too many roads, too many chances come and gone, too many stories, too many lives. Give it enough time and all things will happen. Good, bad, love, hate, joy, pain.

All but death.

I sit on the ground, the sun gone now, faint remnants of color tainting the horizon. Past the artificial glow of Astraca, a few stars dapple the sky. I sit on the ground, pluck the tin smoke box out of my breast pocket and roll a cig. Not that vape junk they make especially for wimps. Real tobacco, the kind you have to smuggle in the belly of one of the Stingray ships, the box drenched in oil to make sure the dogs won't sniff it out.

I sit on the ground, watch the lights go off inside the house and smoke my rolled-up cigarette.

I could knock on the door, but I don't.

I could just walk on the porch and make myself heard and somebody would get the door, I'm sure.

But I don't.

I sit here in the humid grass and think of Rose the way I last remember her, her flushed cheeks and lemongrass breath, the thin hair that she refused to braid because she's always been a stubborn one. That one freckle on her upper lip, the cutest thing ever; the way she pouted and then instantly laughed. Rose, the most beautiful thing that ever happened to me, worth living a million years just so it would last forever.

Forever, they told me when they jabbed my arm and said, "This will work, brother. This will bring you back to life."

I'd survived the riots within my own city, dodged death when my own brothers had killed one another in the name of justice. And when I left, I went to fight wars that weren't mine, to kill enemies I didn't hate, to defend ideals that weren't my own. I'd drunk water muddled with blood when there was nothing else to drink, and burned human flesh when there were so many bodies the crows and the rats couldn't eat them fast enough. I'd survived my city's destruction only to find myself dying in a foreign land, my ship taken down by the opponent's fire.

Somebody else's land, somebody else's enemy, somebody else's war.

I was broken inside out, my face a mask of blood and my skull cracked open. I yelled my copilot's name but he wouldn't reply. He was sitting in the cockpit, his head snapped backwards and his eyes sprung open, yet the man wouldn't move, empty eyes staring into nowhere. And then more explosions, the sting of smoke, the cockpit filling up with dense fog, the ship spinning nose down, me realizing, *This is it*, and then thinking, *Oh shit. Oh shit, oh shit, oh shit.*

I didn't care that I was dying in a foreign land, away from home.

Death didn't scare me.

Yet in that one moment, when the ship crashed deep inside the forest, its metal body collapsing around my body, an image flashed before my eyes.

Rose.

Rose with her hands stretched out toward me, Rose resting her head against my chest, her hair soft against my rugged skin.

Rose.

I could lose my life and I wouldn't care.

But I couldn't lose Rose.

I had to see Rose one more time.

"This will bring you back to life," they said, the doctors whose names I couldn't pronounce. They made me their guinea pig, me, a mercenary desperate to serve in a foreign army. What did I have to lose?

"This will fix you forever," they told me, and all I could think of was Rose's skin, soft and milky and innocent, and so I shut my eyes and let them poke my brain, because all I wanted was to hold Rose in my arms one more time. Nothing else mattered.

Nothing else.

* * *

The moon makes its milky appearance behind a thin veil of clouds. The night is warm and velvety, the air mellow and sweet. A soft breeze rushes through the tall grass and makes it whisper. The hum of the city is still present yet distant, like a recurring thought.

One by one, the lights in the house go off. All but one. A silhouette comes to the window, a whimsical appearance, so brief I wonder if I just imagined it.

I don't know why I'm still out here doing nothing, thinking nothing. Why I haven't knocked again on the door or simply left instead. I just sit out here, roll another cig, and listen to the crickets chirping. Waiting is something one grows accustomed to, eventually. When you've lived as long as I have, waiting is all you've got left.

I hear a creak, then a long squeak. I turn and in the silvery moonlight watch the blue door open up a notch. A ghost in a white nightgown steps softly out of the darkness and shuffles down the porch. One step at a time, as though time no longer exists, as though waiting has lost all its meaning.

I scramble back to my feet, drop the cigarette, and squash it in the damp grass.

She's so fragile she clasps the railing at the end of the stairs and almost faints. I sprint and catch her before she drops to the ground, her delicate frame like glass in my arms, the scent of her hair, now white and sparse, so oddly familiar to me.

"Rose," I whisper.

She grasps my hand with her knotty fingers, her paper-thin skin mottled with liver spots, and then turns her head up and looks at me for the longest time.

Wrinkles blemish her face, bald spots glisten under wisps of white hair.

The sight is overwhelming. I cup her cheek—her skin surprisingly soft under my callous touch—and once again murmur, "My Rose."

"Hey, Dad," she wheezes, yet underneath the strain in her lungs, her voice is crisp, and her eyes still sparkle.

I suddenly feel it inside, the monstrosity of this, me, the father who held her as a baby, who followed her first steps, her first words, now holding her again, so close to death. She, at the end of her path, and me still here, still with a long way to go.

Too long to know.

I let her lean against me and we sit on the porch stairs, side by side, her arm wrapped around mine. She could be my grandmother, but she's my daughter.

"Meg wouldn't tell me it was you," she says. "But I recognized you just the same. You haven't changed a bit."

"Except for the lumps," I reply. "The lumps and the scar."

She raises her chin and stares at the lump growing on my throat. "Is that from when—"

I nod. "They told me the procedure would make parts of my body grow forever. They said all immortal cells eventually become tumors. That's what they did to me. They made me—my cells—immortal."

A faint tremor takes hold of her body. Her breathing is shallow and intermittent, her concave chest rising at an odd rhythm.

How much longer do I have with you, my child?

"If I could, Rose…if only I could, I would give this to you. So I could be buried out here, in the same ground I broke when Dad and I first built the house. I want to give this to you, so you can live forever, enjoy your children and grandchildren and—"

Rose puts a finger to my mouth. "No." She swallows, thin lines pulling at the corners of her mouth. "Death is natural. What they did to you—is not."

And then she leans her head against my shoulder and squeezes my hand. Together we watch the moon move across the sky. Her breathing becomes slower and shallower as the minutes tick by, until she says, "Goodbye, Dad," and everything stops, the moon, the breeze, the grass, the crickets.

Even the city, watching from the distance, stops.

For a moment I think my heart has stopped too and peace comes over me as I squeeze my daughter's hand and think, *This is it. You've set me free, my child, free to die with you.*

But it's only one ephemeral moment, after which my heart, my old, battered, resilient heart, resumes beating.

Tha-thump. Tha-thump. Tha-thump.

Rose feels limp and soft in my arms. I pick her up, so light in my arms, as light as the day I brought her home, the day after she was born.

The blue door doesn't offer any resistance as I push it open. Dim lights installed along the stairs come on as I trudge up to the first floor and down the long corridor interrupted by doors I no longer recognize, rooms I've long ago lost count of. Voices resonate with my steps as I once again walk these floors, voices from the past, maybe ghosts, voices I once knew and loved and made part of my life.

Rose's room is the last on the left. Still is, has always been, even now that the house has morphed, shrunk and reshaped itself. A small lamp on the bedside table is on, casting a yellow glow on old picture screens. I lay Rose on the bed, but the heat sensors don't go off as her limp body touches the foam board.

The monitor embedded in the wall blips. "No heartbeat detected." A red light flashes on the screen. I touch it and close the dialogue box.

Feet drag on the floor behind me.

"She's gone."

I turn. Rose's daughter—my granddaughter—stands in the doorway, bracing herself. She presses her lips together and inhales. "She chose when and how."

I nod. That's all I have. A nod.

My daughter's heart has frozen forever and yet mine won't stop beating. Lumps grow all over my body, yet my cells will keep dividing forever. One day the Earth will become so hot only bacteria will be left to inhabit its surface, yet my cells will still keep dividing. Long after my body ceases to exist, my thoughts scattering like ashes in the wind, my cells will still keep dividing.

I only wanted to see you once more, Rose.

Instead, I lost you forever.

I leave the room, the long corridor, the house. I don't stop to say goodbye, I don't turn around to see the house one last time.

Immortality, not death, is in the end the most complete negation of life.

A WORD FROM
E.E. GIORGI

When Samuel Peralta asked me to write a story for the *Immortality Chronicles*, I immediately said yes. One, because you never say no when Samuel Peralta asks. Two, because my all-time favorite short story is *The Immortal* by Jorge Luis Borges. Three, because I'd just met Rose.

Real life Rose is a lovely lady who's lived a long life and, like all people who've lived a long life, she has many stories to tell. Listening to her is like reliving history you've read in a book. Her eyes twinkle with pride. This small lady is sharp, witty, funny, healthy, and you wouldn't believe it, but yes, she's very much strong and fit. And as she told me the story of her life I couldn't help but think, "Where do I sign up to age like her?"

Until she told me about her daughter and I suddenly changed my mind. Her daughter died of lymphoma when she was my grandmother's age. Despite the disease, she aged gracefully and lived a good life. She enjoyed her children and grandchildren. And her mother too, given that Rose took care of her elderly child until the end.

And that's when I thought, *I don't want that. I don't want to live so long that I'll see my children age and wither away.* A long, strong life like Rose's is a blessing and a burden.

I hope you've enjoyed my short story "The House on the Cliff". You can find out more about the Gaijins and what happened to the city of Astraca in my new series *The Mayake Chronicles* (*http://www.amazon.com/Akaela-Mayake-Chronicles-Book-1-ebook/dp/B00WTTSQ42/*).

I am a scientist by day, a writer by night, and a photographer in whatever spare time I have left. All my stories spur from some cool scientific premise, genetics and viruses in particular. A complete list of my published works—mostly thrillers and science fiction mysteries—can be found on my blog: *http://chimerasthebooks.blogspot.com/p/books.html*.

Subscribe to my newsletter to get a free story and exclusive content before its release date: *http://eepurl.com/SPCvT*.

Many thanks to my first readers Mike Martin, Kat Fieler, and David Bruns for their valuable feedback, to Carol Davis for the insightful edits, and to Samuel Peralta for making me part of yet another epic installment of *The Future Chronicles*.

A Long Horizon
by Harlow C. Fallon

SPACE IS A MISNOMER. If humans weren't blind to it, they'd see that space is full, teeming with enormous creatures that float and skim through the blackness in the same way that phytoplankton fill the warm waters of Earth's oceans. I don't know why humans can't see them. I see them all.

Even now, they glide and wheel past me, translucent, blinking, some bright and disc-shaped, others pale with whip-like appendages that lash the darkness. I can see the stars through them. They move away and then return to hover. I know they see me as I stand here at the port window. They're curious, not only about me, but about the ship that confines me.

The ship is my prison.

I am a convict aboard the *Lonecross*; a crew of ten also shares my fate. We are all sentenced to death, but a small, bright hope holds their hearts and minds—a hope for freedom, for an extension of breath and length of days. Their hope is my certainty, but they don't know that. What we all know is this: their deaths are kept at bay for as long as possible by my isolation. My immediate company would be fatal to them all.

These are interesting times, full of ironies and paradoxes. The aristocracy has found itself with too much prosperity and too little desire to dirty its hands when dealing with commoners. It's grown an odd skin of politeness that insists on humanely dealing with its worst dregs, so as not to offend the offenders. This is nothing new; I've seen it played out over and over through the years. The people in power change, the justifications change, but underneath the masks, the faces are always the same.

As for the worst lawbreakers, those deserving death, the benevolent method of dealing with them arrived later. A hundred years ago, eyes turned to space and desire to break free of Earth grew. The death penalty was abolished. In its place: a one-in-a-million chance at winning the lottery of the disgraced. Criminals were cajoled into volunteerism, that they might contribute something to give their hopeless, pathetic lives meaning.

These make up the crew of the *Lonecross*. They're trained and made useful, then launched into space on a one-way journey, put to work whether they like it or not, for the good of a society that has cast them out like trash into the abyss of space. They'd like to believe they're explorers of our vast galaxy, but in reality, they're only maintenance workers on a vessel programmed to observe, record, and send back information as it searches for new worlds that might be habitable. They forget about death—until fate snips the final threads of their existence by one cause or another.

But always dangling before their noses is the small hope

that they will find that new world where second chances wait to embrace them.

And what of those who deserve the worst death, but are unable to die? Who cannot be killed no matter what torture is inflicted upon them? There is only one such soul on this ship. And I am locked away, isolated. My movements and activities are quietly documented by a computer's cold eye for the duration of my so-called humane journey. I am the only prisoner ever to meet that description in the past nine hundred years.

I've never understood very clearly what sort of monitoring is done, what sort of notes are collected about me, or even why. I imagine some scientists at home want to know about my end, if there is one. It's always best to be mindful of one's enemies and keep a careful eye on their whereabouts.

And so I remain alone, or almost alone, monitored like the stars and planets along our course. I don't mind. I'm quite used to it by now. One crewman keeps me company, albeit by voice only. The pulsating diatoms of space keep me company. So does the life maturing inside me.

Sometimes I close my eyes and imagine I'm on that other ship, the *Prospect*, where I first met my fate. I can almost feel the dizzying rise and fall of its bulk as it succumbs to the troughs and peaks of waves. I smell the pungent tang of salt and ocean decay. I hear the creak and whine of the hull, the thump of wind filling its sails. I close my eyes and I am almost there, where it all began.

* * *

I'd lived in London all my life. My name was Kate then;

I'd just turned eighteen, straining at the fetters of drudgery and poverty in my overcrowded family home, eager for escape, for the freedom of adventure. It arrived in the form of an advertisement. Brides were wanted in the New World; women who were strong of bone and mind and lean of soul, because one had to be of that disposition to survive life in Virginia, let alone the journey there by ship. I felt qualified on all points. And so, without my father's blessing, I responded to the advertisement. Soon I received a letter from The Virginia Company of London accepting my application and granting my fare to a new world. My mother and father did not say good-bye. I never looked back.

The journey was horrendous. I became so sick I truly thought I would see death before I saw land again. Halfway through the voyage, during a particularly sadistic storm, I considered pitching myself overboard and letting the sea swallow me. I didn't think I could take any more. I hadn't eaten in days because the mere thought of food made me retch. I was weak and feverish.

Then the sea calmed. The passengers embraced the relief it brought and slept. But I couldn't sleep.

After twisting and turning in my bed, I had a brief, disturbing dream: a man had kidnapped me, stripped me naked and tied me to a bed spread-eagled, where he proceeded to probe my body with a glowing instrument. When he looked into my eyes, I felt a burning sensation at the back of my head. I was terrified, but finally he untied me and said, "You'll do."

I woke in a sweat, and realized my fever had finally broken. I rose and made my way to the deck for some night air, hoping it would bring calm to my frantic heart.

The ship rocked gently in the small swell of the sea. There was no moon, but the stars were so bright and numerous, I thought it might be possible to touch them. I stared out across the dark surface of the water. It was then I noticed a strange glow in its depths.

* * *

"Time to eat, Kata," says Ruhan through a speaker in my door. His voice startles me from my thoughts. He calls me by my name, and he's the only one. I know the others only by combinations of numbers and letters. Ruhan is CR7. I'm CK3, and in my files I'm told I have a suffix: 22, which means I'm extremely dangerous. The crew isn't allowed to talk to me, although I've heard their voices from time to time. They've whispered through the speaker: "Hey, CK3, what you got going on in there?" or "Suck my dick, bitch." Ruhan was no different at first, when he sought me out twenty years ago. But there was something about him that caught my attention. His snide remarks quickly gave way to curiosity; then, as time went on, to friendship.

Ruhan fills me in on the goings-on of the crew. I never ask, but he talks as if I want to know. He told me once that I'm the subject of many discussions among the men. They wonder what I am, and why so much effort has been made to send me away and keep me separated. Why didn't the judges make a special ruling in my case? Why didn't they humanely euthanize me?

I never say anything. They don't need to know. I suppose it doesn't matter. Regardless, Ruhan talks to me. I think he feels sorry for me. Perhaps it's because I'm the only female on board. Or he's simply curious. I never ask him why. I'm grateful for his friendship.

"I have some meat for you," Ruhan says.

I know it isn't real meat, with blood in it. It's a block, processed and shaped to look and taste like meat. But I'm not hungry. I haven't been hungry in years. I can't remember the last time I tasted cooked food. I know this is a phase that will soon end. The cycle will come around and I'll need another kind of food, as I have many times before.

"No, thank you," I say.

"You have to eat, *osita*," he insists. *Little bear*, he calls me. If only he knew.

"I'll eat later," I tell him.

A brief silence hangs beyond the door. "How about we eat together?" he suggests. "Me on this side and you on your side. We'll eat and we'll talk. How about that?"

I smile, but of course he can't see it. Perhaps he hears it in my voice. "CJ9 won't be too happy with that," I say. "What if he catches you?"

"CJ can kiss my ass," Ruhan replies. "What's he gonna do? Send me to prison?" He laughs at his own joke.

I don't say anything. Outside, the creatures swim languidly past my window. A sudden, incoherent longing rises in my chest, leaving me feeling fragmented and jumpy. I reach over and push a button. Portal shades descend and hide the view.

A series of clicks and hisses announces the arrival of my meal. A small door in the wall slides open to reveal a plate of food and a cup of water in a steel-reinforced box. I remove them both and set them on the table by my bed. Later I'll drink the water, but I'll send the food back to recycling. I don't need it.

The life growing in my womb feeds me, and in turn eats me. Together, we live.

"Tell me a story, *osita*," Ruhan says. "One I haven't heard before."

We've been on the *Lonecross* for twenty years. I've been telling him stories for the past ten. Perhaps he is the observer after all, the collector of information. He knows more about me than anyone else aboard the ship.

"You've heard them all, Ruhan."

"Guess I have," he says. "You sound tired."

"I am."

"Are you ill?"

"No."

"Old age, eh?" His concern is brief. Through the speaker I hear him take an eager breath. "Tell me about the alien in the sea, then," he says. "I like that one."

I've told it a hundred times, it seems. But I comply. "The year was 1620, and I was eighteen," I begin, as I always do. Ruhan chuckles.

I stop. "What's funny?"

"That always gets me."

We've discussed this countless times, but he won't accept it as truth. "You never believe me."

"That you're 900 years old? It's a good story."

I want to argue with him, to convince him of the truth, but the urge passes, and I continue my story. "I was one of many young women hoping to become wives," I continue, and I'm transported back once again.

* * *

I wasn't the only person who saw the glow under the waves. I was one of a hundred or more passengers looking for opportunity and perhaps love in Virginia. Several had joined me on deck that night, as well as a few of the crew, all of us staring down into the depths, curious and maybe a little frightened of what we saw. One of the crew said, "It's only the phosphor glow of tiny sea creatures. They cluster together and sometimes they grow in number to the millions. We've seen it before."

That reassured us a little, but still we watched. Soon we realized that the glowing object was rising rapidly and would soon break the surface alongside the ship. We all stumbled back, stifling cries and gasps. The crewman who had offered the explanation leaned over the railing and said, "Damn." It was all he was able to say before something from our nightmares rose up from the water and rocked our vessel so violently, we lost our footing and fell, grabbing for anything to prevent us from being catapulted overboard.

It was an oval-shaped thing and huge—almost the size of our ship—with a ring of shining eyes pulsating in colors of blue and green. The object slowly circled our vessel. When it completed a full circuit, it stopped, as if considering what to do next. It moved sharply to the left and then to the right, finally hovering a few feet above us, perfectly still and silent. I felt all those eyes scrutinizing, examining, sorting. The others on deck shouted and screamed, scrambling away, but I remained, paralyzed, transfixed by the sight.

A long appendage appeared from beneath the object and lowered itself closer to me. I felt the sensation of heat in the back of my head just as I had in my dream. In my weakened state, the shock and terror were too much. My ears filled with a high-pitched ringing, and all the stars in the night sky winked out.

* * *

"What happened to the ship?" Ruhan asks. "After you were abducted."

I realize he's never asked that question before. "I don't know."

"Kept on sailing, maybe. Minus one passenger, eh? Must have been like a hammer to the head: that whole experience, the whole ship telling wild tales of aliens. You think they went crazy after something like that?"

"How would I know that?"

"Seems like it could've happened. Maybe the ship sank and they all drowned."

"Maybe."

"And that sumbitch dropped you on the beach like nothing happened. What did it do to you?"

"You know what it did to me…what *he* did to me."

"But you don't remember."

There's much I remember. But to Ruhan I lie and say, "No. I don't." I choose not to share the details of an encounter with a creature so foreign and yet so humanlike that I wanted to both flee from and embrace him. He was altogether beautiful and entirely repulsive, an outsider in the fullest sense of the word, trapped on a world not his own, who knew he'd never see his home again. He did what he needed to do. He made a way to escape, if not for the whole of him, then for a piece.

I knew none of this at the time of my abduction. I was convinced I had died and been carried to hell for my sins. I thought I was facing a demon disguised as an angel of light. Only later in my dreams did the revelations come. But at that first encounter, I thought only of eternal torment. He studied me with a piercing, ferocious gaze that dissected my soul and stitched it back together. His touch burned, but stirred in me an intense longing I couldn't begin to comprehend. It didn't ease the pain and terror that overwhelmed me at the insertion of some part of him into my womb.

"So when did you know you had a baby inside you?" Ruhan asks.

"Not for a while."

"Until the natives found you."

"Yes."

"And you turned cannibal."

I cringe at the word. I don't need human flesh. I don't need blood. I did it for the life within me, my enemy lover who required a particular type of nourishment. I had no choice but to get it for him. I tried to stop myself, but I could no more prevent my burrowing into a brain or a neck or an abdominal cavity than I could prevent my blood from coursing through my veins. At the time I didn't know the names of those things I craved, but now I can name them: the thymus, pituitary, thyroid, pancreas, liver—those parts rich in vitamins, amino acids, and hormones.

"I don't consider myself a cannibal," I say.

"I read your file. It goes back a long time. Hundreds of years. You've always been a cannibal."

"I thought you didn't believe I was that old."

He chuckles.

"It's all true, Ruhan."

"Yeah, okay, whatever. Let's just say it is true—"

"In the twenty years we've shared space on this ship," I push, "have my stories ever changed?"

I hear nothing on the other side of the door.

"Do those files lie?" I ask.

Again, nothing.

"Have I wavered in any detail? Added or subtracted? Embellished?"

He considers this, I know, because the tone of his voice changes. Uncertainty, even anxiousness, shades his words. "How can you be that old? Are you immortal?"

"He preserves me," I tell him. "As I've said before. Perhaps he will forever."

"A baby can't do that."

"Not a human baby. But he's not human. Or a baby."

"What the hell is it, then?"

Now I hesitate, uncertain myself. "I don't know."

"You've never tried to get rid of it, then?"

Our discussion is moving into forbidden territory. I won't answer such questions, no matter how many times he asks. "I'm tired, Ruhan. I need to sleep. Go join your companions."

He doesn't argue, because he knows it won't change anything.

* * *

Ruhan was an enigma, not so much in his character but

in the way he made me crave his company one moment and recoil from it the next. I had spent most of my life in isolation of one form or another, ever since the day I woke up and found myself alone on a rocky shore. Twenty years on the *Lonecross* has been nothing out of the ordinary. But Ruhan changed everything when he took an interest in me. Not as an oddity, but as a person.

Initially he was no different than the other crewmen who slipped away unnoticed to try to engage me through the speaker with snide remarks. I ignored them and I ignored him too. But then one day he told me his name.

"Everyone knows me by CR7," he said quietly. "But my real name is Ruhan."

I didn't respond, but I pondered this new tack. What did he expect from me?

"Are you lonely in there?" he asked in a strained voice.

I hesitated, then spoke. "No."

He didn't seem surprised that I answered. I heard a small sigh in his voice, and then he said, "I'm lonely."

Over time, Ruhan and I settled into a peculiar relationship. He talked and I listened. I rarely asked questions, but when I did, he devoured them like a hungry animal. He needed to tell his story. He shared how his older brother had been responsible for getting him hooked on phreno, a hallucinogen. He mentioned his grandmother and her effort to keep him at home, away from trouble.

"What did she look like?" I asked. I don't know why I asked. I can't remember my own grandparents. Perhaps I wanted an image to fill that hole.

"Ah, *mi abuela*, she was such a beauty, even in her old age," he said with a smile in his voice. "She had hair black as a raven, even at seventy. Barely any gray at all. And even though she was *mujercita*—a little lady—she had these eyes that would put the fear of hell into your soul with one look. She would tilt her head to one side and put her hands on her hips, and her mouth would turn into a hard, thin line. Those eyes would drill right into you. That's when you knew you might as well give up, because there was no escaping her wrath. But she was good. So good. And she loved me. I wish I'd paid more attention to that."

* * *

Before he began begging me for stories, Ruhan would often tell me about the crew. He'd share conversations, altercations, weaknesses and strengths. Later, after we'd become more familiar with each other, he'd tell me what the men said about me; wild speculations, some of them humorous.

"CN8 says you aren't a woman. You're a machine, or a program or an AI-bot to make us think you're real. He says you're spying on us."

I smiled at that. "What would be the point?"

"That's what I said. But it makes more sense than what CV10 says."

"Which is?"

"You're an alien."

"Maybe he's right," I said, but I didn't want him to know how close they were to the truth.

As the years crept by, he shared more troubling experiences. Infighting became worse. Twice, a crewman attacked and killed another. One by one, their numbers dwindled, until there were only five. Their tasks took longer to complete. Eventually, repairs were neglected and chores left unfinished. Ruhan began avoiding the others as much as possible.

Once, he came to me in the night, his voice tight with pain. "You awake?" he asked, gasping.

I rose from my place at the portal and moved to the door. "What's wrong?"

"They beat me."

My chest tightened. "Why?"

"They found out I've been talking to you."

For the first time I felt a protective rage rise up inside. I wanted to make them pay for what they'd done to him. I might have even said something to that effect, although I don't remember.

"I...I won't be able to visit anymore, Kata," he whispered. "Sorry."

And he didn't. Not for an entire year, by my feeble calculations. It was the longest year of my impossible life.

* * *

Time passes for me without an identity. I struggle to recognize its markings of minutes and hours. I try to make my own but they constantly shift and change. I sleep and I wake. I shower, read, write on a small tablet provided for me. I talk to Ruhan and Ruhan talks to me. And then I sleep again.

I dream I'm in the box. It's a steel coffin and I watch, bound and helpless, as the seams are welded shut. It's so hot inside; I can't breathe. I'm jostled severely, my head and shoulder slamming from one side to the other. I know what's happening to me. I'm being transported once again on a ship, but this time it's a barge filled with cargo containers.

I can't stop screaming. Pounding. Kicking. There's a violent impact and thunder. At once the temperature changes—cool, cold, freezing. The pressure builds in my head and lungs. This is the end. I won't be miraculously released this time. But I am. Always I'm protected. Shielded. Freed.

I wake up panting for breath. This is a nightmare I've had more times than I can count. The worst of my tortures always revisits me in my dreams.

When I find sleep again, he comes to me. He's a thunderstorm that takes me by surprise each time. He rolls across my dreams and covers me, a shadow over the sun, an eclipse. He knows I can't turn away. He's a coiled adder, a stinging hornet, a hungry panther who devours me and I let him. He's all I have.

I hate him because he's stolen from me every precious thing I've owned or ever hoped to own: a family, children, a home, friendships, companionship, dreams, ambitions, all the things that have never had a chance to come to fruition because of what this creature has done to me. I love him, because he's been my family, my child, my home, my lover, my companion, for nine hundred years. And when he visits me in my dreams, I lash out like a cornered animal, then I yield. More—I welcome him.

Always sorrowful, Kata, he says. *Why do you resist?*

I'm tired.

I am stirring inside you. I am growing now.

I know.

Are you ready?

No.

A woman is given nine months to prepare for birth. I have given you nine hundred years. Is that not enough?

No. How could I ever prepare for something like this?

Ah, Kata, my river of souls, my stream of dreams. Do you love me?

You're cruel.

No, only pragmatic.

When you're released from my body, will you let me die?

Is that your wish?

It is, more than anything.

Do you wonder if there is something more for you?

No, because I know there isn't.

Has it been so dreadful that you welcome death?

Nine hundred years is too long for anyone to live.

I could give you something more, something fuller, richer.

I only want release. I want peace.

Do you love me, Kata?

You're a parasite. I'm a mere host. How can you ask that question?

You are more than a host. You are my eyes to the stars, my ears to the music of the spheres. You are my heartbeat and my food, you are my breath. Do you love me?

Yes.

Afterward, I sleep and do not dream.

* * *

When I awake, I'm hungry. It's a sensation I haven't felt in a long time. The cycle has begun again as it has hundreds of times before, but this time something is different. The life in my womb is growing and changing. It's ready to be born, to emerge from this shell of a body, this swollen belly that has housed it and nourished it for far too long. It needs to be fed, more than what I can give. I think of the crewmen who've died in the past twenty years, whose internal parts could sustain me if I had them now. Space has devoured them instead.

I shower, lingering under the hot spray a little longer than usual. Afterward, as I dry off, I study my image in the reflective surface of my bedroom wall. I notice how much I've changed. All my body hair is gone, including my eyebrows and lashes. My eyes bulge slightly, as if too big for their sockets. Over time, he's replaced my blood with a blue fluid, and it gives me a deathly tint, the color of a body pulled from icy waters. My skin is translucent, but also coarse and leathery. I look as though I could crumble at the slightest touch. But I'm stronger than ever. I'm impenetrable. The irony of that is not lost on me.

I don't bother to dress. No one but the cold, impartial observer in the ceiling sees me, and the freedom of nakedness is one of the few small pleasures I can enjoy.

Ruhan comes with breakfast. "Did you sleep well, Kata?"

"No," I reply. "I had bad dreams."

"Tell me about them." The speaker crackles. I'm sure after so many years it's beginning to break down. The crewmen are nothing more than maintenance men, but they are few now, and there are priorities. Speakers are likely at the bottom of the list. I'm only grateful that Ruhan still comes to me, that he found a way to visit mostly unhindered. He's never told me how it happened, what arrangement he made with the crew, or what threat he may have held over their heads. Ruhan doesn't seem like a strong man, but I think he wears it as a disguise. I think—after the beating, after the long year passing—he took that disguise off and showed the crew who he really was.

The speaker hisses. I remember my loneliness without Ruhan's conversations, and a tiny spark of panic flares in my chest at the thought of another long, empty stretch with no communication. But it passes.

"I dreamt that I was in the steel coffin, the one they put me in to try to kill me."

"Ah, yes. A long time ago. When did you say?"

"I don't remember exactly. I've tried to forget over the years. I think it was sometime in the mid-twentieth century, maybe around 1960."

"You have that dream a lot."

"Yes."

"I can't think of a worse way to die."

I have to laugh at that.

Ruhan laughs with me, but he seems puzzled. "What's so funny?"

"You don't see?" I reply. "It *is* the way you will die. You're in a box, sealed in, cast out into the vast ocean of space, with no control over where the ship goes or what your end will be."

Ruhan is silent for so long I think he might have left. Then he says, "It's not so bad, I guess. It's different than a steel coffin. I can breathe."

"You can breathe," I say. "Yes, there's that."

He changes the subject. "CL6 won't make it much longer. He had a stroke yesterday. That means just four of us now."

His news means nothing to me. CL6 is a number. I've never seen him. I don't know if I've ever heard his voice. Ruhan only mentions him in passing. But I think about his death, of the possibilities it might offer me.

"Will you do it this time?" I ask.

Ruhan knows what I want. "I can't," he says. "You know I can't."

"Just the pancreas, the liver and the thyroid glands. That's all I ask. Is it so much from a man who will end up ejected into space? What difference will it make to a dead man?" There's a desperate tone to my voice. I don't want Ruhan to hear it, but I *am* desperate, and I need the organs. The life in me needs to be fed again.

"They'd never allow it," he says. "They might kill me if they found out. They're scared of you, Kata."

"Aren't they scared of *you*?"

"Not enough. Not anymore. But you…it's different with you."

"They have every right to be scared of me."

I hear Ruhan's shallow breathing. "Would you kill us and eat us if you could?" he asks.

I want to say no, but I can't. "It's out of my control, Ruhan. He's like a demon possessing me. I do whatever he wants."

Ruhan thinks about this. "My *abuela* believed in demons."

"Did your grandmother believe in aliens?"

"She believed in everything," he says, then tries to change the subject. "Have you named it? The thing in your belly."

He doesn't want me to push about the organs, because it frightens him. So I let I go. "I call him the wasp."

"No shit? What kind of name is that?"

"It's not a name. Just a label."

I tell him another story, one I haven't shared before. "Once, sometime around the early 1800s, I broke into a house. I'd been wandering in the wilderness for months, maybe even years. Time gets lost when you live so long. The natives there kept me fed and covered by making me offerings of animals and furs so I would stay away from their villages. They called me the River Witch. Sometimes Red Boar.

"I needed real clothes, something more than furs. I'd been watching this particular homestead—a woman lived there with her husband and three young sons. She was similar to me in size and build. So one day, when they'd gone to town, I broke in and took one of her dresses and a blanket.

"I allowed myself a moment to explore the house. It had been so long since I'd been inside one. The house was small but cozy. I noticed a small stack of books on a table—children's books. One was about insects, with pictures carefully detailed and colored. There was a wasp with indigo wings, which I read about…it laid its eggs inside living beetle grubs.

"This was a revelation to me. For the first time I had some way to identify what had happened to me, no matter how grotesque the comparison. I hadn't become pregnant, as I'd shamefully believed all those years. No, I was the captive host to this creature, a slave to his whims while I nourished his offspring with my body. The alien I encountered was humanoid; in fact, there was nothing about him I would define as insect. But what he did to me was very much like the wasp in that book. So I called him a wasp after that. It seemed most appropriate."

Ruhan lets out a low whistle. *"Jesus."*

There seems no good reason to hold back anything anymore. "He was stranded," I continue. "Wounded. Abandoned. Dying. His ship would never again break the chains of Earth's gravity. And so he waited for the time when Earth developed the technology to travel into deep space. Nine hundred years. He's on his way home."

Somewhere, out in the vast reaches of space, we're drawing closer to what's familiar to him. It's an exchange, of sorts, between us, and also something we share. Against his will the wasp gave up his familiar home for an alien one; and now, ironically, I find myself doing the same. A slave to the will of one who could no longer direct his own fate.

Three days later, when it's time for my meal, I find a bowl of organs, the ones I've asked for. I can't eat fast enough.

* * *

Weeks pass before I hear from Ruhan again. When he shows up, I feel more relief than I want to. But he sounds tense, even frightened.

"How are you?" he asks, his voice shaky. "Are you okay?"

"I'm fine. I was worried about you."

"Worried about me? Ah, *osita*, how nice." His words don't line up with the fear I sense from him.

"You got in trouble for bringing me the organs, didn't you?"

"Oh…yeah, some trouble," Ruhan says. "Kept me locked up for a few days. But…you don't want to hear about that. Talk to me, Kata. Tell me how many different ways you were tortured."

I'm startled by his request. Does he wish to identify with me somehow, or are there darker, perverse urges at play? "I don't understand what you're asking," I say finally.

He's quiet for a long moment. "I think, sometimes, that if you went through so much, I can face it too, you know? I can handle it."

I reluctantly rattle off a list of unsuccessful attempts by others—and myself—to end my life: drowning, burning, impaling, poisons, acids, bullets, explosions, radiation, lasers. And when nothing worked, confinement to small, dark rooms, exile to wastelands, separation behind impenetrable fences... Then I stop. "Is that what you wanted to hear?"

"Yeah, I guess. Are you scared, Kata? Scared of the end?"

"You mean, scared to die?"

"Yeah."

"No. I'll welcome death if it comes."

"You think it won't? You think you'll stay alive forever?"

I ponder his question, my answer. "I hope not."

Ruhan releases a long breath. "They want to kill me, Kata."

"Who?"

"CM and CJ. They've killed CB."

This news alarms me. *"What?"*

"We're close to a planet. Looks like it's habitable. A lot like Earth. Either we'll burn up in the atmosphere or crash. Who knows? But there's only one escape pod. I figure CJ; he's the strongest. He'll knock off CM and me, and take the pod. He might land on the planet; he might not. But he thinks he will."

I open my port window, which I've kept dark for the past few months, and see what I've missed: a large, bright planet fills the view. Outside, the space plankton skim gracefully past, unperturbed by our presence. But there seem to be more of them, gathering close, as if waiting. I understand the purpose of their presence now; they've been guiding and maneuvering the ship through space toward this point. It was never random. The minute the ship launched, it had a destination.

But it's Ruhan's revelation that surprises me most. "The ship has an escape pod?"

"It only fits one person. Files and logs are stored in there. It can be maneuvered and it'll make it to the planet in one piece. That's what CJ said. But who's to know what the atmosphere's like? He says it's good… But what the hell, it doesn't matter anyway. We're all sentenced to death, right? Here it is, ready and waiting."

There's a hitch in his voice. "I don't want to die alone, Kata."

I don't know what to say. I don't want him to die at all. He's been the only human friend I've known in nine hundred years.

Ruhan says, "I love you, Kata. I know that's crazy. But I do. You never once asked me why I was sentenced to this ship. You always made me feel like I was a real person. An innocent man. A free man."

My throat tightens. If I had tears, I would cry. "You've been a good friend, Ruhan."

I hear scratchy, disjointed sounds of screaming, but it's not Ruhan, it's someone else.

"Oh, shit," Ruhan says. "CJ's killing CM. I knew it. He's coming after me next. Jesus!"

Inside me, desperation wells up, one part born of an urgent need to rescue Ruhan, and another born of a craving to feed. I can't deal with it. I cry out and slam my fists against the door.

Ruhan says, "If I open the door, if I go in there with you, will you kill me, Kata?"

I'm shocked once again, not by his question but by this news. "You can open the door?"

"I found the code. It wasn't easy. Years of searching. I thought maybe, someday…"

I want to answer his question with a no, but I'm afraid I won't be able to control myself. "Ruhan, I don't know what I'll do. The wasp, he—"

Ruhan is yelling now, and suddenly the door slides open. Warm air rushes in, with terrible smells—the odor of blood and shit, of fear. Ruhan stares at me, wide-eyed, and the color drains from his face. "Oh, God," he says. "You *are* an alien."

I realize with a jolt of astonishment how shocking my appearance must be. Until this very moment I never understood, but now I do—now that I see myself as Ruhan sees me for the first time. I've been remade—the alien has recreated me in his image, so slowly and so minutely that I simply accepted the changes without question. But more than adapting my body to carry his seed, I'm now perfectly adapted for life on this new planet, the alien's home world. He never had any intention of letting me die. He'll keep me with him, and I'll live in his world, as though I belong there.

I smile ruefully and say, "I'm not. I'm still me. Am I so awful?"

He shakes his head, breathing hard. "I'd rather die by your hand."

I'm not sure why he says that, and I don't believe him.

From the corridor behind Ruhan, I hear someone yelling. I know it must be CJ. Here's my chance. I rush toward Ruhan, who screams when I grab him, but I merely fling him aside and make my way out the door. I'm filled with anger and a need for vengeance. But I'm also hungry. CJ will get what he deserves.

I sprint down the corridor and turn a corner, almost slamming into him. CJ stumbles back at the sight of me, his eyes wide and full of fear. He's splattered with blood. It drips off his gray beard and runs down his arms. The iron bar he's gripping falls to the floor with an echoing clatter, and he runs, but I catch him with little effort.

"Don't kill me, please!" he pleads, but I must. I throw him to the floor, rip out his throat and pry him open like a clam with a strength I'd forgotten I possessed. Hungrily I feed, finding everything I need by instinct. When I'm finished I get up and look for Ruhan.

I find him cowering in a corner of my room. He knows there's no use hiding from me. I must be a sight now, blue, naked, and smeared with blood. For the first time that I can remember, I feel self-conscious. I don't want him to see me this way. And I don't want him to be afraid of me. "Do you still love me, Ruhan?" I ask, almost as a joke, a feeble attempt to break through his terror.

He's shaking, breathing in short, shallow puffs. As I approach him, the crotch of his trousers grows dark with a wet stain. "I don't want to die," he says.

"I didn't think so." I grab him by the wrist and pull him up. "Where's the escape pod?"

"Two levels down."

"Take me there."

We hurry down metal steps and along dingy corridors until we reach a small storage bay. Ruhan points to a door. "There."

"Get in," I tell him.

He stares at me, trembling, unbelieving. "No, Kata, I can't do this." He thinks I'm giving up my chance of escape for him. He doesn't understand the real reason I'm putting him in the pod.

"You have to, Ruhan."

He shakes his head firmly. "I won't make it."

He's made it this far. I haven't killed him yet. Perhaps the wasp has done this for me. I don't know. But I'm sure it's a short reprieve. Already I feel the beginnings of need blooming in my gut. "You might," I tell him. "But if you stay here with me, you most definitely won't make it."

Ruhan's eyes grow wide, and then soften. "What about you, Kata?" he asks. "Do you want to die so badly?"

"Yes. But I won't." I know what my destiny will be. The ship may crash. But I'll live because the wasp will keep me alive, just as he has for 900 years. I'll emerge unscathed.

Ruhan looks at my swollen belly, then at my face. I see a new strength in his eyes. He relaxes, smiles. Then, without hesitation, he pulls me into his arms and holds me tightly. It's the first prolonged human touch I've felt in hundreds of years. I cry; my body shakes with deep sobs, but no tears. Ruhan takes my face in his hands and searches my eyes. "You aren't alien, *osita*," he says. "I was wrong. Just like you said, you're still you." He wipes the blood from my lips and kisses me. Then he turns and keys in the code to the escape pod.

I watch as he climbs in. The door closes and seals shut with a hiss.

"See you on the surface," I tell him, even though I know he doesn't hear me.

A WORD FROM HARLOW C. FALLON

One day I was doing some research on mail-order brides, and discovered that as early as the 1600s, there was a call for women to journey to Jamestown, Virginia, and wed the many single men there. In their records, the Virginia Company wrote: "a fit hundredth might be sent of women, maids young and uncorrupt, to make wives to the inhabitants."

As I did more searching on the subject, I found myself following a rabbit trail (as I often do) about early accounts of UFO sightings. Christopher Columbus wrote that he had seen something strange from the deck of the Santa Maria:

"...a light, but so small a body that he could not affirm it to be land...appearing like the light of a wax candle moving up and down."

Well, that sent my imagination into overdrive. How would the passengers and crew of a ship react to seeing a UFO if it approached? What if it came up out of the water?

"A Long Horizon" came about as a result of my wild imaginings. It tells the story of one woman who becomes the unwilling host of an alien creature who cannot leave Earth and therefore keeps the woman alive for 900 years until Earth's technology advances to the point where deep space travel becomes a reality. Now he has the means to travel home, and she carries him there, still the unwilling host. But the passing years change her in many ways. This is her story.

I'd like to thank Samuel Peralta for the opportunity to write for *The Future Chronicles*. It's an amazing series of anthologies and I feel honored to be included, especially in this volume, where the proceeds benefit a worthy charity: First Book, a nonprofit organization that helps provide new books for children in need.

Although science fiction is my first love, my debut novel (in two volumes) is a fantasy. You can find them here:

http://www.amazon.com/All-Wild-Places-Elmwyn-Journey-ebook/dp/B00TT4Q01O6/

http://www.amazon.com/The-Reach-Hand-Elmwyn-Journey-ebook/dp/B00VR8X4J8/

Follow or friend me on:

Facebook: *http://www.facebook.com/harlowcfallon*
Twitter: *http://www.twitter.com/HarlowCFallon*
Website: *http://www.harlowcfallon.com*

A Note to Readers

Thank you so much for reading *The Immortality Chronicles*. If you enjoyed these stories, please keep an eye out for other titles in the *Future Chronicles* collection, a series of short story anthologies in speculative fiction. Currently available titles in the *Chronicles* include:

The Immortality Chronicles
Alt.History 101
The Z Chronicles
The Dragon Chronicles
The A.I. Chronicles
The Alien Chronicles
The Telepath Chronicles
The Robot Chronicles

Available later this year will be *The Time Travel Chronicles*, *The Galaxy Chronicles*, and *The Cyborg Chronicles*.

Please see *www.futurechronicles.net* for a full list of titles.

And, before you go, we'd like to ask you a very small favor, if you please: *Would you write a short review at the site where you purchased this book?*

Reviews are make-or-break for authors. A book with no reviews is, simply put, a book with no future sales. This is because a review is more than just a message to other potential buyers: it's also a key factor driving the book's visibility in the first place.

More reviews (and more positive reviews) make a book more likely to be featured in bookseller lists (such as Amazon's also-viewed and also-bought lists) and more likely to be featured in bookseller promotions. Reviews don't need to be long or eloquent; a single sentence is all it takes. In today's publishing world, the success (or failure) of a book is truly in the reader's hands.

So please, write a review.

Then tell a friend. Share a link to us on Facebook, or maybe even a Tweet—link to our books at *http://smarturl.it/future-chronicles*. You'd be doing us a great service.

Thank you.

Samuel Peralta
www.amazon.com/author/samuelperalta

——

Subscribe to *The Future Chronicles* newsletter for news of upcoming titles, and to be eligible for draws for paperbacks, e-books and more – *http://smarturl.it/chronicles-news*

www.ingramcontent.com/pod-product-compliance
Lightning Source LLC
Chambersburg PA
CBHW060356260626
47160CB00006B/2331